Sparks

Ablaze, Volume 1

Trisha Thacker

Published by Desert Cats Publishing, LLC, 2024.

SPARKS

First edition. February 16, 2024.

Copyright © 2024 Trisha Thacker.

ISBN: 978-1963337020

Written by Trisha Thacker.

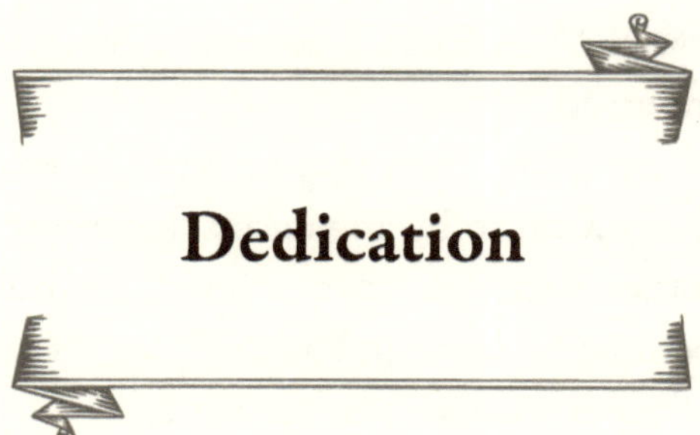

Dedication

This book is dedicated to my mother, who never gave up on me publishing my book and to my friends, online and off that have supported me with reads, edits and rants. Also thanks to Jenna Moreci for her videos of what not to do; Sarra Cannon for all her help in publishing. You're all the best.

Chapter One

The Shadows hated the smell of the chemicals and gasoline released in the air and Fateh privately agreed. The air was breathable again. As they walked through the mist of the forest, the smell of crushed leaves was potent. Any trip into town was an adventure; it was practically an all-day affair, complete with backpacks and water bottles for the hike. When Fateh was younger, they'd just drive into the city, but no one drove cars these days. This part of Wales was isolated enough, and not having cars just made it more isolated.

"Why do we live up in the hills again?" Fateh asked, adjusting the straps of his bag, making the records, DVDs, and salt lay a little easier on his back. His mother had the old tapes and her CDs. He was willing to give up CDs, but not his other music. The salt helped to protect their way to town, but he was also going to use it as his major bargaining chip for the night. Salt repelled the Shadows. Spreading it around your house or yourself could protect you from them.

"You know why," she said with a grin.

Yes, Fateh knew why. Hippie grandparents were the least of it, but they had their own host of problems living out in the wild. The fae that were out in the woods were numerous. He eyed the creatures dangling in the trees above. They were snickering, with whispering voices that echoed across and blended into the sound of the wind. "There are just more of the little fae out here," he said. "They're creepy."

"Hush," she scolded him. "They're just living like we are at the moment and haven't harmed us." She bit her lip and lowered her voice, though no one was around to hear her. "They've made life a little more difficult, but who's to say we can't all get along eventually?"

"Holding hands, singing, and skipping along the forest trails? This isn't a kid's movie, Mom." Fateh was easygoing in terms of the way the world had shifted and that was his mom's fault. He was still more cynical than his mother would ever be. She rolled her eyes at the comment and he huffed. "Well—I mean—they're not ..."

They were careful where they stepped, not wanting to intrude in anyone's path. There was faint snickering coming from all around them and Fateh's body went tense with fear. He could see the Shadows, but that didn't make them any less menacing.

"I'd rather stay on good terms with our new neighbors, Fateh. They might not talk to us or be as obvious as the fae are in town, but they've still made a home out here." She paused. "Unless they try and bite my ankles off. I'd have no remorse in salting the little bastards at that point."

Fateh grinned at her threat but stayed quiet. He hadn't ever told his mother how clearly he could see the fae shifting through the trees or a flash of silver teeth underneath an old rabbit burrow. His mother saw very little, but Fateh saw them so clearly that he could practically give them separate names.

As they walked further into the woods, they heard more snickering. They walked more carefully than before, making sure not to step on something that was more than just a shadow. Fateh took a small breath but the snickering continued. He felt his mom tense next to him and he reached out to squeeze her hand, getting a return squeeze to reassure him as well. As he turned his gaze up to the trees, he caught the sulfur glow of their eyes shining like demented fireflies.

It wasn't something he'd ever mentioned to anybody and nothing that he let the Shadows know of either. People who had originally seen the Shadows coming had vanished early on. He didn't plan on being one of them. He suspected his grandparents were among that group. If it wasn't the people who fought, it was the people who saw the truth for what it was before everyone else came to their senses as well. The Shadows were like the fae, but not like them at the same time. They were creepier, more indistinct, and could appear in the most unlikely of places. She noticed his silence and the way his gaze moved around the forest but did nothing except wrap her arms around his shoulders and tug him down the well-worn path into town.

It takes so long to get back and forth from town. It's a good thing that we can stay with Meira and Tobias.

"Before we go and do our shopping and see my friends, I've got a birthday dinner to arrange for you." He grinned broadly at her wide-eyed surprise. "I know just how to bargain, too." His voice was quieter at that; to reassure her that he knew what he was doing.

"It's not my birthday for a week," she protested. "Trying to usher in my old age already?" She ruffled the dark, curly strands of his hair, plucking out a leaf lodged in the tangled strands. "I'm worried, Fateh ..." she said. "Anything you buy in town requires a high price, but I know you're a smart kid with a brain under that mop of hair."

"I'll make sure of it." One didn't ask favors lightly of Shadows and he knew what it meant to do such a thing, how much to ask, and what to offer. "I promise I'll be careful." He smiled and shoved the leaf down the back of her shirt, then darted ahead, leaving her shouting behind him.

———

It had only been two years since the Shadows—a type of the fae—took over, but the Felinheli had already changed so drastically. He had only been fourteen when the Shadows came and the Shadows that ran the town were unlike the ones that were in the woods.

They were vaguely human-shaped, tall, and terrifying in the way they seemed to follow in your own shadow whenever you got near them.

The houses that were nearest the forest were abandoned, covered in vines and other brush. Fateh knew that nothing could grow that fast in a house after only a few years left alone. He knew the Shadows had something to do with it. Fateh wasn't sure what the purpose of that was. To intimidate? To show that they could do this to all their homes without a thought? It *was* rather sobering, and it gave the Felinheli more of a neglected look than it ever had before. It had never been large; walking from one end of the main street to the other end took only a few hours. The signs of ruin put it right up there with an urban explorer's paradise.

As they walked further into town and along a line of businesses, Fateh deviated from the path and tugged a streamer of creeper vines loose from what used to be the old roller rink, twining it around his fingers. Nothing could skate in it now—not with the entire building practically collapsed in on itself. Old, rusted skates lay abandoned around the entrance and Fateh could only wonder what lay inside. As if his thoughts conjured them up, he saw a glimpse of eyes in the high windows and he quickly turned away. It was best not to think about it. It could be humans *or* Shadows, but either way, it was too dangerous to investigate.

> There were a few businesses that were up and running that *weren't* run by the Shadows; small stalls that sold plants, and others that sold groceries. He and his mother weren't the only ones who grew their own food and sometimes they came into town with vegetables from their garden to sell.

"The Shadows act so human," his mother said. There was a restaurant next to the roller rink and it was filled with the Shadows. She leaned against his head, arms folded. "They laugh just as we did in that same place, but you know they aren't ..." she sighed.

Fateh's gaze followed hers and lingered on the group that hung out around the restaurant. They had called themselves Shadows, but one was outside the restaurant and was brightly flickering, like a sparkler on a dark night.

"Don't stare at them too long, Fateh. You know how they can trap people ..." His mother was cavalier about the small Shadows, but like any real predator, the larger ones invoked fear and his mother wasn't immune to it. There was talk about 'getting along with your new neighbors' and there was knowing to be careful of the predators in your midst. Common sense won.

"I've never been trapped, you know that," he snorted. He had something to do here. This had once been his mother's favorite restaurant to go to and while he hated to see the Shadows there, he wanted to give her some small gift. There were humans there as well, and he relaxed a little. It couldn't be so bad if there were humans with the Shadows, right?

The smile he tossed at her was reassuring, even if it didn't reach his eyes. "It's okay, Mom," he murmured. "I'll be fine, I promise." He squeezed her hand once before he ambled up to the door, aware of all eyes on him. Not only from the Shadows from within but also from everyone else who lived in town and guessed at what he was going to do. Whether they thought he was stupid or not, no one tried to stop him.

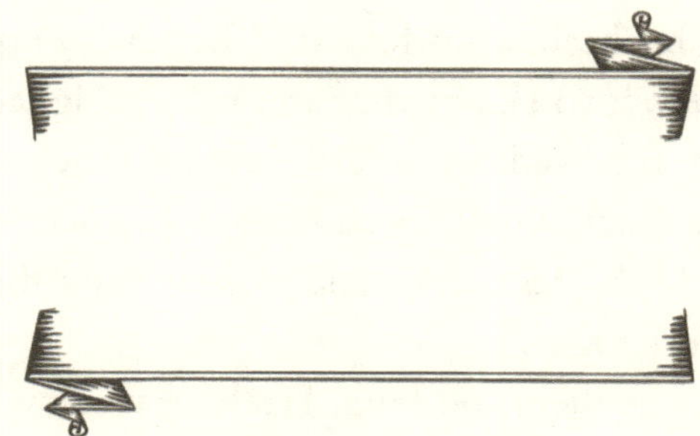

8

Chapter Two

Being treated like they were slightly more intelligent than dogs was insulting. Using the fear of the unknown against everyone was worse. Fateh simply didn't see a need to react outwardly and give them what they wanted. They wanted fear and submission, but Fateh had noticed that they treated humans much better if they *didn't* completely cower and lick the feet of their so-called masters. He took a strident step forward, body straight as an arrow as he made his way to the front door.

They can bite me, he thought crossly, tapping on the door frame and waiting for someone to come to the entrance. He wasn't just going to barge in. That would have been unforgivably rude in their eyes and if he was going to come out of this with what he needed, he had to be on his best behavior. He was met at the door by something that was vaguely feminine; smoky bits straggling into an almost recognizable shape.

"A little human decides to grace us with his presence?" Her voice rasped like dry leaves. She had more in common with a human than some of the other Shadows he had seen. Her appearance still sent a shiver down his spine. There were no real features, just a hint of sharp, jagged teeth and bright, acid-tinged eyes. She was as tall as the door frame, fingers stretching down into thin, sharp talons. "I wasn't told the humans here were so bold."

No matter how brave his words from before were, Fateh was very aware of how much danger he was in at the moment. "I'd like to negotiate dinner." He thrust his hand in his pockets and watched her, making sure that he was far enough away so as to not be intrusive, but casual enough so that it didn't look like he feared her. She wasn't known to him and it chilled him slightly that they were still being invaded, bit by bit.

There was a conversation from the back, pitched too low for him to understand, and the woman turned to listen to the unseen speaker before turning back to Fateh. "You are coming to us for a favor? How amusing," she murmured, leaning close. The smell of blood and rot was strong on her breath. Fateh fought to keep his gag reflex from engaging. "Little treats for the little pets that still hang about?"

Fateh scowled, arms crossing against his chest. "Even pets like a night out." He held back the worst of his initial reaction. "I request to have a spot tonight and I offer the protection we carry for the night and this night only." He closed his eyes briefly to better remember the words. "Inside your walls, we will not be harmed, nor will we be touched outside of it as long as we hold the peace." He was grateful he had listened to his 'crazy' grandparents so that he could pass these little tests.

He knew he'd surprised her when a thin smile stretched her lips wide. Sometimes the myths had a grain of truth in them. They served as a guide. His family had proved that before and today was just another example.

"Someone's been reading fairy tales ..." she taunted. "What is this protection, human?" She towered over him, pressing close as if trying to distract him. "Do we get to play with you tonight? You are the most protection that your little family can have, with all your smart words." Fateh's hands tensed with the effort it took to not shove her away as she continued. "I can make it good for you. Hardly a price at all to pay ..."

"Sorry, no. I have something that I'll enjoy giving away more." Fateh fished through the deep pockets of his backpack to pull out the salt. It was their one real protection and the one thing that Shadows feared. "Payment in advance," he said shortly. "I know that you will honor any deals you make with us and I am giving you this early as a token of my trust."

It was a hefty price to hand over the salt that they used when they walked to and from their house but he wanted his mother to have a nice night. She did deserve it. She was working herself to pieces at their home, growing enough for them to live by, cleaning and cooking and just taking care of him, although he didn't need to be taken care of as much as he used to when he was younger. Now that he was sixteen, he could take some of the burden off of her. He had a feeling there was much more that was going on with his mother than she was telling. They could replace the salt at some point.

She took in his words but didn't take the salt yet, eyes narrowed and expression looking almost human for a moment as she considered it. She then smiled coldly, tilting his chin up with sharp-tipped fingers. "I think I shall agree to this little proposition, *Fateh*." She held out her hand, fingers curling inward to cut at her palm. Strange silver blood gleamed and dripped down from the cut, landing on Fateh's open palm. How could something that looked like smoke *bleed?*

He couldn't help but jerk backward at the sound of his name. This bothered him more than her odd advances and veiled threats because she didn't know him. He managed a nod, and he heard a snicker behind him. He tried to save face, hoping he sounded sure of himself and not scared. "The words?" He raised his eyebrows. "I'm not doing this without your bond."

"Very good," she whispered, stroking down his face hard enough to raise a thin line of blood, licking it off her fingers. "With a taste of my blood, I and those within these walls are accountable for any mishaps that occur. You will be safe while you dine and while the protection you have offered in return lasts."

It took almost everything Fateh had not to wince or grimace at the blood seeping into his skin as if it were being absorbed. She smirked and patted his cheek. "Run along now, little human." Her expression shifted to one of delight. "Or not. It seems you have a *nuisance* attached to you."

Fateh blinked and tried to twist around, but something pressed up against his back, warmth leaching through his coat and arms resting on his head. *What is it with these people?*

"Did dinner arrive for us already?" Breath was warm against his ear and Fateh watched with narrowed eyes as a skinny hand traced its way down his chest. "Can I play with it before we serve it to the guests?"

Fateh growled at the threat and tried harder to shove the creature away. He had a feeling he knew who it was and he gave a mental groan that the idiot had been able to find him again, and so quickly this time, too. He found the strength to shove at the arm holding him down. "I'm going to be a guest, not be a menu item for you," he snapped.

"Well, it isn't like you'd be much of a meal anyway. You're so small you'd hardly be an appetizer." The presence pulled away and twirled him around.

The first thing he noticed were eyes that were a vivid, unnatural shade of blue, laughing down at him. Jaggedly cut hair, reminiscent of flames, topped a bony face. It *was* him—that annoying, insufferable, had to bug him at every opportunity Shadow. He was the most human of them all, and he had been around the longest. Fateh gave an internal growl. He had thought Tabor was a friend until he had revealed himself as a monster, and now Tabor wouldn't leave Fateh alone.

"It's not like you're that much taller than me," Fateh snorted. "And I'm sure you've had *so* many more years to work on it." His temples throbbed and he just wanted to be away from here, away from Tabor and his idiotic taunts. He didn't treat Tabor like an ordinary Shadow; there was too much history between them to do so. He wouldn't dare talk to one of the other Shadows this way.

"Mmm ... did you just get sassed by a human, Tabor?" A smaller Shadow, looking more inhuman than the rest, peered out the door and laughed up at Tabor. His hair crackled like a thin bolt of lightning, light flickering in and out of the hazy outlines of his body. "Poor baby; can't even get respect from the trash." There were snickers and mocking tones from the crowd inside the restaurant, and Fateh almost felt sorry for Tabor for a moment. He couldn't start thinking of Tabor as a friend again. He hadn't ever been one. It had all been a trick.

Tabor's smile didn't quite reach his eyes and his entire tone changed as he looked toward the assembled Shadows on the porch. "Oh, I just haven't had enough time to play with him yet. It'd be a shame to turn him into firewood so soon."

Fateh kept his face carefully blank so as not to give away any of his fear at the real threat in Tabor's voice, but he couldn't help his reply. "Yeah, whatever—you keep on thinking that. I guess your ego needs a lot of fuel to run. I won't be contributing to it, though." He gave Tabor a warning look, showing him that he wasn't amused by this turn of events. Part of him wondered why he was reacting this way. Fateh felt he could stare down Tabor like he wouldn't get chastised or hurt for it later. Maybe it was that old thread of friendship, or maybe it was just not caring anymore.

"He wasn't hurt by you, Tabor," the hostess murmured, half wrapped around Tabor. Fateh was the only one who saw Tabor's wince as the creature touched him. He could have almost pegged Tabor as human—but he was good at playing that particular role. Fateh wouldn't be tricked again. "Strange little human, hmm?"

"You really expect me to break the rules so quickly, to give you an excuse to hurt me?" Tabor murmured, eyes meeting Fateh's for one moment. A shiver worked its way down Fateh's spine, especially when Tabor gave him his own warning look before the other Shadow tugged him into the restaurant. There was something Tabor wasn't saying, as if there was another reason he hadn't been hurt. Tabor always acted like he knew something. Either he really did or he was pretending so he could mess with Fateh's head. Fateh barely caught Tabor's final words as he was lost from sight. "Humans have their own protections that I won't be breaching just to make you smile."

But what could he be warning me about? Fateh swallowed hard. When the enemy was trying to help you out, things had to be very bad indeed.

He didn't notice the people walking around him, almost avoiding him, as if he had a disease that they didn't want to catch. *What the hell does he have to gain by messing with me?* He couldn't figure it out and almost didn't want to, but he knew that it would gnaw at him until it drove him half-insane. *I'm just reading too much into it.* But Tabor had ceased to be his friend once the other Shadows appeared and now Fateh just put up with him and tried to stay away from him.

Usually, the Shadows didn't stick around one person so much. They'd taunt their target, waiting for them to slip up so that they could take someone who was unprepared. Most were like the creature at the restaurant, smoke and darkness and sometimes iridescent with a rainbow of colors, but others were just inky darkness, swallowing up the light that surrounded them.

Fateh swallowed and jumped at his mother's hand on his arm, so lost in thought that he hadn't seen or heard her come up. "Ready to go meet your friends?" she asked softly, not saying anything about what had gone on. She would talk to him later, he knew—when they were inside and away from prying ears. When it was safer.

He ignored the snickers from the Shadows still watching him. He was still thinking about how they'd acted toward him. He didn't know what they meant, and he wasn't entirely sure he wanted to find out. It had changed since the last time they were here. The 'politics' of the town had shifted, and he was very much out of his depth. The stories his grandparents told wouldn't help him against the people of the town. Their advice had been more of the fairy tale variety.

Fateh didn't say what had gone on or what was said. She didn't need to know. As he shifted his bag higher onto his shoulder, he let his thoughts drift. Before they did more exploration, they needed to find out what had changed. *It's a good thing that we do have such vigilant friends here*, he mused. *They'll be able to give the answers we need to survive.*

He was aware of all eyes on him as he left the area, not just the eyes of Shadows who frequented the restaurant. There were people in the town who were giving him covert looks. He knew he was being categorized in the same light as those who gave into the Shadows. He would have to find out what that meant before things really went south.

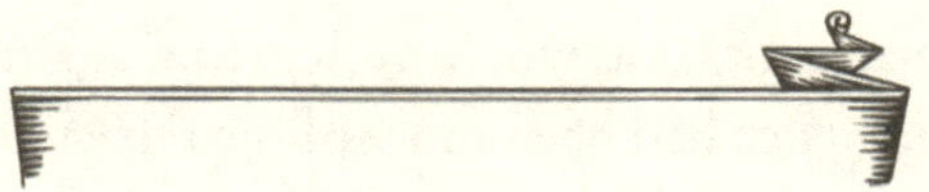

Chapter Three

Tabor sighed when Fateh walked away, shoving at Ilianda with one hand. "I'm not in the mood to play today," he snapped. "Go torment someone else." The humans did their best to avoid the Shadows and the other fae, but Tabor was still aware of them. The town had changed since he first came here; the fear was almost strong enough to see.

"Oh, but we missed our precious little flame," she murmured, stroking a finger down his cheek. "You were so close to joining our ranks. Can you blame us for wanting to draw you into our little circle?" The titters all around echoed oddly and Tabor grimaced. He had barely escaped them and it had saddled him with a debt that he wasn't sure he would ever clear of—if he was even given a *chance* to clear it.

"I was never yours," he snapped, real anger coloring his words as he shoved with power this time. "I am not the simple child I was." He had been young and foolish and walked straight into their trap. That they had come here, to his territory, did not bode well.

"Not the child you were, but still a child," she taunted. She didn't seem bothered by his show of power, but she backed off from touching him. "Such a shame you had such ... allies." Her eyes narrowed. "It's a pity we cannot meet him again to thank him for his kindness."

"Yes, do thank him." Tabor's expression brightened with vicious humor. "I would like to see the price he would hold over your head for such simple words." Even the scáthach were bound by such rules; all of their kind were. No matter that they were the dregs of life, the rules still, thankfully, bound them. Whatever they had been before, they were of the Otherworld now.

She tilted up her nose at that taunt and took her companion's arm in hand. "We're done playing with you for now. We'll reserve our energy for your *volatile* little friend when he comes. He seems *so* smart, but it's so easy to slip up." Her expression was calculating and Tabor resolved to keep around Fateh as much as possible. He didn't realize the true danger that the scáthach represented to him.

"I'll be back tonight," he warned her. "With humans actually eating *real* food, someone has to watch over him."

"Oh, the little protector, as always." She snickered. "So determined to watch over your little playthings that you'll wander right into a trap again and this time your little friend won't be able to save you." Her expression hardened. "We've already made certain that the pathways are closed to him and his kind."

Tabor narrowed his eyes. "You've no chance in fighting me now. I weave my own protections that your shadows cannot touch."

"So you say. But it's dangerous when one walks in shadow, Tabor. You never know what might be waiting for you in the dark." Her eyes held the eerie, lamplight glow still that all the scáthach seemed to have when they were first created, but Ilianda was not young; she was older than he and vicious with her threats. Her form was as indistinct as the others, bleeding into the shadows at her feet. There were flickers of colors in her form, the only sign left of the lives she had absorbed.

"I have my own pathways there, too," he said smugly, enjoying the look of shock on her face. "It must be so sad for you that you don't control everything." It had taken a long time and several sacrifices to get a safe passage, but it was worth it to have an escape route. More of the scáthach were gathering, and he guessed that he'd have to use it sooner than he thought.

"We'll see, Tabor," she murmured. "You can give in any time, you know. Just ask all the others who joined our ranks. Fighting is so ... in the past."

"Your kind is the trash they left behind," he retorted snidely. "Pardon me if I don't want to nest among the sewage." His smile turned cruel. "You wouldn't want to know what I'd do to redecorate the place this time."

She gave him a baleful look and spun around, looking almost human again for a moment. He supposed some traits remained, even when the soul mutated beyond all recognition. The way she seemed to drift into the seeping darkness evaporated that line of thought, though. No matter what she had been once, there was nothing left of that now.

"And we get to deal with the resulting mess," he mumbled under his breath, hurrying away from the place. There would be more chances to observe and bring back information. For now, he'd take what he had and work with it, planning his defenses and attacks. An escape route sounded best right now.

What was more interesting was what Fateh was planning. It was brave of him to come into the lion's den and all for something so simple as a meal. Fateh had changed little since Tabor first met him. He had only appeared to be a few years older than Fateh. He had shifted his appearance so that it reflected the relative human age. He wasn't much older than Fateh was.

It was a shame that the friendship had ended when the scáthach arrived, outing him as being otherworldly. He had been interesting, full of opinions and sass, and scared of nothing. Two years ago that friendship had cut off when Illianda had wrapped herself around him, cooing about how good it was to see Tabor 'playing with the little humans already.'

Two years ago the town had been *his*, his nest with the humans to watch over and protect. He'd never dreamed that the scáthach would come and take over. He knew that this town wasn't the only place that the scáthach touched, but this was the only place where they were so obvious. In another part of the world, the fae had come forward, some more dangerous than the scáthach.

It didn't bode well for the humans, but Tabor was only one. He couldn't even save his town, much less the humans who lived outside of it. The most he could do was continue to watch over Fateh and make sure that his deals wouldn't get him in trouble. There was something about Fateh that Tabor couldn't quite put his finger on, but he knew it would come to him eventually. He would never get the chance to ferret it out if he let the scáthach take over Fateh as they already had other *stupid* humans.

Fateh was a mystery to be solved and Tabor was ashamed that he hadn't taken the time to solve that mystery before the scáthach came. This time, he'd stick around to figure it out and save at least one human in the bargain. He wasn't the only one interested in Fateh. The other scáthach were keeping a hungry gaze on him as if he were a meal they were waiting to consume. They only did that to people with power; it didn't matter if they were human or fae. There was something about Fateh that he needed to figure out before it was too late.

21

Chapter Four

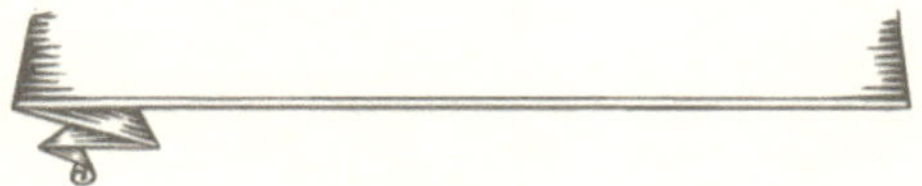

It was later in the day when Fateh finished up in town and went to Meira and Tobias's house. They were his oldest friends and Fateh and his mom often stayed with them when they came into town. He wanted to invite them to dinner tonight and so he was explaining what happened in town with Tabor and the other Shadows. He was proud of his bargaining and standing his ground. It didn't go quite as planned.

"Why did you go and talk to them, Fateh?" Meira leaned close to him, expression defiant, almost hostile. "That's just ... baffling." She made a face, handing him a hot cup of tea as she talked. "I mean—I don't know anyone who's actually gone to a restaurant. No one's brave—or stupid—enough to do that." She pushed straight blonde hair out of her eyes, her fair skin flushed with anger. She and Tobias were twins and he shared her coloring, but he wasn't worked up like she was. Fateh was a study in contrast, with his tanned skin and dark curly hair.

Fateh shrugged, feeling uncomfortable. He wished he hadn't told her about his little adventure with the Shadows. "We don't come into town that often, and I wanted to do something nice for my mom," he muttered, staring at the drink cradled in his hands. "She deserves to have something nice and they ... Well, I made sure I went to the one place that had humans on staff. They can't hurt us since I bargained." If he told himself that it was just about dinner, then it would be okay. He clenched his jaw and shuddered as he remembered the lightning-filled shadow. "If you've got something to offer them, they'll listen." The taste of jasmine filled his mouth as he took a quick swallow of tea.

Meira sat up, exchanging a look with Tobias. "So, you bargained for our safety to come along with you?"

Fateh couldn't read the look, but something about it made him slightly uneasy. He didn't question it, though. "Of course I did. I couldn't leave my best friends out of dinner."

"That's really outstanding of you, Fateh." She kissed his cheek. She had been his friend since they were young and she was the only one that he would let get away with such affection. "Even if you did invite us to dinner with a bunch of soul-sucking leeches, you did it to be nice."

Fateh made a face. "Gee, hold back the appreciation, would you? They won't harm us. They did that stupid spell thing that showed us that if break broke their own rules, they'll be the ones that get harmed from it." He grinned. "It seems the crap that was in those 'myths and legends' books was true. Don't do this, don't do that ... and they're bound by their word, even if they don't really have any honor."

"At least we can count on something as obvious as *fairy tales* to guide us." She rolled her eyes. "Still, it's difficult, Fateh. I can hardly stand to be around them when they fade in and out so much. You can't tell what they're thinking at all."

"It's not that hard to make nice with them on a regular basis, guys." Fateh snorted and crossed his arms over his chest, filling his voice with bravado. He wanted to seem like it wasn't a big deal. "You just have to remember what they said at the beginning and bribe the bastards. They love half of the crap that we invented if they can get it to work for them." He was quiet for a moment. "But they love us without our little protections." He had bargained away his salt, but he had a bit of metal on him he really didn't want to use unless it was a last resort. There was being safe and there was exposing all his tricks at once. The Shadows hated metal almost as much as they did salt. Salt would repel, but metal would *burn*. It was one of Fateh's most treasured possessions and a gift from his grandparents. They had seen the need to have metal on hand.

"If you can get near enough to them without them trying to fry you or choke you or whatever," Tobias muttered from a prone position, one hand over his eyes, "then sure, you can bargain all you want. Meira's not all that bad at bargaining. I let her do it when we need to shop." He grinned suddenly. "At least there are a bunch of stores still open—and a good thing, too. I think your clothing is trying to unravel itself at this point."

"Whatever." Fateh snorted, waving that away. "It still works. It covers me and I really don't care. As long as the fees haven't changed, I've got a mess of Broadway musical crap that we had in the barn."

"You'll need to shop at some point." Meira looked over at him. "You're here and you've got the time." She smiled at Fateh, tugging self-consciously on a strand of pale blond hair. "I know of one that's really interested in old records and stuff..."

Fateh noticed that while she hated the Shadows and talked so badly about them, she was just like everyone else when it came to finding something to bribe them with. It was survival behavior, no matter how degrading they were made to feel. Still, instead of him hunting for a Shadow to deal with, she could take him right to one.

"Thanks," he murmured. "I'd rather not go into that crowded mess of overpriced merchandise, but even my mom scowls over my clothing now."

"You're so weird, Fateh." Meira ruffled his hair, smiling at him. "But we like you anyway. And look—" Her grin stretched wider than before as she handed him and Tobias a hand-held video game. The screen was tiny and the controls stuck, but it was something fun. "We can play for a little while. Just like old times, right?

Fateh smiled, forgetting about the encounter earlier that afternoon, and brushed the edges of molded plastic as the tinny video game opening started. It was just like old times—if only for a short while.

"So, Fateh—you want to head over to the mall now?" Meira peered over a pile of boxes at him. "I heard that besides clothing without rips and tears, they sell books as well." She grinned. "We have time to kill before dinner, after all."

Seeing humans in a restaurant was exciting because humans rarely bargained well enough to go to the places they once frequented. It was a hefty cost these days to go to a restaurant; you were bargaining with more than just salt. You were bargaining with your life. It was a little extravagant to go to a restaurant for dinner when they could have just eaten at Meira and Tobias's place, but he knew it would mean the world to his mother.

Fateh blinked, looking outside. Dinner would not be for a long time, that was certain. "Sure." He shrugged. "Why not?"

"Good." She nodded at him as she knelt down, tossing a few socks, a battered-looking unicorn, and her old school uniform aside before pulling out a crumbling box that held her collection of CDs. Bands that had long ago vanished into obscurity, disks that wouldn't play on the amount of power they had available to them. "Here." She tossed him her school bag. "Start filling that up. We'll go with these. We can at least bargain to get you some new shoes. Not everyone likes records and you may want to save those for clothing, too." She wrinkled her nose. "Really, Fateh—why haven't your shoes crumbled yet? They're a disgrace."

"You and my mom." He made a face at the dig against his shoes. "They still work," he protested, but he did as she said. She flipped over the cases of the CDs, looking at what was inside. He wondered if they'd ever be able to listen to music like this again.

"For now," she snorted. "But one more trip back to your house and they'll turn to dust. Shoes aren't that expensive."

He hauled his own knapsack over his shoulders, grimacing as the records he had brought dug into his back.

"Guess you're right." At least someone who would appreciate the varied sounds of Broadway could play the music they could not enjoy. Getting something to read out of it, even if it was old, was something nice to have as well. *It doesn't hurt to have something for yourself,* he thought absently. The shoes would be something to appease his mother.

"Of course she's right," Tobias snorted as he came back into the room. "I learned that before she started talking." He and Fateh shared a grin as Meira faked a punch at him. "Are we ready, then?"

"Yeah—we've got enough to at least get something decent." Meira tossed a bag identical to hers at Tobias. "You're not having sex to get inside the mall," she lectured. "God knows what you'd bring back with you."

"That sounds like bad sci-fi," Tobias protested, trailing after Meira, bag hanging limply from his fingers.

Fateh snorted, feet thumping dully on the metal of the stairwell as they left the apartment. He blinked and shaded his eyes in the bright sunlight. "We won't have our hero in a bad suit and trainers to come save us from this invasion."

"I'm still waiting for that one." Meira grinned. "Of course, I wouldn't want to deal with the rest of the mess that usually comes with that storyline ..."

"Depends on the episode," Tobias and Fateh said in unison.

Meira rolled her eyes, jumping over a gap in the sidewalk that led towards the mall.

"Boys," she huffed. "It still would be a mess no matter what." Her tone changed, becoming more wistful. "And it's still fiction. No one will save us." Her tone changed a moment later, expression turning determined. "And that's why we need to fight."

Fateh gave a worried look around at her words, worried that someone would overhear and report them or a Shadow would hear and come after them. He reflexively looked down at their own shadows a moment later, relieved that it was only theirs that the bright sunlight showed, and not one of the enemy.

He stayed behind until they came to the low, sprawling building of the mall, their eyebrows rising at the creature that guarded the gates. She was as ... blue and well-endowed as Tobias had mentioned. She was also completely naked. *Doesn't she get cold?* Fatah thought idly, watching her cautiously as the three of them approached the gate together.

"So, little humans want to come in?" she murmured, slinking around. Her skin gleamed iridescent colors in the sunlight; she was more snake-like than human as she circled Tobias, sliding a hand down his face. "What sort of offerings do you have for Luchi?" A forked tongue flickered out, tasting Tobias's skin. Fateh shuddered, but Tobias didn't seem too bothered.

Luchi was not a Shadow, but she was one of the fae and was not to be trusted. He didn't know what kind of fae she was. It didn't matter if she was smoke and wind or a snake; the fae were their enemy. It was unusual to see a fae that wasn't a Shadow in this town, though. Tabor was one of them as well, but he hung out with the Shadows so much that Fateh forgot that he wasn't one.

"Not that type of payment." Meira shoved her brother away from the creature, grabbing Tobias's bag and waving it in Luchi's face. "We have other stuff to offer." CDs spilled out of the bag to land at Luchi's feet. "See?"

"Mm ... you bring delicious currency—but a shame, though. The young ones are so tender ..." She actually looked disappointed as Tobias stumbled back into Fateh. "But I will allow this for the three of you. Just realize—" She reached out to stroke Fateh's face as he edged past her. "You can get so much more if you want to play."

"Uh ..." Fateh tripped over his own feet in his haste to get away from her. Her face turned down, lips pouting, but he wasn't having any of it. Hopefully, they'd find another exit out of here. He took one last glance back before the glass doors slid open—Luchi had cornered another visitor; this one seemed all too happy to be dragged into the small booth next to the entrance. He shuddered and followed Tobias and Meira in. They knew how to navigate the changed interior and they knew the rules.

Meira turned towards him. The Shadows were operating the stores, and now that they were in the mall, they were just customers. They'd passed the hard part of the trip. "Well, it won't take us very long," she said as she gestured widely. Most of the stores were gated, the contents stripped. "It's not like we have a lot to choose from."

Fateh was grateful for the almost-echoing corridors. Too many people gave him a headache. "Not like we need to spend hours in the mall," he said, rolling his eyes. He still wanted his books. His mother would never forgive him if he didn't buy new shoes and clothes, but it wasn't something that would take a lot of time. He wanted to be home, where he knew the garden variety of annoying Shadow. He had his own methods for dealing with those. The ones that looked vaguely human didn't bother him quite as much.

Tobias was snickering and he bolted down the line of shops. Meira gave chase. Fateh sighed and followed them more slowly. Meira had most of the bargaining items and knew the amount to give and how to present it. *I hated shopping when we used money*, he thought crossly.

Fateh grabbed a hold of Tobias's hood before he could run any further. "Stop chasing and let's shop." Meira's breath came in little pants as she gave Fateh a playful shove.

"Now look at who's all serious and not wanting to have fun." She was clearly in her element here. "Come on, Fateh—lighten up. The only Shadows are running the shops and we're protected here. They won't harm us and we can buy stuff."

"Oh, joy," he deadpanned. "My thrill in life."

"Spoilsport," she huffed. "Come on." She grabbed his arm, dragging him into the nearest store, ignoring the stares and giggles of some of the other shoppers. More people were relaxed here—that was almost astounding in a place run and guarded by Shadows.

It was more bare than he remembered the store being. The shelves and racks were half-empty, but he could at least find a pair of shoes, satisfy Meira's nagging, and then vanish for a couple of hours while she ran through the full line of what all the other stores had to offer. *Girls,* he thought in disgust. *Why can't we just get what we need instead of trying on every last thing around?*

He headed straight for the shoes, picking a pair up, flipping them over to check the size, and then handing them to Meira. "I'm done," he said shortly. "Can we leave now?"

"Fateh." She made a face. "No, we're not done yet. We still have to get you something else to wear and I need something nice if we're going out to eat tonight." She stuck her lower lip out, grabbing his hands. "You can't have me looking like I can't get anything, right?"

"It's not like this place has the latest fashions," Fateh snorted. She lost the pout and smacked him again. "Ow, hey—jeez, sorry. Go find something frilly and girly then. I'm going to buy the stupid shoes and then find a bookstore to hide in for a while."

Meira really was the type to be into ribbons and lace and curl her hair. It was a shame that she couldn't get the outfits that were in her years-old magazines. She'd had a few of the outfits when she was younger. They were all fluffed-out skirts with cute patterns on them and shiny shoes. She had long outgrown such outfits and the stores didn't stock that variety of clothing. At least, not anymore.

"You really aren't any fun," Meira muttered, stomping away from him. "Come on, Tobias."

Fateh sighed and went up to the counter. He'd lost his bargaining tool; Meira didn't look willing to help him at the moment. "So." His voice was dry and he ignored the smirk on the cashier's face as he put the shoes on the counter. "What will you trade me?"

He dumped out the records, smiling inwardly at the look of glee on the clerk's face as her fingers streaked over the plastic, music pouring into the air from them. *That* was a little creepy, but if she took the music, who was he to complain about it? He tried to ignore the falsetto of the 'hero,' keeping a polite look on his face. "I think one record will do it since it pleases you so much."

The clerk knew when she had lost her advantage and huffed, sliding the shoes across and taking the proffered record. At least he was able to do something and get something out of it. The music followed Fateh out of the store.

He could catch up with Meira and Tobias later; it wasn't like they'd leave without him and if they did, he knew where they lived. He didn't want to be dragged from store to store; he wanted to spend time with his friends, joking like before. Shopping gave him a headache.

Fateh barely glanced at the wisp of Shadow that guarded the counter of the bookstore. He relaxed a little at the sight of it. This was the type of Shadow that he was used to.

The bookstore was stripped of most of what it had carried. He wondered how the authors felt about not having their work sold. *Well, you don't know that. They can still print stuff, but not mass-produced like before. Maybe somewhere, it's finished.* For all he knew, it was completely normal outside this town. They had just been swallowed up by the Shadows like some magical black hole.

This was one of the places he felt at peace and he lost himself in the smell of paper and glue and ink. His fingers brushed over familiar titles he had read before. It didn't take him long to take a few books from the shelf. It was like a thrift store; if he didn't take them now, they might not be there the next time.

It would take more to buy the precious few books; it would be obvious what he wanted and the bargaining would be harder. *At least there'll be less stuff to cart around, and less Broadway to clutter up the barn.*

This Shadow didn't speak, just held out one hand for the purchases and the other for the payment. Fateh silently thanked his grandparents for the special edition Broadway books—glossy photos in hardbound books that detailed the lives of the actors in that particular show, the history of the musical, the scores—anything that a musical-loving nut could wish for.

Still, it took three books and a record for him to get what *he* wanted and he was never so grateful to leave a bookstore in his life.

"There you are!" Meira smiled as he came out of the store, apparently having forgiven him. "I knew you'd still be around the books."

"Like I said I'd be." Fateh raised his eyebrows. "Did you think I'd run off to shop for anything else?"

"No, and it's a good thing." She hugged him around the shoulders, pretending not to notice him tensing. "Because you need my expert opinion to get you something else to wear tonight."

"Meira ..." he protested. "I don't ..." He wanted to protest the clothing, but if he was going to be around creatures that looked down on them so much, it probably wouldn't hurt to have something decent to wear. "Alright, fine," he said, giving in.

He was rewarded with her smile as she dragged him along, Tobias trailing this time. He still needed to get his mother a dress, after all. It wouldn't do for her to be left out of all the shopping. He would use Meira's advice in getting the right thing, but he wanted to ultimately be the one who chose.

———

He placed most of what he bought into his bag but carried the shoes. It wasn't like there were plastic bags on hand and while he was certain there used to be tons of them lying around, the Shadows seemed to have found some way to dispose of them. *Better on them.* He shifted his shoes to the crook of his arm. *We've been trying for decades and haven't been able to break away.* It wasn't like there hadn't been such a thing as reusable bags, but plastic bags had always been a staple.

Meira was practically skipping, hugging her outfit to her. Fateh didn't see what was so special about it, but then again, he wasn't a girl and didn't see why a shred of fabric was all that great to have, either. As long as it wasn't falling apart or accidentally indecent, then what was the point of buying so much new crap? And for a dinner that you didn't even want to go to in the first place?

"Who are you trying to impress with that?" He winced; he couldn't believe he actually asked that out loud. She was going to beat him with her pointy shoes eventually.

"Jeez, Fateh—you're really thick sometimes," she huffed. There were less people on the street now, and the sky was starting to creep towards the pink and gold streaks of sunset. Fateh watched for a moment, eyes following the shifting of the clouds, stretching out and blending a multitude of colors together.

"Come on, Fateh—" Tobias grabbed his shoulder, jerking him out of his observations. "We shouldn't linger outside. Tonight'll be bad enough when we go to the restaurant. I don't want to push our luck too much." He grinned. "Besides, Meira will throw a fit if she can't make herself all done up."

"Girls," Fateh snickered, punching Tobias in the shoulder as he raced ahead of the twins, letting the shoes dangle by their laces. He heard an outraged shout and then the others sped after him. He was about to put on an extra burst of speed when he tripped, elbow landing painfully on gravel. There were no Shadows around to observe the mishap, something Fateh was grateful for. Sometimes the Shadows could be weird about blood, as if some of them were vampiric in nature.

Meira giggled as she ran up to him, toeing his shoes with her foot. "Told you those shoes would fall apart on you completely one of these days. You should have just dumped them in the trash and worn your new ones. I don't think there's anything but the laces left."

Fateh grimaced and tugged off what remained of his shoes. "Guess this is as good of a time as any to try out the new ones, then," he huffed. He rubbed at his elbow briefly. "You were right, I was wrong. What can I do to make it up to you?"

"I'll think of something." She practically leered at him. "Just you wait."

"Yeah—I'll do that." He grinned, shoving his feet into the new shoes, dumping the old ones into a nearby trash can, and walking the rest of the way to Meira and Tobias's apartment, where his mother was waiting.

"Do you think your mom will like the dress?" Meira asked softly, leading the way up the narrow metal stairs to their apartment. "I mean, it's not really fair that the rest of us got *something* and your mom stayed behind." She stroked the light-colored fabric of the dress, expression uncertain.

"Yeah—that you thought of her, that's really important." Fateh smiled and gave her an awkward hug around her shoulders. He tapped on the door before letting himself in. "Mom?" he called out. He could feel himself relax when she came into the room. He wouldn't admit it out loud, but every time he left her behind, he worried about her, just as much she worried about him.

"We've got presents!" Meira sang out, pushing past him and holding out the dress, the folds of the skirt swinging out. "Now we can *all* get dressed up." She giggled. "Even Fateh is dressing up." She snorted. "For him."

"I got new shoes and Meira bought me some clothing." His voice was low as he shoved his hands in his pockets. "Let's all get ready, then, right?" He couldn't help the smile on his face as his mother took the dress, stroking it and holding it up to herself. He was glad he had sacrificed the live recording of his favorite band and his grandparents' high school yearbook to get the dress for his mother. Meira had done the bargaining, but Fateh had paid the price. Memories were important, but ... "Happy Birthday, Mom."

Her answering smile was enough for him.

Chapter Five

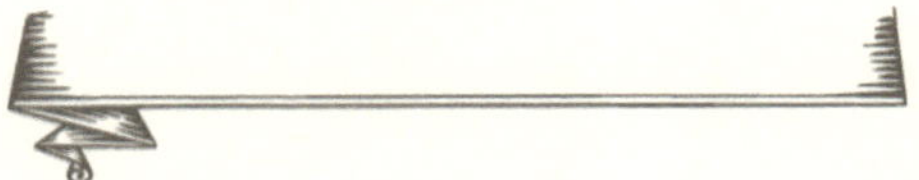

Without any operating streetlights, it was dark as they made their way to the restaurant. "You look just fine," he replied to Meira's fussing. "I don't know why you're so concerned, anyway—you said that you didn't even like them." Meira was looking more like her old self again and she seemed to gain a lot of confidence from that. It may have been the new outfit, but Fateh didn't press. He was just glad that she wasn't angry with him anymore.

"Dense, Fateh—you are so dense." She flushed and looked down. "I still want to look nice. Like I said, like old times. We can pretend that things are normal, right?" She gave him a pleading look, begging him quietly not to mess this up or state the obvious. The ragged skirt was half lace and so were the leggings she'd bought. They were new, but they looked used and worn out and Fateh wondered *why*. The thick stitching of bright blue against the black looked intentional, but it emulated his own home-sewn fix-ups.

"Man, it's chilly out here," she murmured. She rubbed at her hands as if that would fix the problem of her outfit—which Fateh personally thought was stupid for someone who got cold so easily. He rubbed her arms quickly, trying to warm her up a little. She always said that he had warm hands and if it would distract her and stop her shivering—he wasn't that much of an idiot and knew that she was still worried, no matter how she talked.

"Let's go up," he murmured as he pulled away, ignoring the hopeful look she gave him.

He wasn't as dressed up as Meira or his mother, but Meira lived to dress up and it was nice for his mother to wear something other than dirt-covered overalls. At least the jeans he wore were new and so was the shirt. The dress his mother wore complimented her eyes, and he grinned a little at how pleased she seemed with it. She still liked nice things, it seemed, and he couldn't wait to tease her about it. Later, though—not when she looked so happy.

Businesses that would have been lit up a few years ago were dim now, but houses still displayed yellow squares of light that spilled onto the street. Fateh caught a glimpse of a pale face pressed against the glass before it was snatched away by an unseen presence.

"It's so ... different." He grimaced. "Does seriously no one walk around at night anymore? Nothing's running at all?" They were some of the town's few humans out on the street, but the majority of creatures were the Shadows and he could barely tell them apart from the shadows on the street. They blended in so well that only hints of them were visible.

"Ah!" Meira smacked into him. His breath hitched in his throat as she momentarily stunned him. He blinked and squinted to see what scared her and he kicked away the hissing creature that was still trying to wrap itself around her ankles.

"Jeez, we can't even go walking to eat without being attacked," Fateh complained. "You can eat what you want if you bargain for it, but you have to make it there alive first." It was no wonder that not a lot of people were out at night—not if this was the type of creature that was common.

Meira was obviously freaked out about seeing the small Shadow. With glowing lambent blue eyes, it was small and inky black. It reminded Fateh of the small Shadows that hung around the woods near his house.

Meira's hands dug into his arm for a moment longer, her pulse still pounding against his skin. "Thanks, Fateh." She pulled away as they walked into mellow light spilling from the windows of the restaurant. "Guess we get our reward now. We made it safely. What exactly did you give up for us to have this night?"

"Just gave up some of our protection," Fateh murmured. "Strange how far a bag of salt will go ..." He made a face as he took his mother's arm. They walked up the stairs together. The sound of their shoes against the wooden boards echoed loudly and soon they were attracting all sorts of attention, including faces that were decidedly more predatory than that of the person in the window before. His chest hurt as he looked around, unsure of what they would do next.

The Shadows did not precisely run the restaurant Fateh chose, but the Shadows were the ones that allowed it *to* run. They also used it a great deal, and they said that half the staff was shadow-held. There was a heavy price to pay for being so determined to keep 'what was yours' and the Shadows didn't really negotiate when it came to deals like those.

It had been his mother's favorite place to eat before the Shadows came, which was the main reason why Fateh had made the bargain he did. Hopefully, there would be no Shadows here that night; it wasn't every night they came, after all. He hoped they could enjoy a normal meal together. Even though Fateh saw no point in it, he would play pretend and act like everything was normal. Maybe his mother would lose some of her worry and strain. Even just for a little while.

So, it was a nasty shock when he saw Tabor moments after they entered, leaning against a battered and slightly singed host stand.

"Ah—look who is here. I almost expected that you wouldn't show." He stepped forward, each moment deliberate, and his accent was more pronounced as if he were showing off for more than just Fateh tonight. "You don't look too pleased to see me, though—and after our lovely interlude today." He shook his head. "I would say I'm heartbroken, but it's rather rude to lie to ladies." He gave a mocking bow to Meira and Fateh's mother. "I am here to make sure that your safety is assured."

"We didn't ask for ..." Meira began, eyes narrowed. "Fateh didn't say anything about getting a Shadow to ensure our safety." She grew uncertain, looking at Fateh.

"Fateh bargained for protection and since I know him oh-so-well, I volunteered to make sure that none of the rules would be broken." He bowed in Meira's direction, a mocking smile on his lips. "I'm sure Fateh has told you all about me, even if it was just to complain. My name is Tabor." He looked rather unconcerned about the whole matter. "Besides, most of those who were here when you made the bargain are off ... amusing themselves." His expression turned dark for a moment and for a second, Fateh saw Tabor as the dangerous creature he was. "So, I'm here to assure you that no harm will befall you with those that remain."

Meira practically scrambled away from Tabor and Tobias frowned at Fateh for being on a first-name basis with a Shadow. "We didn't know." Fateh's mother drew her son closer to her. "I just thought the salt was enough." She looked down at Fateh as if asking '*What have you gotten into now*?' but didn't voice that thought.

"There had to be someone held accountable," Tabor said dryly. "I'm a good choice for it. You trusted that you could just waltz in here without someone to watch over you? Accidents happen, after all. I'm here to make sure even a minor occurrence doesn't occur."

"Sounds logical." Fateh gave Tabor a distrustful look. "Even if it does say something about the people I made a deal with."

Meira was fidgeting again and Tobias stayed close to her side, his expression wary.

"Well, let's go back to your table," Tabor said brightly. He hung back next to Fateh, pulling him back a bit to whisper in his ear. "Accidents," he murmured, "can go both ways."

Fateh frowned at him, keeping his voice to a whisper. "You think that *we'll* be causing trouble? We just want to eat and get on with our night."

"I'm sure *you* have the best of intentions," was all that Tabor replied before he led them to a small table, smirking faintly. "For now, I'll leave you to discuss your dinner plans, but I won't be far off." He dropped off the menus. It was surreal, seeing him act like someone normal as if he had been Fateh's friend all along and had never come out as one of the enemy. "Be good, children," he said and with a small wave, he was off into the depths of the restaurant.

The mood immediately lightened and everyone was more relaxed about what they said without Tabor hovering over them. "I didn't realize we'd have a watcher." Fateh tried to apologize. "The fact never came up during the negotiations. I guess it's better in a way, though." He stared down at the menu instead of his friends. "I was wondering how they'd work out the 'no humans on the menu' deal. I wouldn't just take their word for it."

"Lucky for us to have a babysitter." Meira looked annoyed. "Watching us, reporting back our words—it's like eating in jail."

"Hush, Meira. He's all the way over there and he's just here to protect us. Think of it as having a bodyguard." His mother was obviously trying to look at the whole situation from the best angle. "We don't have to pay for dinner and we're protected like no one else is." It was obvious where he got his balanced points of view from, even if his mother always put a more positive spin on the matter than he ever did.

Meira switched to another tactic. "How do you know that Shadow, Fateh? He seemed really friendly to you. Didn't look down on you as much as he did the rest of us. Even called you by name."

"You haven't been around me when he latches onto me, either," Fateh mumbled, putting down the menu, shedding the pretense of reading it, not eager to talk about this part. "And ... I knew him a few years ago, right before the Shadows came. He pretended to be a human; you see how he blends in. His little game was given away when the other Shadows addressed him by name and were ..." Fateh paused; they hadn't been exactly *friendly.* "They knew him, that's all."

Tabor still didn't look like the other Shadows. It wasn't the first time Fateh wondered just what Tabor was. It made him more dangerous, not being able to categorize him like the rest of the Shadows. It was like the fae that guarded the shopping area. She wasn't a Shadow either. It was easier just thinking of them all lumped together as one singular threat.

"Still," Meira tried. "Now that you know, you shouldn't encourage his presence." She placed her napkin in her lap and seemed determined now to enjoy her meal, enemies be damned. They were eating in a nice restaurant and Meira wasn't going to let one Shadow ruin her night. Not when Fateh had sacrificed so much for it. She raised her glass, listening to the comforting and now unfamiliar sound of ice clinking in it. "Let's just forget about it."

"Sis, do you really want to see what happens when Fateh tells that creepy Shadow no?" Tobias shuddered. "He might set Fateh on fire or something. I've seen what that one can do and no one tells them to go away." Tobias's expression was more serious than before. "Let it go, okay? Fateh just tries to get by like all of us. He's not the only one the Shadows take an interest in."

"I *was* letting it go," Meira muttered. "Come on, let's just enjoy our meal." She smiled winningly at Fateh's mother. "After all, it is a special occasion."

Fateh didn't tell them he had told Tabor to go away before and in much ruder terms, too. He had since the start of it all. Fateh held onto the theory that the Shadows had a perverse sense of humor. He couldn't fathom why Tabor was still around. After all, the fae had played his little trick and that should have been the end of it.

"Well, what if we stood up for ourselves? You know, fought back?" Tobias didn't seem to want to let this go. "There's gotta be a way. There was always a way in the stories, like a trick or someone that is trained to fight the monsters." His chin stuck out, mulish.

"Like the priests and warriors of old?" No one had heard Tabor come up and everyone jumped at the statement. "Sweetheart, faith has faded since we first wandered freely here and your weapons—well, most of them have been taken care of." He didn't elaborate on how or why; he simply looked smug. "But feel free to look so indignant and fierce. It's always so amusing to have some people act as if they have spines left. You are right about that. It's those with a bit of *spark* to them that interest us the most."

"We don't need your approval," Meira snapped, but her voice wasn't as strong now that they had Tabor next to them. She could be outspoken when the Shadows weren't around.

"Again, so amusing." Tabor laughed. "You're lucky you have me, little spitfire. The others that I work ... *with* ... wouldn't take your words as jokes." His expression warned her against saying anything to the contrary, and the warning was enough to silence even Meira.

When he was certain of their attention, Tabor smiled broadly. "Now, as I won't be dining with you, let me explain some rules. You do notice you are not the only humans here tonight, yes?" He barely waited for affirmation before continuing. His expression was deadly serious. "Do not interfere with anyone, no matter what you may see. Some are not as good of bargainers as Fateh here. This includes the staff. Your protection ends if you compromise your safety for others."

"So, you mean to say that if someone is getting hurt, even if it's right next to us, we simply ignore them?" Meira's voice came out in a shocked squeak. "You want us to be like you? Be a monster?"

Fateh kicked her from under the table, trying to get her to shut up. He didn't want to be in the middle of enemy territory without any protection and didn't know how far Tabor would let the back-talk go from someone who didn't amuse him as Fateh did. He tried to cover it up.

"It's like in the streets, Meira. You said that you don't interfere if someone's being hurt in town; you never want their eye to turn to you next." It almost hurt to say that and to see the betrayed look in her eyes when he turned her words against her.

It was apparently the correct thing to say as Tabor just patted him on the head as if he were a puppy that did a good training session for once. "Good." He smiled. "You understand that you accepted this when you walked in here. If you forget, I'll be forced to stop you to protect you." The heat coming off of him seemed to increase. "I'll leave it to your vivid imagination how that will end up." Tabor gave another mocking bow. "Your actual server will be over shortly," he murmured. "Remember—*no rescuing.*"

Fateh didn't even get to respond when Tabor left with a little wave. They weren't sure what to say or do anymore. It was obvious that Tabor could sneak up on them easily, with hardly a thought.

Meira was looking uncomfortable again, staring down at her plate as if it had all the answers. "I wish we didn't have a human server," she whispered. "It can't be good if they're working here. I mean, yeah—it's a job and stuff, but ..." She grimaced. "It doesn't seem like the best environment." She meant the lingering Shadows; there had been a lot more during the day than there were now, but there were still enough around to make anyone uncomfortable.

What do Shadows even eat? Fateh wondered idly. *They don't seem solid enough for actual food ... Of course, their intangibility could be an illusion.*

Fateh didn't really think that working at the place could be too bad; it was a job like most others. "Like you said, people still have to work—and this doesn't seem all that bad." Even with Tabor's warning about no rescuing, there wasn't an overabundance of humans here. There *were* other fae, not Shadows. He snorted. "You'd rather have one of the Shadows bowing over you and handing you who-knows-what on a plate?"

"It's not like they hired them off the street and they have a normal job." Meira huffed. "Remember how we talked about the Shadow-held?" Meira fiddled with her fork. "You'll see what they're like firsthand." She scowled at her plate. "You can't trust them." She sighed. "Even the ones that seem like victims report everything back to the Shadows. They practically *are* Shadows." Her expression was distant as she continued. "It wasn't their own choice at first." She was willing to concede that much at least. "But eventually, they're willing victims."

He remembered something vaguely about those unfortunate enough to get caught on the wrong side of a Shadow's displeasure, and he wasn't sure he wanted to see, but Tobias and Meira grew quiet after that statement. All of them jumped when the waitress came over. She looked human, but there was something about her that twisted Fateh's insides. It was something about the smile, it was too insincere. He trusted *Tabor* more.

"What would you like?" There was no expression in her voice and it was completely at odds with that smile and the odd look in her eyes. "We have so many specials tonight for people lucky enough to get to our restaurant."

He stared at her in shock as memory kicked in; he knew this girl. He had gone to school with her, she had been in his class. Seeing someone he knew so broken inside made him hurt and he snuck a look at Meira. She had been friends with the waitress. Her name was Amanda.

Meira wasn't looking at her or any of them, focusing just on the menu. Only Fateh saw how she was clenching her fist against her thigh, trying to keep her emotions in check.

"Fried chicken." She choked out the words. It was sad, Fateh realized. It was hard to see Amanda in the girl now, but it was hard to be so complacent at either her bad luck or willing servitude, too. Meira nudged Tobias who held up two fingers. Was this going to happen to all of them eventually? Was that what the Shadows wanted to make them into?

"Um, the burger and fries?" Fateh said, looking to his mother, but here at least, she seemed as confused as he was. The waitress nodded, then took his mother's order as well. She got the fanciest thing on the menu; steak and lobster. Amanda stepped away after getting everyone's order, moving to the kitchen. Loud laughter echoed as she slipped into the kitchen, steam rolling out, clouding the air for a moment.

"Sooo ..." His mother fiddled with her silverware, brows raised. "No greetings to your old friend, no conversation, and is it just me or did she look a bit ... off?"

Meira swallowed hard. "That's no longer Amanda. She's one of them, practically. Listen how she was laughing with them!" She looked sick, cheeks pale, as she continued. "That's no longer my friend and none of the Shadow-taken are the people we knew. I hate them!" she spat out, roughly wiping the tears from her eyes.

Tobias rolled his eyes. "What she's saying is that they have no souls because they sold them. They're traitors because they gave in instead of giving up. That's what the Shadow-held are." He shifted uncomfortably, meeting Fateh's eyes for a moment before looking away. "It's not all of them, but some people think that the Shadows are cool or they think they can overcome them and make deals. Some deals don't go all that well and things ... break." He gestured. "Like Amanda. Dealing with them changes your soul and she's almost like one of them now." He grimaced. "When she dies, she'll turn into them. I've seen it before."

"You know the stories, Fateh." Meira's voice was sharp with impatience. "This is just the nastier side of it—they don't take the whole body, just the part that matters, and the part that gives them life. She's a result of what happens when you think the Shadows are trustworthy. Amanda's father sold out the family first." Her voice went flat.

"And history repeats itself," Tabor said with a yawn. All at the table jumped at the sound of his voice; again no one had realized he was there until he started talking. He shifted plates from his hand to the appropriate person. "One group covets what another has and they take over and shift things. In this case, dear child, we were here far before you and went on a small vacation. Just look at what happens when you let the pets out when the owner goes for a walk." He looked amused at their reddening faces.

"We aren't pets," Fateh snapped, glaring at his burger. "At least we're not the type of assholes to take someone's soul and change them so that they're more acceptable."

Tabor laughed and ruffled Fateh's hair, which Fateh winced away from. "You keep on telling yourself that. It's not the only thing that's out there, and one day you might see that it's not all that bad to be a pet sometimes. Better to be a pet and safe than a wild animal and hunted." He was more bitter than amused at the situation.

"Let's just eat and get out of here." Fateh's words were rushed. He didn't want to owe Tabor for his so-called protection.

"Well, you have fun, kids." Tabor snickered as everyone nodded quickly, distrust on their faces. "Hate to have you thanking me for anything." The warning was clear, even as he looked amused. "Stay safe, little pets."

Chapter Six

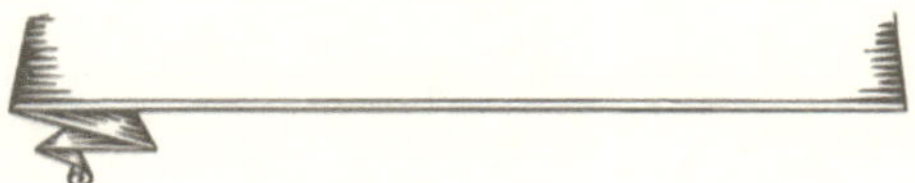

Dinner was better after Tabor left, although Fateh couldn't help but keep an eye out for him. It was impossible not to look at the other diners, as exotic as they were. Fateh wondered why the 'no rescuing' rule was in place for such an obvious assortment of fae, but when Fateh looked closer, he noticed the Shadows menacing what was supposed to be their 'kin.'

"So, how are you enjoying dinner?" he asked his mom, sipping his drink and speaking as casually as possible. As long as one ignored the background, it was possible to pretend that this was an ordinary night where they went into town and treated themselves.

"The scenery is lovely," she said dryly, eyes flicking around the room. "Next time, let's eat at your friend's house, hm?" she asked. "Your mother doesn't need a fancy meal to feel loved by her son."

"Yes, but we're enjoying the fancy meal." Meira grinned. "Real steak and potatoes and fresh vegetables?" she asked. "Yes, please. Let there just be dessert and I'll be in heaven." She tapped her glass. "And an actual cold drink! I think I've died and gone to heaven."

"Well, as long as *you're* enjoying yourself," his mother said with amusement. "I have to admit that it is nice." She smiled at Fateh. "Thank you for treating your mother. It sure beats veggie casserole, right?"

"I *like* meat," he said plaintively. "I'm not going to turn down a good burger when I get one." He hadn't gotten as fancy of a meal as everyone else had, but he had simple tastes. Besides, he had been craving a burger. *Sometimes a burger is better than a steak.*

"And if you lived in town, you'd have better access to it. Unless you plan on butchering the cow that gives you milk." Tobias grinned.

"Perish the thought." Fateh wrinkled his nose. "I like my fresh milk, too."

He took another big bite of his burger and then let his attention wander to some of the conversations around him. There was one other human couple there; they were obviously on a date. They were holding hands and looked like they didn't notice anything in the room but themselves. *It must be nice to have that sort of single-minded focus.*

"Milk or burgers." Tobias continued to tease. "Which is better?"

"Butter and cheese," Fateh said promptly. "You really haven't lived until you've had fresh butter and cheese." It took them ages sometimes, but the payoff was worth it.

"Spoiled." Meira grinned. "Fresh vegetables all the time, fresh cheese and milk—the other thing you're missing is the canned good glory that is our lot in life." She was eating her steak with gusto, hardly slowing down between bites.

"You could live that life too," he pointed out. "We've invited you enough times."

"We're fine with visiting." Meira spoke for her brother as well. "But no way could we live so far away from people. You and your mom can live like hermits all you want; I like having people around me."

"Suit yourself." Fateh grinned. It was nice and normal and it felt comfortable and *fun*. Just as long as they didn't see anything that they couldn't interfere with, things would be just fine.

They finished their meal without any incidents; Fateh was grateful for that. There was a commotion after they left, but in unison, they all ignored it in favor of getting out the door. No one wanted to *see* what was happening; if they didn't see it, it didn't happen.

It was even darker when they left the restaurant; the moon and stars were the only brightness in the sky to light their way. Fateh stopped in the middle of the street, staring up at how beautiful everything was. How long had it been since he had been outside long enough to see the stars again? He was picking out constellations, tracing them with his hands when his mother jerked him out of his gazing.

"Fateh!"

Fateh blinked up at her and the hand on his arm and flushed when he realized everyone was waiting for him; the stares of Meira and Tobias were more than a little shocked and worried. Judging by the shifting, darker Shadows on the ground, pooling near their feet, they were attracting the wrong kind of attention just being outside.

"Let's go, Fateh. You can't. We can't just ... I mean, the town is worse than where you are, you know. Hanging about like this is asking for trouble." Meira was obviously trying to get something through to him.

Fateh was surprised she didn't rip her skirt with the way she was tugging at it.

"Yeah, I'm ... I'm sorry," he murmured, rubbing at the back of his head, resisting the urge to look up again. It had been too long since he'd seen the stars and they were so bright without the trees covering them up. If it wasn't so thickly wooded where he lived, then he might have seen the stars more often. It wasn't like they had a ton of ambient light where they lived.

"It's a bit much to walk home tonight, especially since you bargained away our protection," his mother said. Her teasing grin let him know that it was okay and the tension drained from his shoulders. "It's a good thing we already have a place to stay."

He grinned up at Tobias and Meira. "Just like old times again, right?" he asked. "Thanks for the crash space."

Tobias shrugged, walking faster now that they had Fateh's attention back. "What sort of friends would we be if we didn't take care of you, huh? It's not a problem, Fateh—you'd do the same for us ..."

Now his grin grew wide. "If you didn't live in the middle of nowhere, that is."

"Hey, don't knock it until you've tried it." Fateh laughed. "I like it just fine. Fewer people and ..." He didn't see any less of the Shadows. They wanted more of a target, people who lived out of the main area. "It sucks not being around you guys as often, though." He was looking forward to tonight. Being around Tobias and Meira made him feel normal again, like some of the bad wasn't creeping around the corner.

"I did try it." Meira made a face. "I got that terrible rash from when we decided to build a fort out of poison oak, remember?" She rubbed at her arms as if recalling how badly she had been taken by it. "I wouldn't do that again for the world." She practically ran up the steps to their building, not even looking as she pushed in the key to unlock the door. "You can keep it."

"More space for us, then." Fateh wasted no time in following the others in; the Shadows were darker here, the feel of them sending unpleasant chills down Fateh's spine. Maybe this wouldn't be like old times. The air felt charged with uncertainty.

"Yeah, yeah—" Tobias laughed. "You keep telling yourself that." He fell on the couch heavily, one hand over his eyes. "Man, I'm just glad we're back in our safe little apartment." Uncovering his eyes, he looked over at Fateh. "So, what the hell was going on in that restaurant, Fateh?"

With one arm still caught in the sleeve of his coat, Fateh stopped and stared at Tobias, caught off-guard by the question. "I should be asking that as well. I didn't realize that was what happened to some of our classmates. What are you questioning *me* about?" he asked, expression wary.

"Why haven't you mentioned that Shadow before? And how did you not know he wasn't human when you met him? Why does he still bother you?" Tobias looked more upset.

Fateh sighed. "How the hell should I know why that sadist does what he does?" He snorted and crossed his arms against his chest protectively. "I'd be happy if he never crossed my path again."

"Lay off him, Tobias." Meira rolled her eyes. "You know the Shadows don't need an excuse to screw with us. So, he got Fateh when he was gullible and decided to keep at it." She looked at Fateh. "As for ... that girl," she didn't say Amanda's name out loud, "you're right that she's not the only one. Some are worse off than she is." She scowled at her brother. "At least Fateh is annoyed by it."

"There has to be more of a reason a Shadow went out of his way to help Fateh. That's all I'm saying."

Fateh grimaced, hating that the attention was put on him. "Look, I have no idea why he's sticking around me either, or why he helped out so much. He probably does it to be funny or out of some misguided sense of ... whatever he was playing at when I was a kid." He was looking distinctly unhappy. "Maybe he felt bad because I'm not from here."

"He's not a normal Shadow, Fateh. He looks human enough that most people would be tricked by him. It's no wonder that you were." Meira looked briefly fascinated. "Did he look your age when you first met him or did he look the same as he does now?"

"He looked my age," Fateh said uncomfortably. "Until the day he didn't, and he was hanging around with the Shadows that came." Tabor had been there before the Shadows came. Fateh was about to relay that when a hand landed on his shoulder.

"Children." Fateh's mother stepped between them, eyes focusing on each of them in turn as she stifled a yawn with one hand. "It's late, we're all tired, and I think bed will do us all some good. Stop squabbling like toddlers. That Shadow was just doing what their kind does best—making trouble. Think about that, forget about the rest, and let's just get some sleep."

Fateh flushed, staring at the ground, and Tobias and Meira didn't look any more comfortable than he did. His mother had that type of effect on people.

Tobias coughed and nodded. "Um ... yeah. Sorry, Fateh," he whispered. "I'm just tired, I guess."

Meira nodded as well as she ran a hand through her hair. "Let's get everyone settled."

Fateh listened to the words, but as Meira talked, he couldn't help but watch her and listen to her—and realize the matter was far from settled. The uneasy feeling stayed in his stomach as Meira led him to the spare bedroom to set it up for him and his mother.

"We hardly ever see you anymore, Fateh," Meira whispered, shaking out the blankets for him to use. It was obvious that hardly anyone used the bedroom and the mattress was bare. "It's nice to have people over again and I'm sorry we ruined it all by arguing like we did. Tobias and I get out and stuff, but since everything's changed, we usually stick to our safe spots." She gave him a rueful smile as she dumped the comforter onto the mattress, sitting down on it and smiling down at him. "So, it's kind of stupid to ruin it by acting like five-year-olds, huh?"

Fateh tilted his head questioningly at that, tossing the pillows on the bed and narrowly missing her. "What do you mean by sticking to your safe spots? I mean, it's not like you'll go for a walk out to where we are, but you're in town and surrounded by all our old friends. I mean, I like the woods and all, but it's not like we're surrounded by people. You are."

"Not really," she murmured. "The Shadows don't come into our homes, so most people stay there, except when we have to go out and buy stuff. Even home's kind of a cage," she muttered. "Especially when they say all this stuff about how humans have to be penned up. It's like we're animals to them."

The comforter bunched up under her hands as her voice rose. "They really don't like when we're out all that much. It's disgusting." She punched the pillow hard, denting it almost in half. She looked ready to cry again. "And you saw what happened to our friends. We can't trust anyone anymore. They're turning us against each other, too." "Hey, at least we're alive," he said softly. "Come on—it's okay." He gave her a half-hug, feeling awkward as he tried to comfort her. He was never very good at offering comfort to anyone.

"It's not okay!" She jumped up from her sitting position, striding back and forth. "They came and trod all over us and they're like creepy and some of them are nothing but shadows and they do weird stuff and hurt us." She sniffled, some of the fire going out of her; Fateh couldn't help but notice that with all her brave and angry words, she was really scared.

"Well, humans aren't all that great either." Fateh tried again to comfort her. "We've killed each other for ages and don't act all that nice to each other. We're racist at times and judgmental ..." His voice trailed off as he registered the look that Meira was giving him. "What?"

"You ... that's not ... the point. What is the point is that they're treating us like animals when they're the freaks of nature. We were here and living just fine and now we have to duck our heads and act like we've dropped three levels just because they're here and think that they're better than us?" She had worked herself up, face flushed and lending color to her pale cheeks.

"This isn't a game," Fateh snorted, amused at her references to 'dropping levels.' He was unsure as to why he was defending the Shadows at all, but ... some things he couldn't help but point out. "Look, like my mom pointed out, we're all alive and as long as we don't piss them off, they won't do anything to us. You've got your brother like I've got my mom and maybe ..." He shrugged. "Maybe things will settle down and we'll co-exist or something." He looked out the window, where he could see the Shadows moving through the streets. Some of the more colorful ones stood out like fireworks against the night sky.

Her face was set in an expression of mulish stubbornness that Fateh knew all too well. "I'm never going to live side by side with such ... such ... evil creatures," she spat out, the bravado back. "They ruined all of our lives, Fateh, can't you see? We can't live like them or with them. Who knows if they'll just eat us one day?"

"They could have killed us all at the start," he pointed out gently. "And they didn't. They've let us live in our homes and with our families—that's good, right?" he asked. "We can still work if we want to. Sure, we don't have some of the same stuff that we had before, but come on. We'll get used to it; we'll figure something out."

His smile was half-there and a little shy. "We're adaptable, aren't we? We can overcome anything. Look at how we've survived all these years." He looked away for a moment, biting his lip. A sudden memory of Amanda and her blank expression rose in his mind. She had been such a vivacious girl, popular with everyone. Now she was just a husk.

"But it's not okay, is it?" he asked her. "They infest the woods where I live, they ruined everything that we loved and upended our lives." It was the first time he let himself speak so bitterly and she seemed a little shocked at his words, but he wasn't done. "At first it was like a story; having the fae show up and grant wishes; then the Shadows came and everything became twisted."

She reached out to give his hand a squeeze. "Yeah, it sucks," she commiserated. "I'm glad that you see the truth of the matter, Fateh. I was starting to worry about you for a moment there."

He didn't like the look in her eyes, but he pushed away his unease. He gave her a tentative smile back and shrugged. "Gotta look on the bright side until the dark side kicks you in the ..." he paused. "Teeth."

She wrinkled her nose and smacked at his arm; she knew what he had been about to say. "Thank Fateh," she murmured. "You get some sleep now; we'll talk more in the morning." She exited the room and Fateh was left to wonder just how he had helped her and if it was just admitting that he was scared, too. His mother came in a moment later, wrapping an arm around his shoulders in a half-hug. "Don't worry so much, Fateh," she murmured. "Holding the weight of the world only gives you gray hair."

"I'm just worried as to what's going to happen next, how we're going to handle the next thing that gets tossed at us."

"We all do that, Fateh." She sighed. "You just weren't meant to do it so young." She squeezed his hands. "Let's get some sleep and hopefully it will all look brighter in the morning." Her expression was strained, and he could understand why.

She was a mother who had to watch as her son tried to shoulder burdens he wasn't meant for yet.

"Yeah." He kicked off his shoes, crawled under the covers, and stared at the ceiling, trying to calm himself down enough so that he could sleep. So much had happened today that it was hard to relax his thoughts long enough to get his body to relax as well. "Let's see what the morning brings."

Meira's voice talking to Tobias in the next room woke him up in the morning. No matter how much he knew it was bad manners to eavesdrop, he couldn't help but edge closer to the door and listen in. He was especially interested when he heard his name mentioned. He took a quick glance at his mother, but she was still sleeping, arms flung wide as her mouth opened in a soft snore. He crooked a grin and slipped out of bed, creeping to the door. He pressed his ear to the door, biting his lip as the muffled words came through.

"Fateh doesn't understand." Meira's voice came in the clearest, sharp with anger. "He was defending them." Her words snapped.

Fateh could picture her expression, and she was probably still wearing that hideous nightgown his mother had sewn for her three years ago. Clearly, she had focused more on his defending of the fae than on his worrying about their lives with the Shadows.

"Come on." Tobias's voice was harder to hear, but Fateh strained to hear it anyway, wanting to know the response of the saner half of the twins. "He's always been fair like that. You know—a natural sort of scale, right?"

"It's not like settling disputes on the playground," she snapped. "These are demons, Tobias. I thought he'd work with us and understand it, but he's not from here. He doesn't know what it's like to actually live in town and deal with the monsters all the time. The big monsters aren't out there in the woods, because there isn't anyone to bother except people like Fateh's family."

Fateh frowned; she made it sound like he was diseased or something. So what if he didn't live in the town with the others? If it made him think clearly to live out in the middle of nowhere, then he was fine with that.

"So what, Meira?" Tobias demanded. "We can't drag him into this—he'll get hurt, you know he will. We've already decided that we can risk it. We're our own family." His voice grew softer and Fateh had to strain to hear him again. "He has his mother; it's not fair to drag him into this."

"He needs to be dragged in, to get some sense smacked into him," Meira huffed, but her voice had softened somewhat, losing its sharp edge. "He's human, no matter how he acts or how ... strange he's become. He's not one of them."

Strange? Fateh crossed his arms against his chest, almost losing his balance as he tried to stay pressed against the door. *I'm not strange.* Meira couldn't have noticed all the stuff going on with him lately. It wasn't ... He wasn't strange. He waited for Tobias to defend him, but he was shocked by Tobias's next words.

"I know that he's not one of the Shadow-touched, but if he ever becomes one or sides with them, we'll take care of him, Meira. I won't let him hurt you."

Fateh fell back, feeling his stomach churn and twist with shock. He jumped in the air when his mother put her arm around him, eyes soft and sad as she pulled him away from the door.

"Now you see why eavesdropping is bad," she murmured softly. "Come on, put on a cheerful face, kiddo. We'll say our goodbyes and go home, hmm? Maybe it's not as bad as all you've heard." She tried to reassure him. "They're just scared." She hesitated and then shook her head. "Never mind me. We'll talk about it later if it comes up, hmm?"

He knew the look in her eyes; she would ferret out what she could and then confront him later. He was fine with that. He didn't want to deal with it now. He'd do as his mother said, but he could already feel the walls going up.

Fateh waited until it grew quiet again before he opened the door. He obviously didn't want Meira and Tobias to know that he had been listening in, but he didn't want them coming after him, either. Fateh didn't even bother to tie the laces of his shoes as he shoved his feet into them, barely waiting for his mother as he left the room.

Meira *was* wearing the nightgown and he tried to hide his grin at how odd she looked in it—it was some strange shade of pink that had faded over the years with purple butterflies straggling down the side. It was fine for when she was sixteen, even if it was too young for her. At eighteen, she looked absolutely ridiculous. Meira looked up from her bowl of cereal, hand knocking it over as she jumped when she saw him there.

"Good morning?" Fateh raised an eyebrow, kneeling down to help her scoop up the mess. "I didn't know I was that startling."

"You're just so quiet." She gave an uneasy laugh as she scooped up the small kernels. "I think we should tie bells on you or something so that people know when you're on your way."

"Yeah—'cause that'd look just *awesome*," he said dryly, taking the bowl from her and plunking it on the table. "Mom and I won't take up much of your time today. We've got to finish up in town and then we're heading home before it gets too late." He grimaced. "We don't want to stay out late again—that was just too weird, watching all the Shadows go by."

"You mean you didn't like our nightlife?" Meira's voice was equally dry as she poked at her cereal, and then made a face as she pushed it away. "I told you that they're creepy as hell in town." She looked behind Fateh. "So, where's your mom? Don't tell me she slept longer than *you*."

"She's just packing up so that we can get out at a decent time." He poured himself a bowl of cereal, shrugging. "I was planning to buy some seeds and stuff. I swear that Mom's garden is bigger than our house, but at least we eat fresh when it comes up."

Meira snorted. "Don't tell me your mom's expanded *again*." She laughed. "I swear—she could supply half the town if she wanted to."

"Mm—I've told her that, but she says that it's better that we just feed ourselves and stock up in case the next great fallout occurs. Mothers—" He tried to smile, but it was strained at the edges. There was already the first major fallout and talking about another, even jokingly, was too much like ill-wishing.

"Tobias is the worrywart of our family." Meira snickered, getting down another bowl as sounds from the back indicated more people joining them for breakfast. "He practically buys clothing in bulk in case the stores completely go out of business."

"Hey—it's practical," Tobias and Fateh's mother spoke in unison, grinning at each other.

"I think it's better for us, anyway," Fateh's mother continued, chair scraping along the floor as she settled next to her son. "We don't have the chance to go to the store, so having a stockpile of the home-grown is more practical."

"We get our stuff from one of the local farms now." Meira looked thoughtfully at Fateh and his mother. "You two should think about selling your stuff, too." She raised an eyebrow. "I've seen your garden; it wouldn't be a hardship at all. Plus, you mentioned fresh butter and cheese and milk—people would *love* that."

"That'd leave less for us." Fateh grinned. "Plus, we'd have to drag boxes of vegetables down the hills, and without a car, it'd be a pain in the ass." It wasn't like they hadn't sold in town when cars were still running. Now they'd have to literally cart the food down the hill.

Meira snorted in agreement and turned her attention back to Tobias. "They're heading out today, by the way—going to expand their garden even *more*."

Fateh nodded. "Yeah—and we figured we can't take up more of your space than we already have." He looked outside and grimaced briefly; there were more Shadows out wandering the streets today. It was no wonder Meira was so adamant in describing her fear. The ones outside blended in with the long stretch of shadows on the ground, formless—shapeless—except for a few.

"You know you're always welcome here." Tobias frowned. "You never acted like a burden before and you don't need to start now, you know."

"Well, you know Fateh." His mother squeezed around his shoulders as she leaned close. "He's so determined to stride along on his own that he doesn't want to mess up his master plan by leaning on anyone else."

"Idiot." Meira punched him lightly. "We're always here for you, you know. We'll always stick together, no matter what."

Fateh nodded, but he couldn't help but think back to the conversation he'd overheard and wondered what would happen if he ever did something that they didn't agree with. "Of course." He grinned as he ate the last of his cereal. "The pact we made when I was in the third grade was supposed to last until I was at least twenty."

"And since you're not quite seventeen," Tobias snickered, "we've got a few years yet." His bowl clattered in the sink as he tossed it, grabbing his coat. "Well, I'm going out, too—meeting up with Mikel." With a wave, he headed out the door, and Fateh stood up as well.

"Hate to leave you alone, but Mom and I should get going, too. "

Meira waved at him with her spoon, shaking her head. "Are you kidding? I get the place to myself for once. Party, party." She grinned. "Like Tobias said—don't keep away, alright? I miss having you around, Fateh. You always make things interesting."

"With his rapier wit and good looks, I don't know how you could let go of him." His mother returned from the back, dumping Fateh's backpack in his lap. "We won't stay away as long this time, I promise."

"S'cool—see you soon, Fateh." Meira gave him a tight hug.

"Yep, see you soon," Fateh murmured as he left. *I only hope you'll still see me as your friend and not some bogeyman in the dark.*

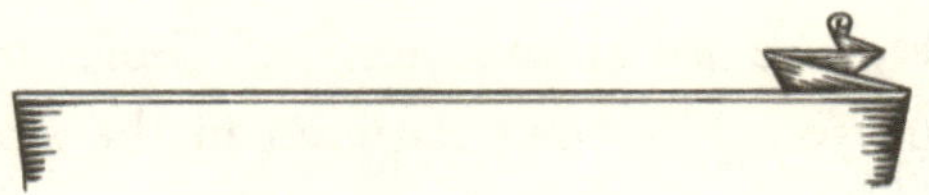

Chapter Seven

"It'll be fine, Fateh," his mother reassured him once they were far enough away from the apartment that they could talk without Meira or Tobias overhearing. "They're just worried. You know that, right?" she asked.

"It doesn't mean that they have to treat me like an enemy when I've been how I've always been," he whispered.

"It's not easy," she pointed out. "You know what we deal with at home; the small Shadows burrowing in our carrot patch, but they're a lot more restricted in what they can do and they have those human-looking ones around as well. You understand all too well how they feel. They'll start to treat you the same if you *open up more* and stop being the eternal optimist that you are."

"I hope so ..." He sighed as he looked up at her. "Well, I'm going to go buy the seeds and stuff at the farmers market—didn't you say before you needed to pick up *icky personal* stuff?" he teased her, changing the subject.

He only laughed when she smacked him on the back of the head. "Yes, I have to get *icky* stuff, as you've phrased it." She wrinkled her nose at him. "I'll meet up with you outside the market when you're done. It shouldn't take me too long."

He nodded slowly, arranging his bag more carefully on his back, the contents much lighter without what he had traded at the store. "Yep—I'll try and haggle for the best." He smiled and waved at her as he hurried off. He also wanted to finish up as soon as possible.

Oh, jeez ... not him ... Fateh tried not to stare as his eyes caught a glimpse of familiar red hair in the crowd of shoppers. *I was hoping I wouldn't see him again.* He just wanted to shop and get home and not have to interact with Shadows any more than necessary. It didn't seem to be his day, though, as Tabor strode closer, expression amused, one hand in his pocket and the other holding a familiar-looking sack as he watched Fateh.

"Wanted to talk to you, little appetizer."

"Appetizer today? I guess that's about on par with Spark or flame bait, if slightly less appealing." Fateh edged away from that acid-tinged smile. He never trusted it; there was no reason to trust it. "What do you want?" he asked, keeping the bored tone obvious in his voice as walked up to the aisle that had the plant seeds and seedlings. He trusted this booth, and they traded plants, both offering clippings from each other's garden.

He picked up several packets, passing over the carefully wrapped seeds that he had saved. He ignored Tabor for a moment as he turned to Lira, the owner of the stand. "My mom had the best tomatoes out of this set." He smiled at her. "I think you'll like them."

"I always do, Fateh." She grinned, and then her smile faltered as she took in the Shadow watching the two of them. "Who's your ... friend?" she asked, her tone warier than before.

"Someone I'm trying to ignore," Fateh mumbled. "Do you have any of the herbs this time?" He steadfastly ignored Tabor as he stepped closer to him, but he noticed the reaction the fae was having on the plants. Some were starting to wilt and he couldn't help but glance back, wondering if Tabor was the one doing it.

Lira had opened her mouth to reply when Tabor draped himself over Fateh, halting whatever she was going to say. She backed up into the wall behind her booth, eyes wide. "Should I just leave the two of you alone?" she asked. "Fateh—just take those seeds over there. What you gave me is enough." Her look clearly stated that she wanted Tabor out and since he was attached to Fateh, with one staying the other would as well.

"He's just being an idiot," Fateh growled, but her fear was obvious, the whites around her eyes showing. "Every time I wander into town, he finds an excuse to be annoying. I don't know why he's still hanging around; he should have had his fill of bugging me last night."

Tabor grinned widely, making himself comfortable against Fateh as he talked. "You left so quickly after your meal last night. I was disappointed."

"And let me guess," Fateh deadpanned. "You hate being disappointed."

"No, no." Tabor laughed, running a hand through bright strands of hair. "You are so quick to jump to stereotypes of fantasy characters, aren't you?" It was clever of him to throw back Fateh's words in his face. "We didn't even get to really talk. I expended *all that energy* making sure your friends didn't run off and ruin their meal."

"I told you that I don't live around here and contrary to popular belief, I don't find you as interesting as you think you are."

Steam began to form on the glass surrounding some of the more heat-needing plants as Tabor leaned against it. "Oh? Then should I be bothering the ones that do live here?" His voice took on a more dangerous, taunting edge. "I could look at other options, of course, such as that pretty little girlfriend of yours with the smart mouth." He smirked, tugging on Fateh's hair and pulling him out of the shop.

Fateh didn't miss Lira's look of relief as they vacated her place. "She would make for a good tumble and a little snack on the side ... and I saw how much she wanted it, even with all the glares she gave me."

Fateh wanted to hurt him, his hands curling into fists. A shiver ran down his spine, accompanied by a searing flash of hatred. He settled for a nasty look as he uncurled his fists and gently placed the plants into a bag and tried not to jerk away from the tight grip Tabor had on his hair. He didn't want Tabor to pull out his hair. He didn't appreciate being threatened or dragged around. "Leave them alone," he growled. He didn't bother to say that Meira wasn't his girlfriend. "Why don't you just stick with your own kind?"

Tabor started laughing again, eyes bright with amusement as he tightened his grip on Fateh's hair. Fateh tensed even more, one hand going to shove at Tabor. He might get in more trouble for hitting a fae, but he was tired of this.

"You have a smart mouth, too—but you don't look as if you'd appreciate a tumble from me. Why is that, little Fateh? Are you that disgusted that you spurn the chance, the thrill of being with one of us? Are you a good little Mama's boy, living dutifully from day to day with no adventure singing along your veins?" He shook his head. "And you've read the stories, little creature. Haven't you heard that beguiling your kind for a quick night is something that we're *supposed* to do?"

"No, I apparently can think with my brain and not my balls," he snorted, lips turning upward in amusement. "Amazing what years of evolution can do, isn't it?"

"Yes ... amazing." Tabor smirked, hand still twined in Fateh's hair. "Look at you, for instance—I can make plants wilt with my amazing presence; you however aren't even singed at all." He tugged one last time, a few strands pulling free. "What is your secret, little creature?"

"Would you stop with the 'little' already?" Fateh demanded. "Jeez, it's not like you're much taller than me even though I'm certain you're *a lot* older." For a moment, he saw Tabor exactly as he had seen other people around him, like his mother or his friends, teasing him about his height.

"Sore because the only ones shorter than you have barely hit their first set of double digits?" Tabor smirked.

"Are you bitter because the only ones your age are already stooped over or dead? Asshole."

"You use such sweet terms." Tabor pressed a hand to his heart. "I'll just hold your hair as a token of your non-affections to remind you that if I want you, I have to grab you first." He smirked and poked Fateh in the chest, hard. "But remember, Spark—you'd best wake up soon before the fire consumes you."

He dumped the bag he had been carrying into Fateh's hands and, with that bit of cryptic advice, Tabor left Fateh alone in the street, bewildered and frustrated and wondering just what the hell Tabor was playing at now. He looked to see what he had given him and he blinked in surprise to see the return of the salt they had used to pay for dinner. He hadn't expected to get it back.

Still, he hoped that the next time he and his mother visited Meira and Tobias, Tabor wouldn't be there. He didn't want to see the supposed fire-Shadow again. The few times he had seen him were enough.

It was a relief when he spotted his mother, bag hanging, weighed down by whatever she had purchased. He took that opportunity to relieve some of his stress and confusion by teasing her. "So—just buying a few things?" He grinned, accepting the small bag she gave him. "I think it weighs more than when we left."

"Just because you're wearing what *you* bought," she smacked him lightly, "it doesn't mean my purchases will go the same way."

As Fateh rearranged the second bag, he showed his mother his purchases from Lira's store, carefully holding the seedlings in his hands before wrapping them back up again.

"Lira had some really good items today." He smiled up at her. "If it wasn't for that ... Shadow following me around—" he scowled at the plants as if they were to blame for him being tagged by Tabor. He barely registered his mother's alarm, but when she stopped in the middle of the street to stare at him, he couldn't help but respond. "What?" He used the excuse of putting the plants away to avoid the look she suddenly gave him.

"I want you to be careful," she said slowly, gaze flicking to the side as if to assess who was overhearing her words. Even as her shoulders relaxed slightly and they started walking again, her voice was still hushed. "I don't like the idea that they're taking an interest in you. It's not ... I know we don't go into town that often, but people might get the wrong idea." She gave him a soft, worried smile. "And I don't want you turning into a zombie, either. Who would tease me about wearing glitter and spandex?"

He laughed at that and then shook his head. "What would they say?" he snorted. "It's not like I'm *friends* with ... it." He made a face. "I've seen other Shadows harass other people here. It's not like I'm the only one." He wanted to believe that Tabor would leave him alone, but ever since he had first shown up, his presence was constantly around Fateh in one way or another. He tried to reassure himself all the time, but it hadn't changed Tabor's habits yet. Even if it was just a smirk or a scathing comment, Tabor always had something to say to Fateh. He was just grateful their trips to town weren't all that frequent.

"It's not like he's a normal Shadow, either. He's ... he's almost human and that is why I worry." Her smile back at him was tired, even as she ruffled his hair. "You said he had been your friend before we knew the Shadows existed. That's the part that worries me, so don't give me *more* to worry about. I'm still waiting for the day when I can perfect my crazy, over-protective parent act when you bring a girl that isn't Meira over."

He played with the small bag of salt, tossing it from hand to hand. "And I don't foresee myself bringing anyone home in the near future."

"Sometimes you can't help yourself." She sighed, settling her pack against her shoulders so that it lay higher up. "I hope you stay the late bloomer that I know you are, but I'll still sleep better at night if I know what you're getting into. You can let your old mother be over-protective for a few more years, can't you?"

"Mm ... I think I can live with that." He smiled up at her. He felt comfortable and relaxed again now that they were away from town and the ever-increasing Shadows.

"At least the ones around their home keep to their burrows and treetops and hardly ever speak to us. It's like having talking animals from some twisted fantasy novel living in our backyard."

"I don't like when they speak to me, either," he murmured. "They're ... they're cryptic and manipulative and treat us like we have no idea of what we've done. Like they've left their pets for years on end and found out that all the housebreaking they trained into us failed because we've piddled on the couch."

He wasn't looking at his mother as he talked and was surprised to hear a muffled snort from her, even as her expression was slightly pained. "What?" he asked. "That's what it seems like to me."

"Yes," she said wryly, "but most people don't phrase it in such a way. It seems my bad habits have rubbed off on you." Her voice was sad, though. "It's easier to deny it, makes it seem like it will all go away." Neither one of them had that luxury; her parents had vanished because of the Shadows.

"Does it make it easier for them?" he asked curiously. He had never thought about or asked about it before; it simply hadn't occurred to him. Being honest with yourself about it seemed to be the best route; nothing was hidden from you that way.

Her smile was still strained around the edges. "I ... yes, Fateh. I suppose it does make it easier. I only wish that I could be that cavalier about it myself, but it's harder to lie to yourself when you're surrounded by it." She shrugged. "It would be nice to be so open-minded with all the possibilities."

"Yeah, I should be like Tobias and Meira, my role models," he snorted. "They're open like a failed parachute." He kicked at a rock and frowned. "They're going to get in trouble, you know. You had to hear the way Meira was talking last night. It ..." He grimaced. "It didn't sound right."

"Don't get involved." She stopped in the middle of the road again and gripped his shoulders tightly. "I know you care about your friends, Fateh, but ..." Her eyes were serious as she tried to get him to realize the importance of her words. "If you think you hear or see anything, you need to get away. I can't lose you." She didn't have to speak to him about how Meira and Tobias's parents had died. They were the head of a rebellion back when the Shadows first came.

"I'm not stupid," he growled, flushing. "But ... we're already their friends." He looked sad. "They already know who we are and if they do something—" He shrugged. "We'll be taken if they do something." His gaze mirrored his mother's. "I don't want that to happen to you, but ... they're still my friends. If they got taken because of something I did, I'd go after them."

"Fateh ..." his mother pleaded and reached a hand out to him, but he was already walking at a brisk pace back home.

"You'd do the same for me," he pointed out and then blanched when he saw her expression. Just what was she planning?

Chapter Eight

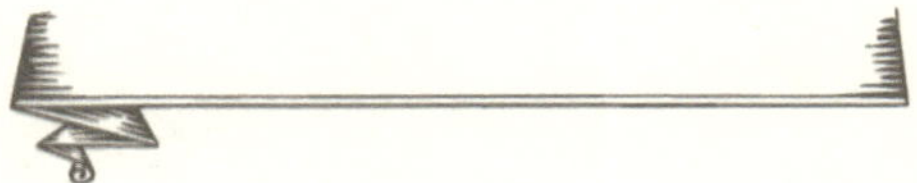

They didn't have to go to town for a month, but the moment they entered it Fateh instantly knew that something was wrong. The entire atmosphere of the town felt as if it was teetering on the edge of something unpleasant. It didn't look all that different, but ... something was off. It was just a hunch, but his gut said something was wrong. Maybe it was that there were fewer Shadows and more humans but somehow, the sight was not a comforting one. The buzz of conversation was tense and people were looking over their shoulders more often than before.

"You feel it too, hm?" His mother looked down at him, eyes dark with worry. "I think we've been away too long."

"You'd have to be blind not to." Fateh crossed his arms against his chest, frowning as he watched people mingle more freely than they had before, but something about them was ... strange. Narrowing his eyes, he focused on one person in particular, wondering about that carefree laugh she had. *No one* had laughed like that after the Shadows arrived.

He blinked as something shimmered in his vision briefly, almost like the links of a chain. *Now I know I'm going nuts,* he thought to himself, more alarmed that he wasn't seeing false things, but something that was real. Whatever it was faded too fast for him to trace it, but if it was real, it certainly eased the minds of the people in town.

If the Shadows allowed it, it couldn't be a good thing.

"Mm ... maybe your friends have some information." She didn't look as if she wanted to ask Meira or Tobias, though. "Or I can check the gossip line and see if they have anything." She crossed her arms against her chest. "The Shadows don't control everything."

"Can't imagine the Shadows listening in on gossiping." He grinned at his mother. "Guess it's a sneaky way to get around the Shadows leaning over your shoulder all the time."

"You do it too." She swatted at him playfully. "You just don't call it that." She was watching people too, and Fateh had to resist the urge to ask her if she saw what he saw, but he wasn't entirely sure of what it was.

"Here—you go find what you can from your friends," she paused briefly, "but carefully, Fateh. You don't want them to blow up again and you certainly don't want to get caught up in anything."

"They probably know a lot and we can trust them," Fateh protested, even if last time didn't lend a lot of strength to that statement. "I'll be careful and I'll keep my mouth shut this time if it turns out to be a bad thing." He thought again of that flicker and he winced internally.

"You do that." She rested her hand briefly on the top of his head and sighed. "I don't want you to get hurt. Not in any way."

Fateh was grateful to see that Tabor didn't seem to be around on this trip—*maybe he finally found someone else to bother*—and he was able to make it to his friends' apartment with relative ease. The number of people all around made him twitchy; it was just too bizarre after what the town had been like last time. He caught snatches of conversation as he walked, filing them away for later.

I'm not as scared to go out at night—they won't harm me now.

It's like everything's turning more normal. Maybe they're getting bored with us.

Fateh grimaced and took the stairs two at a time; he didn't believe any of it. *Bored with us? Not likely.* He hoped that his friends had something solid to work with and possibly more of a reason for him to avoid the town. Maybe he could even convince them to leave town if the situation was dire enough.

Meira looked more than pleased to see him and practically yanked him through the door to get him inside. "Good, you're here—we *really* need to talk."

"I was going to say the same thing." Fateh raised his eyebrows as Meira slammed the door shut behind him, locking it with what looked like newly added locks. "Things have ... changed in town." He looked out the window, watching the crowds. "If I didn't know any better, I'd say it's improved." His tone was dry as if he didn't believe his own words, but Meira didn't catch on to the sarcasm.

"Well, it hasn't," Meira snapped. "And you *should* know better, Fateh. You're not dumb like most of them out there are." She closed the curtains with a snap and Fateh edged away from her, wondering what could have put her in such a mood and what he could do to avoid getting on the wrong side of her temper.

"Jeez, calm down, would you?" Fateh held out his hands in surrender. "I haven't been in town, remember? At least I'm not so numb in the head that I didn't recognize a problem right off." He huffed. "It was like this since we were kids and I know a positive change is not going to happen."

"It'd happen if we got rid of them," Meira muttered under her breath. "Made a stand ..."

Fateh kept the words of how that would be stupid inside his mouth this time. He didn't want her to really get angry at him. "So, what's actually going on here?" he asked carefully, watching for her reaction. "Come on, keep me updated at least so we don't make any stupid mistakes out there."

Meira sighed and rubbed her head. "It's ... " She bit her lip, shoulder sagging for a moment. "They've started something new, the Shadows. They say it's for our protection and stuff, but I don't trust it, Fateh."

"*What's* for our protection?" Fateh was starting to get irritated at how Meira was dancing around it.

"Contracts." Her voice was bleak. "If we ... allow ourselves to be taken care of by a Shadow, for them to do to us whatever they want, we'll be safe from the rest of the Shadows. They'll never be able to hurt us. The Shadow we would be ... *owned* by," now the disgust was thick in her voice, "can't kill us, but he can do a lot of other things, depending on the type of contract you sign."

Fateh thought again of that wisp he had seen earlier and tried to shove it into a corner of his mind. "You've got to be kidding me." He had to say the right thing this time, to make sure that Meira wouldn't think he was on the side of all this craziness. "They're going to chain us like dogs?"

It was apparently the right thing to say; her entire posture relaxed, and she gave him a tired smile. "It happened not too long after the last time you were here," she murmured. "People don't know the truth of it; they just think that if they pretend to play nice, we'll relax our guard." She smacked a fist into a cushion. "I won't let down *my* guard."

"At least you warned me. How can they be so naive?" *Yes, how dare they want to try and hold onto something safe?* Fateh kept that cross thought to himself. *Even if it's not real, it's the illusion that they're clinging to.*

"All they're doing is aligning themselves with the enemy." Meira scowled. "As long as enough of us oppose them, they can't get rid of us. With more people on *their* side—" the implication was clear in her voice, "there's more of a chance they'll turn Shadow-touched."

Fateh snorted at this optimism. It wasn't like anything was stopping the Shadows. They certainly couldn't oppose them; all their weapons had been taken away. "Meira ..." Fateh tried to keep the alarm out of his voice. "Let's just ... stay out of their way, okay?" he asked. It was his job to oppose the Shadows and deal with them, not hers. He didn't want her or Tobias to get hurt like their parents had.

He could be smart about it, whereas Meira and Tobias could be reckless.

"No." Her entire stance was stubborn. "It's time we did something about this, Fateh."

"I thought you weren't going to tell him, Meira." Tobias walked in from the back, toweling his hair dry, eyes narrowed. "You said ..."

"I said nothing like that," Meira retorted. "Fateh needs to know what's changed since he lives so far away. He's untouched by most of this nonsense; if he doesn't know, he'd wander right into the arms of a Shadow so that he was protected, not knowing what was going on!"

"Hey, that's not fair," Fateh huffed. "I knew something was coming before any of you did."

"That's because your grandparents were nuts." Meira grinned at him. "Nice nuts, but still a little nutty all the same. Fairies in the bottom of the garden sort of nuts."

"They weren't wrong," Fateh pointed out. "We got a nastier sort of tylwyth teg." He had grown up on the stories of the fae, both warnings and folktales. "At least they saw something coming." *Just like I did, but I was only a kid. I thought I was skimming off of my grandparent's weirdness.* "So, why didn't you want to tell me?" he asked Tobias directly.

"Well ..." He looked a little uncomfortable. "With all of how you talked last time, we didn't want you to run off about how 'at least they're happy' or 'this happened before' sort of thing." He made a face. "You're too logical sometimes, Fateh. I hope you realize that *this,* at least, is wrong."

"I'm not an idiot," Fateh snapped. "You think I want to be led around like I've got a leash on me? You've got it all wrong." He huffed.

"We just wanted to make sure." Meira stood up and hugged him lightly, ignoring the way he tensed up. "Things are just so strange, Fateh. We don't know who to trust anymore, you know?" she asked quietly. "I mean, you're our friend and all, but like a lot of the people that don't live in town, you're not ... a part of what's going on here. You're separate, you know?"

Fateh sighed. "Who knows when this mess will extend out further?" To know that the Shadows wanted to keep that close of an eye on them—and for what purpose, he didn't know—was more than a little creepy and unsettling.

"That's why I don't have a problem telling you." She smiled and ruffled his hair. "I know you're not the type to bring a Shadow 'round, but if you didn't know and were just offered protection ..."

"Mom'd read every bit of paperwork available to her if that happened," he snorted. "She doesn't go into stuff lightly, you know that. She'd ferret out all the information first and examine it like she was studying for a bar exam."

"Good thing at least one person has a head on their shoulders," Meira teased him. "You'll be safe as long as you stick around your mom."

"Or you guys, leading the way with all the newest bits of information." He gave them a direct look. "I bet this whole contract mess isn't common knowledge yet, is it?" he asked.

Meira nodded, leaning forward to rest her head on her knees. "Sarah Jane entered into a contract. She was happy as a clam and didn't seem like anything could touch her. But she said or did the wrong thing and her soul was taken, just like that." She snapped her fingers. "We only know because we know Sarah Jane. She was in the rebellion with us, really determined, and then just ... nothing."

Tobias nodded and slumped on the couch. "So, don't go shouting it around to people, okay?" he said carefully. "Those who don't have contracts just think that things are getting easier and those who do have them," his mouth twisted downward, "are getting to be like the Shadows."

"We don't really know that." Meira smacked her brother lightly. "We just know that they don't seem to mind the Shadows as much."

"Obviously." Fateh's tone was dry. "The Shadows have retreated, but they're still *there*. You don't see them in the stores or restaurants like we're used to, even if the ordinary fae are still there." He wished that life could go back to normal, that he didn't have to worry about getting snatched or chained or killed.

"The people I saw outside didn't seem to mind that much." Of course, he hadn't seen anything recently; he knew of at least three people who had been taken from their homes and one of them was never seen again. They had friends from school that had gone missing; Michelle and Ryan. Their bodies had been found, but not alive. It was one of the reasons he was so adamant about staying away from town. You got *killed* in town; in the country, all you did was perish of boredom.

"We'll take care of it," Tobias said firmly. "Don't worry about it, Fateh. We've got plans." He smiled up at his friend, eyes bright. "If you'd stay in town, you could help us ..."

"I was actually going to suggest you two *leave* town and come live with me and my mom. You've said it yourself. It's safer out where we are." Fateh looked up at the two of them, watching and trying to understand the newest expression that the two of them shared.

"Fateh, that's sweet of you." Meira patted his hand. "But we'd be wasted out in that wilderness of yours," she teased. "Who'd make sure you had all the latest information or a crash space here?" she continued.

"But ... you'd be safer," he insisted. "None of that contract nonsense."

"We know about the threat and we can avoid it," Tobias pointed out. "You'd be safer in town with us since you know about it now. Who knows what'll bite you on the ass in the woods there, and you won't have any warning of what's coming?"

Fateh winced at that comment; it wasn't something he wanted to think about. "At least they don't *actually* eat people," he murmured. "There's not as much out there as here and they're really small," he tried to convince them. "We'd see anything coming..."

"No, Fateh—" Meira sighed and squeezed his hand. "We're just fine where we are. We're ... busy here and ... well, just don't worry about it. We'll be here for you and your mom when you need it and it's good to know that if *we* need it, you'll *always* be there for us, right?"

Fateh nodded uneasily, but these two were his friends. "Yeah, of course ..." he murmured. He pushed away the thoughts from before. They had just been worried and now that they knew he wasn't 'in league with the Shadows, they'd treat him like they did when they were kids.

They would go back to normal.

He was interrupted from his thoughts by the firm knocking on the door, but he didn't miss the way that Meira and Tobias tensed up. Even he wondered who it could be and edged away from the door, but then he relaxed again when his mother's voice came through.

"Fateh, it's time we were on our way. It's a long walk home. I know he's squirreled away in there." The light teasing was obvious and Fateh grinned, but Meira still looked tense. "Can you let a poor woman in? It's starting to rain."

"Guys, it's my mother," Fateh snapped. "She's not one of them, she's not going to join with one of them—she's *safe.*"

"You can never be too sure," Meira said under her breath, but she opened the door anyway and let Fateh's mother inside.

His mother smiled when she saw him, but it was strained at the edges and he knew that she had found out about what was going on as well. Her next words confirmed it. "Pack up what you brought, kiddo," she said firmly. "We're stocking up and then heading home. I don't want to be in town any longer than we have to right now."

She looked directly at Meira and Tobias. "I'd like you two to come as well," she offered. "It's not safe here. I'm sure you know."

"It was never really safe, not after *they* came." Meira shrugged. "We're used to it, really." She smiled faintly. "It sucks, but we know how to avoid it. Living out in the middle of nowhere, not knowing what was going to come up ..." she shuddered.

"I understand." She sat down heavily on the couch. "So, you both know what's changed?" she asked softly.

"Of course we do." Tobias raised his eyebrows at her.

"Then why are you staying here?" she pleaded. "C'mon—I know Fateh would love to have you around ..."

"We're doing stuff here to help out," Meira said gently. "I know you guys are doing your own thing in the backwoods, but we're doing our own thing, too. People count on us for help, for information—" She grinned faintly. "The information *you* got came from someone who got it from us."

"I doubt it," she said dryly, then waved it off and didn't elaborate when they all turned questioning gazes on her. "Never mind that. The thing is, being what the situation is, I want to get our stuff and get out of here for now."

"But ..." As much as Fateh enjoyed the solitude most of the time, he knew the militant glint in his mother's eyes meant that it wouldn't be a short break between visits to town. They were going to seriously stock up and retreat until word came of some type of steadiness.

She has a point, he had to concede, even silently. *Once word really gets out, things will be hell in town. People will turn against each other, there will be less trust, and neighbors might actually turn in neighbors to the Shadows for a favor. People will die, especially if the Shadows retaliate against any rebellions.*

"No arguments." She pulled him to his feet. "Thanks for warning my son here," she kept a grip on him, "but we really can't stay right now. With things being as edgy as they are, who knows what they'll do to people who aren't from the town?"

"Probably nothing good." Fateh didn't struggle. "They can make up whatever rule they want because we won't know any better."

"We'd make sure you know what was going on as soon as you got into town." Tobias huffed as if he were insulted that they'd think they would let them down that way. "We're your friends, Fateh, no matter how weird you sounded earlier ..."

"Let that one go, okay?" he asked, rubbing his forehead. "I wasn't thinking and of course, we can trust you." *As long as we don't get caught up in whatever mad schemes you and Meira have planned.*

"We've already forgotten about that." She elbowed her brother. "So, just concentrate on stocking up and learning all that you can. When you come back here, you'll be safe." Her expression was strange. "We'll make sure of it."

As he was leaving town, he stopped dead in his tracks, his mother running into him from his sudden stop. The restaurant they had eaten at for his mother's birthday was nothing but a crumbled, black ruin of a building now. "What the hell happened?" he demanded, not expecting an answer. His mother made a sound of dismay behind him.

A girl scavenging nearby just turned to stare at him, her eyes went wide as if she couldn't believe he didn't know already.

"Didn't you hear about the rebels who went after a bunch of Shadows?" she asked, voice hushed. There were no Shadows visible, but that didn't mean anything. They could be lurking in the ordinary shadows that lay stretched across the bare ground. "They died in the attempt, but they took out a bunch of Shadows as well. They found iron and used it as a bomb."

Fateh stared back at her and then at the building. "How did they get that much iron?" he asked in disbelief. Iron was scarce. To have enough to use it as a bomb was unheard of.

"Oh, it wasn't a lot; they didn't need a lot since any iron is fatal to the Shadows." She looked vaguely disturbed, as if she had seen what had gone down. Fateh frowned. He wondered why Meira and Tobias hadn't brought this up. They were supportive of the rebels, so wouldn't a big move like this be something they would have talked about?

"Thank you for the information," his mother said quietly, taking Fateh's arm. "We shouldn't hang around here." She gave the girl a warning look. "It isn't safe for anyone."

"Oh, I'm safe as houses," the girl said with a sunny smile. "My Shadow won't let anyone harm me, no matter what I do."

Fateh almost asked her if that included bombing and killing Shadows, but he looked at her wary eyes and bright smile—both at odds with one another—and decided not to ask. He probably wouldn't like the answer.

Fateh's mother obviously came to the same conclusion as she gripped Fateh's arm. "We need to go," she said with a bright smile of her own. "Be careful, no matter what your Shadow says."

The girl just shrugged and went back to scavenging among the rubble. Fateh was all too happy to make a hasty retreat.

83

Chapter Nine

Fateh wrinkled his nose as the scent of the dirt clung to him. It coated his hands and clothing and he mentally rolled his eyes that his mother thought weeding and planting was good for his character. *It's not like my personality will grow because I've choked the weeds out of our garden. It's going to make me more awkward when I have to speak to real people and not plants.*

"Maybe you should wear gloves," his mother called out, grinning as she held out a pair of worn gloves to him. "You'll get less dirt on you that way." Her eyebrows raised. "Unless you want to go back to making mud pies like you did when you were two?"

"Mom!" Fateh hurried over and took the gloves after wiping his hands mostly clean on his already dirty pants. Even if there was no one around to hear the teasing, he didn't want to be reminded of being that young. He was still sixteen and had *some* pride.

"But you were so cute then." She grinned, ruffling his hair, sweat making the curly strands stick out at erratic angles. "I could never control your hair."

"Yeah—like I really control it all that much now." He shrugged, going back to the section he had been weeding. "Does it really matter, though?" he asked, raising his eyebrows at her. "I'm not trying to impress anyone. We haven't gone into town since that whole contracting mess started up." It had been several months since they had gone into town and Fateh was worried about Meira and Tobias and how they were surviving ... or if they had schemed themselves into danger.

Fateh had never asked his mom where she had picked up her information about what the Shadows were doing with the contracts. He in turn hadn't told her about the chains he saw trailing from certain people in the town. He knew she had a lot of information, though, and he would wait until she was ready to tell him about it.

He'd seen her staying up late at night, reading paperwork long past when they usually had the electricity running and resorting to candlelight. The memory of that made him smile. She had set part of her bangs on fire and after he'd helped trim the burnt parts off, she had agreed to read only during the day.

"You could get an unexpected visitor or just want to impress your mom," she teased, tilting her head back to warm her face.

Fateh snorted, reaching for the spade to dig around the weeds more easily. He could feel the warmth of the metal through his gloves. "I impress you every day by just being me," he teased back. "Aren't you lucky you have me for a son?"

"I can't thank fate enough." Her voice was dry. "Come on and leave that for now. You've done enough. Get cleaned up—there's something I want to talk to you about." She held out a hand, all teasing gone from her expression.

"Does this have to do with the last visit we made and the information you found?" he asked, standing up slowly. He had a bad feeling about this.

"Mmhm." She sighed and ran a hand through her own sweaty hair. "It's kind of important, kiddo. You probably won't even like it, but we've got to talk about it anyway."

"Alright." He kicked off his shoes before he followed her inside, dirt and sweat streaking his face and drying in little clumps. Maybe the foreboding feeling would go away after a shower, the sick feeling negated by cleaning up and resetting his body temperature. He could hope.

It was times like these that Fateh was glad that the Shadows let some pieces of their technology stay. The ability to have running water was the biggest plus; showers weren't something that he would have given up easily. It was the little things that made the unbearable bearable. If he concentrated on something as simple as showers, then he didn't have to think about people going without in town.

If he thought about their garden, he didn't have to think about starving. There was a lot of uncertainty out there right now, and Fateh just wanted to concentrate on something solid. After working in the garden all day, trying to get enough food in so that they wouldn't starve during the winter, he needed a shower. One day he might not have that luxury and they'd end up washing in the creek.

He was saying as much to his mother when he came out of the bathroom, curly hair damp and rioting out of control. "You have to wonder why they left us the shower—you'd think they would have fits, leaving us with such a luxury."

She looked up from the paperwork she was involved in, a faint smile twisting at her lips. "Showers? I've heard it said that they appreciate that we 'know how to clean ourselves now' and that even if they keep animals, it doesn't mean that they have to deal with the smell." Her expression was faintly sour and Fateh mirrored it. "Makes it less of a nice thing, doesn't it?"

"Whatever." Fateh shrugged. "At least we have showers, right? And hot water, at that." He loved his hot showers; the hotter the better. "It could be really bad. They could take away our plumbing and gas." With electricity being sparse, natural gas was a blessing that Fateh didn't overlook.

"Considering plumbing has been around since ancient Crete, I think they'd really have to think about that course of action. If they don't want us to smell, they'd regret that choice in the future. Talk about a cesspit." Her nose wrinkled.

"Don't foul your own nest and all that?" Fateh sighed, staring up at the ceiling. "They've gotten more active lately," he mused. "You see them scurrying about all the time now. I bet the town's even worse, isn't it? With people being chained to the Shadows now. I'm glad we don't have to deal with that. Our place is safer."

"Thinking out loud again, Fateh?" His mother looked over at him. "When we were in town last, I saw what the contracted people looked like. The Shadows did not bother them. She sighed, turning away from him. "Just, never mind. It's not important."

"It's not like I can't see what goes on," Fateh pointed out. Happy and oblivious or not, they were still chained. "If they want to be happy little pets for the Shadows, that's their choice."

"They already see us as pets, Fateh," she murmured, stroking through his wet curls. "I almost thought about signing one. I'm worried that something will happen to you. Sometimes it's best to sign a deal with the devil to ensure safety from them. Isn't it like bribing them with salt and other items?"

"It's not the same!" he protested. "We're free, even if they've changed everything around us. Why chain ourselves to them if we don't need to?"

"Because, Fateh—" She sighed and pulled him against her side. "We can't stay like this forever. We're eventually going to run out of favors and end up in debt. I don't want that happening ... we're living in an uncertain world, kiddo. Why not just ... make it safer, for a little while?"

"We're doing just fine," he said stubbornly, arms crossing against his chest as if he could hold in the emotions that always overwhelmed him when they hit. "Mom ... don't give in to them and those weird contracts they have set up. We've got our garden and our house out here." He was seriously getting alarmed; the fine hairs on the back of his neck stood up, making his skin tingle. It was getting harder to breathe as his chest seemed to constrict. His mother had been the one who had been the most adamant about staying out of town. "We have our stores, don't we?"

"And how long will they let us keep it, Fateh?" she demanded. "You've got to start thinking of the future." Her voice was sharp with worry. "That was only meant to last a family a couple of years. With just the two of us and our garden, we've stretched it out, but ..."

Fateh backed away, eyes wide. She had never been so scared before and had never sounded so frustrated with him before. "You said that I shouldn't worry myself to death over it, that the world wasn't ending! You said that *you* didn't want us to do the stupid contracts, that they were a trick. You can't just change your mind. I don't want to do it. I want to stay here."

He took a closer look at her as he absorbed her words. She was pale and shaking and he'd never seen her like this before. Usually, when things got bad mentally for her, she'd spend time out in the garden, refreshing herself until she could think clearly again. She hadn't been doing that lately, and he worried about that change in her routine. She wasn't taking care of herself in the usual way. She must have been seriously shaken up about where they were right now and the future. *Enough that she's considering moving away from our home and settling in town. Where there are more Shadows and contracts and all sorts of mess. I don't want to move away from here.*

"There may come a time, Fateh, when you're on your own and you might have to strike a deal to at least survive. You're adaptable, kiddo. I think even if you had to give in, you'd bend your way around it all and come out on top."

Fateh shook his head. "I'd rather not put it to the test," he murmured, but his voice sounded hollow, like he was trying to convince himself that it wouldn't come to that. He froze when she gave him a guilty look. He stared at her and then down at the paperwork she had been fiddling with while he was in the shower. "Mom, you're not serious. I thought you were just joking."

"I'm just thinking about it!" Her tone was defensive. "I haven't signed anything yet. That Shadow that always attached himself to you gave me some paperwork and said that it would tell us what we'd need to know." She gave him a pleading expression. "I don't know why he helped, but every bit of an advantage that we get, we need to run with it. Don't be upset with me, Fateh."

"I know," he sighed. "You're just looking out for us in case something goes wrong." He didn't want to think about that. He liked their secluded life here, free from the restrictions in town. He would never like the idea of being chained to some soul-sucking Shadow creature as if they were some sort of exotic pet that needed to be watched over. 'Here, sign this and I'll take care of you. You're not smart enough to do it yourself,' was the way Fateh saw it and it pissed him off.

"You're young, Fateh." She handed him the sheets of paper. "And I'm reading over everything here before I'd even think of putting pen to paper. I'm trying to get the best deal, not to be a snack item at a buffet bar."

"That would be bad." His voice was dry as he looked over the papers, brow furrowing. "Jeez, it's like the legal document from hell. I didn't think they could be that sophisticated." One didn't think of Shadows as having the ability to légalese. The Shadows were things of fairy tales. They were good at making deals and all the stories said so, but he was used to the tales of *verbal* trickery. Having something as mundane as *paperwork* made it seem less mystical. He shuffled through them but read over each line, frowning deeper. "I don't ... It's better than I thought. It's binding, isn't it? They have to honor their own words, right?"

It wasn't anything too dire, at least on the surface. Contract to a Shadow, serve them in a multitude of capacities, and be free from being harassed or killed by other Shadows. The Shadow holding the contract wouldn't harm the human, either. They would take care of all of the human's needs, such as food and shelter if they didn't have any. It sounded all so *simple*, but it was the 'serve the Shadow' part that unnerved Fateh. That could mean so many things and none of them seemed like a good idea. If they contracted to a Shadow, would they have to move to town, or more horrifyingly, would a Shadow move in with *them*? He didn't want his peace shattered by either pos-sibility.

"Mmhm ... but I know how suspicious you are and I've been mak-ing notes." For the first time, Fateh noticed the dark circles under his mother's eyes and the mound of scribbled papers lying next to the contract paperwork, highlighted items, and copies of the original. "

It's straight-forward in the realization you're just a glorified pet, invisible leash and all. If you do something nasty like piddle on the carpet, they can eat your soul." They didn't say anything about the Shadow having to live with them, but there was that damn chain that showed that the Shadow could keep tabs on them from anywhere. They could show up without warning to the house and there was nothing they could do to stop it.

He tossed the papers on the couch and grimaced. "They can de-cide whatever they want as to what is 'bad behavior,' Mom."

"Hush, that's only one of the contracts. That's the one that gives total protection and immunity against the powers the Shadows have." She patted his head. "I was looking at this one—just as long as we or no one that we know rebels against them, we'll be safe."

Fateh blinked and looked over the words. He grimaced and re-membered his last trip into town when he'd seen the burnt remains of the restaurant and the story of the rebels who had destroyed it. He worried that Meira and Tobias would go down that same route and he'd hear the tales of *their* sacrifices instead of random strangers. They hadn't done anything overtly dangerous yet that he had heard of, but it was only a matter of time.

She raised an eyebrow as if she read his thoughts. "Exactly," she said firmly. "I know you're pretty level-headed, so I don't have to wor-ry about you charging into a restaurant, flinging iron silverware at the patrons."

"Yeah, that's me." Fateh's voice was dry. "The Rambo of the dining hall. Watch out for the sporks."

She smiled more widely at that. "See? If it comes down to it, Fateh, no matter what you think, we will be at the dredges of life before I sign something like this. But this is the best route if it comes to that." She looked sad. "Who knows, it may become mandatory at some point. So, it's best to know what the options are before we're forced to make a choice."

"I suppose you're right." As he stared at the contracts, though, Fateh couldn't help but feel a cold shiver twist his insides. He hoped it really would never come to the point.

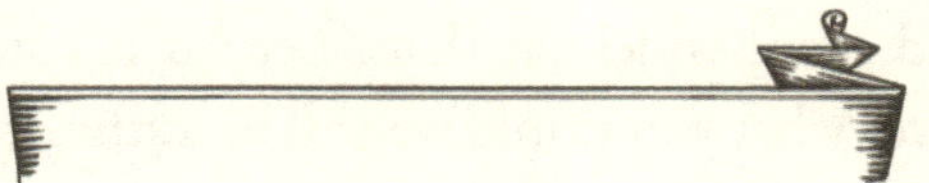

Chapter Ten

"It's more open," Fateh observed out loud, looking around the town. They had finally given in and made their way back into the lion's den. It wasn't like they were lacking food, but they *did* need information.

He disliked how much the town had changed. More buildings had been razed to the ground and all the empty space bugged him. He preferred staying in the closely wooded area where his house was situated. His mother looked over at him and patted his shoulder lightly.

"I know. All this open space is kind of a weird thing, isn't it?" she asked. "I grew up in the forest all my life, too," she pointed out. "It isn't easy not seeing trees surrounding you at every turn." There were only a few patches of trees here—and the gardens that flourished more than the people.

"Yeah ..." He looked up at his mom, biting his lip. "Do you really have to go there?" he asked. "I mean, you said that you didn't want to go. Why now?"

"Because I want to ask questions." She tapped him on the nose. "Asking questions *now* saves me from headaches and unexpected snacking later."

"I think we're getting too skinny for snacking." Fateh gave his mother a critical look. She had lost too much weight recently. "They could probably use toothpicks, though."

"You wouldn't even be that," she snorted. "But I really am not planning on deciding anything today, Fateh. I just want to double-check on things because I hate getting surprised." She ran a hand over the top of her head, strands of hair flying out more wildly than Fateh's did, the sudden wind snatching the tie from her braid.

"Yeah, yeah ... " He stared at the line of people that stretched around the contract office. Ironically, it used to be city hall. "Looks like you're in for the long haul. Hope you brought a book," he teased.

What if I went in her place? Would they even let me sign? He wanted-ed to protect his mom against what was going on instead of her having to be the one to risk her soul. It wasn't fair. *Maybe I can lie about my age.* He filled his head with visions of being the one to go into the contract house instead of his mother. He imagined tearing up contracts and yelling at those inside to *get out* before it was all too late. They wouldn't let him past the door, though. They all had IDs. They would see he was underage and not let him have a contract.

His mind flashed again to that girl in town, the one who told him about the restaurant bombing. She said that she had a Shadow, but she seemed too young to have made a contract on her own. He wondered how she had gotten away with it or if it was her family who had contracted her. Either way, it was sad that she was trapped at such a young age and didn't seem to care.

"Mm." His mother patted her bag. "I've had experience with long lines." She laughed at the look he gave her. "I always have a book on me. It's one that I've read before, but what isn't these days?" She eyed him. "I know you won't listen to me, but stick around this area. I hopefully won't be too long and ..." Her expression changed briefly. "I know you'll want to be with your friends, but I ..." She bit her lip, stopping the flow of words.

"What?" he asked, watching her. Something must have happened between the last visit that his mother and he had made.

"Just be careful." She stroked over his hair, trying to smooth it any way that she could. "There's been rumors lately. I don't want you to be a part of them."

"I won't get caught up in anything like that," he protested. "I'm smarter than that." He was vaguely offended that his mother thought he wouldn't think things through. "I noticed stuff being off with them from the start. I'll watch out, Mom, I promise."

"That's my good kid." Her hand lingered for a moment and then she walked off, leaving him in the street watching after her. He was tempted to go wait in line with her, but he hated being still for so long. He felt the weight of it settle about him all at once, almost making him stagger. Waiting in line seemed trivial when their lives were on the line.

His heart sank as the reality of what was about to transpire hit him. He looked around at the others in line and realized just how far so many of them had fallen. The Shadows finally had the upper hand and he didn't know what that meant. Perhaps Tobias and Meira had the right idea, after all.

"So, little human ..." Fateh scowled at Tabor inserting himself into his way, yet again. He had hoped that he wouldn't have run into the Shadow today, that Tabor would have found someone else to torment and follow around. "Are you going to make a contract with one of the Shadows or would you rather have my protection? Your mom showed you that oh-so-lovely paperwork I gave her?" Fateh winced away as Tabor leaned in, far past his personal bubble.

"Do you realize how desperate I'd have to be to make a contract with any of your kind, much less you?" His mother might end up having one with Tabor, though, and Fateh gave a mental shake of his head at that possibility. He wasn't even going to consider telling Tabor where his mother was. The idiot had eyes and probably spied on him, with the way he always showed up when his mother wasn't around. "You're blocking the street," he continued blandly. "Mind moving?"

"You are just a disrespectful little rat." Tabor shook his head in wonder. "You don't look old enough to use those balls of steel that you're displaying right now."

Fateh winced as Tabor's fingers dug into his chin, Tabor's eyes narrowed and dark.

"You should be grateful that I'm more easy-going than 'my kind,'" he warned. "You could be a puff of ash on the street if I got annoyed by your smart mouth." Fateh swallowed at the threat. He knew sometimes he pushed it, but this one seemed to deliberately seek him out to piss him off. "If we're going for that, you piss me off just as badly," he snapped. "Don't you have other victims penned into your calendar? I can't be the only one that you stop for no good reason."

"Nope, you come into town so little that I drop everything just so that I can make your day that much brighter." Tabor snickered and pulled back. "You're just so amusing that I can't help myself. Who else can stand to be near me without sweating as if they're going to roast?"

"You could probably work on that," Fateh pointed out, subsiding in trying to move past Tabor. It was obvious that he wasn't going to be able to get past until Tabor tired of him, at least. "Tone it down or something." "I wait for you to respond, Fateh," Tabor murmured, voice low and sultry.

Fateh yawned.

Tabor frowned, all pretense gone from his voice. "Now that was uncalled for."

"Upset that you're losing your touch?" Fateh smirked. Now that the initial shock was over, he enjoyed his brief banter with Tabor. It was his way of trying to normalize the situation and since he was pretty certain that Tabor wouldn't fry him or turn him into a grease spot, he felt free to tease in this way. He had an odd feeling that Tabor enjoyed it as well.

"Not likely." Tabor smirked. He was barefoot and clad in only a pair of tight, ripped jeans and even Fateh could see the looks that Tabor was earning as the crowd skirted around them. "You're just odd," he murmured. "But like I told you before, you'll give into my charms eventually. You should feel honored that I'm putting so much effort into seducing you."

"You could stop wasting your energy," Fateh suggested hopefully. "You know what they say about a lost cause. Stop pursuing it or you'll wear yourself out."

Tabor shook his head slowly and Fateh didn't trust the sly smile on his face at all.

"I'll have you one day, little Fateh," he murmured. "And you will be ever so grateful when that day comes."

"I wouldn't hold your breath." Fateh rolled his eyes, pushing past as soon as Tabor moved out of the way. "You'd die of asphyxiation before I gave in." He was about to say more when the rain started.

Tabor winced as a drop of water splashed in front of the two of them, followed by several more in quick succession. "Mm—I think I'd rather be somewhere dry until this blows over." His expression dropped away with the patterning of drops flattening his hair.

Fateh stared up, cringing slightly. "I hate the rain," he moaned, edging away from Tabor again, searching around for someplace nearby that was enclosed—or at least had a roof. Not that he was going to share with Tabor. He wanted it for himself.

As the rain started falling in sheets, it soaked Fateh, even as he tried to hurry toward the covered market. It would be empty today, but at least there was some kind of roof in the entryway.

"You're looking like a wet cat." Tabor stepped in front of Fateh again.

"I just ... don't like it." Fateh shivered and shoved past Tabor, huddling in the doorway and watching the rain. It was rather too late to avoid the effects and Fateh grimaced as his damp clothing stuck to him, chilling his skin.

"Interesting ..." Tabor leaned closer to him, taking in his shivering figure and the way he was hunched in on himself. "You look so very miserable, little human. I've not seen one of your kind look that disturbed by raindrops."

"Well, surprise," Fateh snapped. "Some of us don't let getting wet outside of a shower." His hair straggled into his eyes and he swatted it away, grimacing. The rain was *cold* and he just wanted to get warm and dry again. The wind was picking up, scattering rain into the entryway and making his already wet clothing freeze to his skin.

"You ..." Tabor paused and leaned closer to him, hands reaching out to grasp his chin before Fateh realized what he was doing so that he could stop him. "Interesting," Tabor mused. "I saw something like this before, but *this* explains a great deal more."

"What are you talking about?" Fateh couldn't back any further away and the thought of going back into the downpour was less than appealing. He unwrapped his arms from around himself long enough to swat at Tabor but paused when he realized how warm the other was. He was dry and warm and Fateh couldn't quite remember why he wanted to push him away.

"A gift, little drowned rat." Tabor smirked, amused. "I can't leave you that way. You might get sick and then how would I entertain myself?"

Fateh had opened his mouth to ask again what was going on when he realized Tabor simply wasn't there anymore. He wasn't *wet* anymore, either. His clothing practically steamed as it dried.

"I ..." Fateh winced back into the entryway. The storm hadn't abated yet. Staring out at it, it didn't seem so bad—to *watch*. He still wasn't going to go back into it, but he felt a lot better than he had before. He wasn't sure *why* Tabor helped him, but he knew that he wasn't so ungrateful as not to show his appreciation somehow the next time he saw the Shadow. *Still, I don't think I want that to be anytime soon. One surprise encounter while in town is enough.*

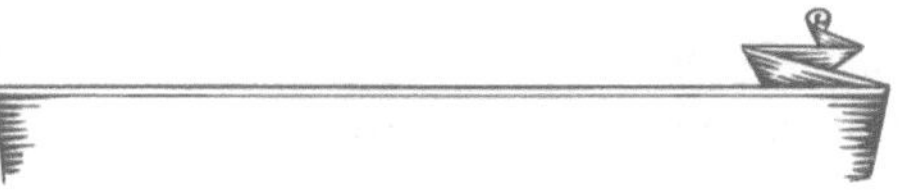

Chapter Eleven

After Fateh ran off, Tabor moved through the town easily, ignoring all who came in his path. They were all so boring after Fateh. It helped that they were simply human with nothing else to spice up their existence. Here in one breath and gone in another. Still, there was one particular human he needed to find and speak with before time ran out.

There—she was unmistakable and he zeroed in on her location, tugging her to the side so that he could talk with her privately. He didn't miss the fear in her eyes or the sweat that suddenly beaded on her brow and he pulled back a bit, cooling his temperature so that he could converse with her easier.

"You—you're Fateh's mother." His expression gave nothing away, waiting to see if she would lie or run. Humans *always* lied, but mothers lied the most when it came to protecting their children. Still, this human woman seemed intelligent, so perhaps she would start by telling the more valuable truth. She gave a cautious nod.

"What's he done now?" she asked, leaning back on her heels and relaxing a little, now that he didn't try and kill her immediately. "I have warned him." The note of exasperation in her voice made him think of his own mother from so long ago and a smile twitched on his face.

"He's going to be in trouble soon," he said bluntly. "You can see the signs and you know your son and what dangers he can fall into." There was no time for prevaricating; if he had any hope at all of pulling Fateh away from this place, he had to give the proper warnings now.

Instead of protesting, her shoulders sagged. The truth was there and no matter how much she had tried to lie to herself about it when one of the enemy was telling her, she knew it was true.

"You have seen some of the effects on the people who have been taken by the dark ones in this town, have you not?" he asked. "What happens to their ... souls, their existence?" He watched her frown before she slowly nodded. "It can be much worse for Fateh. I have seen what else can be done to a person, more than a little mind control."

"Get on with it." Her tone was blunt. "What is going to happen to my son?" She was getting a little bolder and Tabor couldn't help but grin a little in return at her attitude. It seemed that Fateh got his stubborn streak and big mouth from her.

"He's not like the others around here," he pointed out. "You should know the stories."

She bit her lip and rubbed at her arms as if she was cold now. "He is my child," she said forcefully. "He's not a changeling of any sort."

He grinned even wider at that. "No, no—he's not anything of *that* sort, but he is ... well, there is more to him than what is simply on the surface. Thus, his nature is like a shining jewel to the Shadows that run this town."

"... And you're offering to help." The disbelief was thick in her voice.

"I'm offering to help because I know what it is like to be on the wrong side of their interest," he snapped. "Your son possesses many of the qualities that they kill for. He needs real protection, not the false promises that are being offered. This isn't an offer I'm making lightly."

"So, it's coming down to making deals with the tylwyth teg." She ran a hand through her hair. "Mama talked about it. Warned me that it'd happen and that I just had to be smart about which one I made a deal with."

"Your mother had clear eyes as well, hm?" he asked. "Perhaps there's an explanation for Fateh's little quirks after all." He crossed his arms against his chest. "Listen well to this warning, then. If your son is under my protection, the Shadows that roam here cannot hurt him. I have my own patrons and the Shadows are not willing to cross them for the sake of one strange child. However, if that child does not have protection, there is no force on Earth that can save his soul from those abominations."

"Then they're not your companions? You're not all in this to-gether?" She looked almost hopeful, as if she was expecting a rescue from the darkness that had taken over the town.

Tabor barked out a faint, scornful laugh at that hope. He didn't have an army and the higher courts cared nothing for humans except as something to play with. The humans were lucky that the higher courts cared even less for the cast-offs that were created from the humans' own ill-wishing and hopes gone awry. "No." His tone was curt. "There are others of us here that are not tied up with those creatures, but none of us are so suicidal to go up against them carelessly."

"I see. You're just as scared as the rest of us." She shook her head. "So, you're saying that I have to agree to hand protection of Fateh over to you so that something nastier isn't going to snatch him up? Is that it?"

Tabor nodded seriously. "They're starting to push and push—trying to tangle everyone here in their threads until there is nothing left. Unless you want your son to join the list of the casual-ties ... or worse, *their* ranks, you'd best take my advice. When the time comes, you need to hand Fateh over to me."

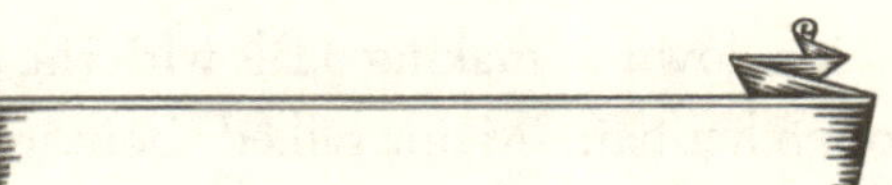

Chapter Twelve

Fateh was still thinking about his encounter with Tabor once the rain ended and he made his way back to the contract office. Hopefully, his mother had made it inside when the rain had started and there was a chance she was almost done. He was almost there when an arm fell around his shoulders and dragged him back.

"Fateh!" He looked up into Tobias's grinning face. "I didn't know you were coming into town. We haven't seen you for a while, you know. Meira and I thought you and your mom would never come down here again."

"Mom's at the contract house." Fateh shrugged it off, but he didn't miss the sharp look on Tobias's face. It only lasted for a moment, but combined with that first overheard conversation ... "Now that it's all public knowledge, she wants to confront them with what she has and get some answers."

It had been several months since the rebels attacked and people were more on edge than ever, as evidenced by Tobias's next words. "I thought you wouldn't ever give into that." Tobias frowned deeply at him. "I thought you wanted to be free."

"I do. Mom's just all worried and stuff. Besides, we might all get chained up anyway. She just ... wants more of a choice than they might give us in the future."

Stuffing his hands into his pockets, he followed Tobias down the street, trying to ignore the stares of the Shadows, most of them hostile and all of them aimed at Tobias. *Just what are he and Meira up to? Whatever Tobias did, I really hope it isn't anything that'll get them in trouble. His thoughts were n*ot just worry over his few friends, but worry that he and his mother would get involved in the whole mess.

"Huh ... she better be careful," Tobias said. "She'll get snatched if she sneezes the wrong way and you'll be stuck in one of those homes for unlucky kids. Taken away from this town and tossed in another. You're still underage, unlike me and Meira."

"Whatever," Fateh huffed. "You're only a few years older and just turned eighteen at that. She's more careful than that and we're not signing anything until it absolutely comes down to the end of it all. We're not like most of the people here. "

"I'm glad to hear it." Tobias's voice was almost frightening in the intensity of his reply. "I always knew that we could count on you not to end up like the bleating sheep around here."

The wording set off warning bells inside Fateh's head, and he had to refrain from taking a step backward away from Tobias. He was afraid of what would happen if he acted that way. He could still hear Tobias and Meira talking about 'taking care of him' if he did anything strange.

"You know me—I never quite fall into the crowd. Too boring." Fateh tried to make light of it, mind racing ahead to find out what was going on before it rose up to haunt them.

"Yeah, always the loner." Tobias ruffled his hair, causing Fateh to duck away from his hands. People were always touching his hair. Meira said it was because it was so fluffy. "Now, let's go drag your mom away from that place before they trick her into signing your souls away."

Fateh gave a slow nod, mind on other things than just what his mother was doing. If Tobias and Meira were up to anything deceitful, it would be more trouble for them than his mother signing a bit of paperwork. He couldn't help but think of the innocents who died in the restaurant and wondered how Tobias and his sister could even consider doing anything against what was going on. The rebels knew what they were doing, but other people got caught in the crossfire as well.

The line outside the contract house was just as long as before, but Fateh didn't spot his mother in it. She had to be inside by now. Fateh slanted a look up at Tobias, wondering what he made of it all. As much as he was disgusted at the idea of being chained, he couldn't say anything against other people doing it. He and his mother lived like hermits; these people had decided on a different road for themselves.

Tobias seemed to be aware of this as well, for even as he glared at the long line of people, he didn't say anything, just stalked angrily down the sidewalk with his arms crossed against his chest. *At least he's smart enough to do that.*

"My, your friend doesn't seem to like the idea of protection, now does he?" Fateh whirled around and was very aware of Tobias staring at him now, as well as a great many of the people in the line. "And it is such a good idea to keep your little minds safe and sound, instead of running like a squeaky wheel in a hamster cage."

"Fateh ...." Tobias's voice was much too calm. "Why is that Shadow around *again?*"

"Why, acting as his protector of course." Tabor smirked. "Keeping him dry and warm instead of letting him freeze himself in that little rainstorm we had." He looked down at Fateh, eyes bright and amused. "All better now, are you? I don't even get a word of thanks for helping you out."

Fateh glared up at the Shadow. "Don't act all put out about it," he snapped. "You left before I could do that." He took a deep breath. "I appreciated that you dried me off. I hate being wet. Now, can you go bother someone else?"

"I'm bothering your friend," Tabor pointed out with a smirk. "You just happen to be here at the same time."

"You asked for his help, Fateh?" Tobias demanded, backing away from him like he had the plague. "You sold out, and you pretended like you didn't? What ... what sort of friend are you to do that?" He was already sweating, even if the air wasn't that warm, still damp from the earlier rain. "You know what it means when you actually *ask* for help."

"No, I didn't ask for help. He did it without any of my *asking* for it. It was raining, he was there bugging me, and he decided, for some reason of his own, to dry me off." Fateh really didn't like the look on Tobias's face, as if he wasn't hearing a single word that Fateh was telling him. "I don't even ask for help from my *friends*, so why would I ask a Shadow? I'm not stupid."

Tobias was still backing away from him. "I've got to tell Meira ... he wouldn't be so casual around you—and you wouldn't be so casual around him—if there wasn't something going on. If you ask for help, it's like a verbal contract." He held out his hands as if Fateh was dangerous or a Shadow-touched to be avoided and feared.

"Jeez, has living in town completely fried your brain?" Fateh demanded. "Do you see a chain between us?" he continued. "No chain, no contract."

Tobias froze where he was, staring at Fateh. "Meira was right. There's something wrong with you. We can't see the chains; we only know about them. What has he done to you?" Tobias swallowed; the sound was almost audible. "I need to go. I need to talk to Meira." He turned abruptly and ran for home, leaving Fateh alone with Tabor.

Chapter Thirteen

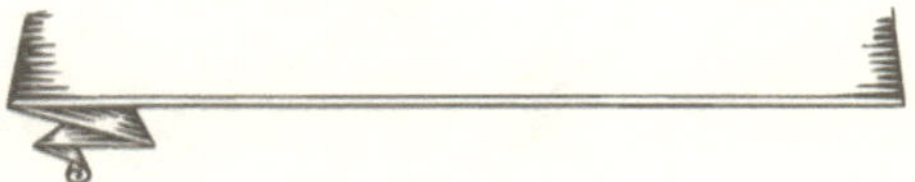

Fateh turned to Tabor, his scowl fiercer than before. "Now see what you've done? You've given him all sorts of weird ideas and ..." His voice trailed off at the strangely pensive look on Tabor's face. It was so unlike his normal, teasing expression that Fateh wasn't sure how to react.

"He's not up to any good, that so-called friend of yours." Tabor turned his gaze downward to Fateh. "I'd be more careful in who I associate with, Fateh-of-the-clear-eyes. You're already enough of an ... anomaly in our little community here. Add your friend and his dangerous plans and you've not got much of a bright future ahead of you."

"Now you're acting all weird." Fateh's look was more bewildered than angry. "Clear eyes?" He had heard that said about his grandparents and people in stories. "And what was that 'it all makes sense now' crap from before? I don't like getting wet, but a good portion of the world is the same way."

"Don't worry about it, little Fateh." Tabor patted his head absently. "I will offer you a warning, though. Don't speak so loudly of the chains that connect humans to Shadows. Humans know that there is some type of connection, but few can see it. Humans like to pretend it's all on paper and nothing else."

"So, why is it a big deal if I can see it?" Fateh demanded, ignoring the *little* comment. "You just said yourself that I'm not the only one and even if people want to lie to themselves, they still know the truth inside."

"Oh, there are others who are clear-sighted, little one, but none so clear-sighted as you, I'd wager." The cocky smirk was back and

Fateh rolled his eyes. "Your little friend doesn't seem to trust you anymore. Are you sure you don't want to throw in your lot with us and save yourself from being on the wrong end of a fanatic's weapon?"

"No." Fateh's voice was flat and uncompromising. "Like I said, I'd have to be pretty damn desperate to sign a contract with your kind. I like being unchained, thank you." He looked to where Tobias had gone. "I have to explain to my friend that you're just an annoyance, not anything I'm contracted to."

"You really need to rethink the way you speak to me." Tabor shook his head. "One person already had the wrong idea—I'd hate for one of the Shadows you so fear to catch wind of such a mouthy brat. The end result would leave me without such an amusing human to converse with."

"What a tragedy for you," Fateh deadpanned. "But worse for me, I'm sure."

"Much worse," Tabor confirmed. "I'll keep on offering, little Fateh," he murmured. "You interest me too much for me to give you up so easily." He paused and smirked at Fateh, "As long as you come to your senses before it's too late, that is."

"Is this supposed to be a good thing?" Fateh asked, watching him and then turning to the office, hoping his mother would be out soon. "Having a Shadow attached to me that doesn't belong to me?"

Tabor smirked slowly, brushing over Fateh's cheek with a hand that, judging by the heat it put off, should have raised welts at the very least on sensitive human skin. "It's a very good thing," he murmured, "to have one of us speak up for you when the tides turn and all dangers are voted on to be eliminated. Some might appreciate the help that is given, even if one never sees it."

"Dangerous? Me?" Fateh looked confused, shaking his head. Tabor was making a big fuss over nothing; so what if he could see the contracts for what they really were? If he stayed quiet about it from now on, it shouldn't be a big deal. But Tobias knew now and Fateh didn't know how that was going to end up.

Tabor laughed slowly, leaning against the wall of the contract office. "You have friends who are a danger. There are whispers that our smaller cousins pick up and let travel down the line to those better suited to handle it."

When Fateh opened his mouth to protest, Tabor covered it with a thin-fingered hand. "I am telling you this for your own good," he warned. "I'd heed the warning. Those who defy those who own them never end up well. I'm getting tired of you ignoring my warnings all the time. I'm not the only one who notices you."

"You don't own us yet." Fateh jerked away.

Tabor smirked down at him. "Oh, really?" he murmured. "Not all the humans wear chains, little Fateh, but look around. Even if you don't believe you're owned, there are others who believe they hold leashes, invisible, connected, or not. They are the ones who judge what happens in the end." He tugged on a strand of hair. "Are you going to let those you care about get crushed under the weight of their heavy convictions?"

Fateh shook his head again and then bit his lip. He didn't want to agree with the jerk that annoyed him at every turn. But he could see just as well as any Shadow, it seemed. The human race was slowly losing the independence and spark that had carried it through the centuries, at least where he lived. He didn't know what life was like outside of his town. But surely, if things were going well for people outside his home, they would have come and rescued them by now. After this long, he had to assume the worst.

He thought of his friends, who never wanted to give in under any circumstances, blinded so much by their hatred that they couldn't see a friend when he stood in front of them. Clenching his fists, he watched his mother come out of the contract office. "I won't let it happen that way," he promised, voice intense, but quiet.

"You just keep thinking that way, little Spark," Tabor murmured, melting into the crowd with an ease that Fateh envied, leaving him alone until his mother came up to him, brushing wet hair out of her face.

"I don't know how you can stand to talk to him." She shook her head. "Just standing near him makes me want to strip down a few layers to stay cool." She smiled faintly. "At least he was able to steam-dry my clothing a little bit. That was quite a storm most of us got caught in. It looks like you were able to avoid it, though. I know how much you hate getting wet."

"I ... he actually caught up with me earlier. Got dried off then," he muttered, shoving his hair away from his face again; now that it was completely dry, his curls were rioting everywhere. "You look like you're done with your questions. Can we go home now since it didn't take as long as we thought?"

"I actually thought we'd stay in town for a little while longer and think some of it over," she murmured. "It's a bit ... safer that way for now. And I have a few things to talk to you about." Her expression was serious and Fateh felt a nervous twinge; so soon after talking with Tabor ... he hoped it wasn't bad news.

"Mom, about staying with Tobias and Meira ..." He stared at the ground, cheeks flushing. "Tobias saw me talking to Tabor and got the wrong idea." Fateh kept his voice low, embarrassed that he kept getting caught out with the wrong conclusions being made about him. "I don't know if it's such a good idea to go back there."

"Nonsense." Her voice was brisk. "It's best to get there as soon as we can and explain things to them. They're your friends and even if they seem a bit misguided in their views right now, they'll still listen to you. Now, about town and what I've found out, I've seen that in some places, it's gotten better; safer. They might open the schools again—you could be around more people than just me or Meira and Tobias."

"Oh yeah—'cause you know I just love school and all its wonders," he deadpanned. "The endless hours of stupidity that go on during and in between the classes. I prefer you teaching me. At least I'm the only one who's stupid during 'school hours.' I don't have to deal with drama."

"But you can be with your friends again, Fateh." She tilted her head, watching him. "I sometimes worry about you being so far away. I think ... it's giving people the wrong idea about us." She didn't say anything more, but the allusion to the earlier overheard conversation was obvious.

Fateh grimaced. "About that ... I really hope that Tobias is going to listen to reason. Maybe it'll sound better coming from you." He rolled his eyes. "He's absolutely nuts. Just because I was talking with that one that follows me around." His mother already knew that he could see the chains; she had worried over it, but not freaked out as Tobias had.

"Fateh," she sighed. "I know you can't help it, but ... let's just deal with it as it comes. Explaining sooner rather than later would be best; I'd rather not be hunted in the middle of the night because you've got someone tagging you for later." She ruffled his hair. "You're just wanted by everyone."

"Yeah—Tobias knows where I sleep." He gave a mock shudder. "I'd rather make sure he's not going to come after me, either." He didn't really want to think they would do something like that, but he had to wonder ... and it was unsettling to think about the way Tobias acted. But ... they were friends. He couldn't do something like that. "Let's go now."

She looked around first, eyes searching the crowd. "What about that one that keeps hanging around you, Fateh? The one that was at dinner; you know he's the one that gave me the heads up. Are you going to contract with him?" She smiled softly. "You could do with worse if it comes down to it. He noticed you were miserable when you were wet, right? Did he help you out? He doesn't seem all that bad for a Shadow."

"Why would I do that?" Fateh huffed, alarmed at how seriously his mother was considering the possibilities. "I'd have to be desperate to give in. I like standing on my own." He grinned. "Well, with my awesome mother, too." She mocked punching him. "I mean that I'm too young to form a contract. Didn't that paperwork say it was only really off-the-wall stuff that got kids hooked up to the Shadows?"

"I hope it won't come to that." Her expression turned absent as their footsteps echoed on the stairwell leading up to the apartment. "I'm hoping that this will all settle down soon and we'll go back home. There's just ... they've been talking about problems in town lately and they want to keep an eye on everyone."

"Tabor mentioned that as well." Fateh chewed on his lower lip, brows scrunching together in thought. They were close enough to the apartment door that he didn't want to say exactly what Tabor had said, or who he had referred to when talking about the problem. Tobias was already suspicious of him; he didn't need to add any more fuel to the fire.

"We'll talk about that part later." She patted his shoulder before knocking on the apartment door. Her expression changed to one of smiles and an easy-going attitude to try and diffuse the look of suspicion that Meira gave her when she answered. "So, apparently we'll be stuck in town for a few days," she said as she slung an arm around Meira's shoulder. "Mind if we bunk with you again?" She spoke carefully, testing the waters. "I know you said we had an open invitation, but Mama always raised me to be polite."

"Why don't you go with that Shadow?" Meira snapped, pulling away, eyes narrowed. "Or didn't he give you at least a dog house to stay in?" She didn't budge from the door.

"Will you get over that already?" Fateh resisted the urge to shove at her. "Just because the annoying moron keeps on following me, it doesn't mean I'm contracted to him. He'll get tired eventually and find someone else to bug or a new shiny toy to distract him."

She hesitated a little and Fateh used that moment to try and wear her down completely. "Come on—you know they'll latch on to people at times. He probably thought I was great to annoy because I bargained for our dinner that night. If I avoid town for a while he'll leave me alone." Not that it had worked before, but Fateh wasn't going to give up hope yet. Surely Tabor had to get tired of harassing him at some point.

"I ... well ..."

Tobias peered from behind her and his stance and glare seemed to raise Meira's defenses all over again.

"Did he tell you that he can see the chains that the Shadows put on people?" Tobias demanded. "That he can be all casual with them and not get harmed? That creature *helped* him, Meira. He was *bickering* with one of them and the creature just laughed and didn't punish him." It wasn't like they hadn't seen him with Tabor before; this strong reaction had to be because they were getting increasingly paranoid about everything that was going on. "He knows his name and acts like it's *normal*."

"Oh, well, it looks bad if you whip the pets all the time," his mother's dry response cut into the ranting. "You know they don't outwardly punish us like that anymore—they're a little more clever than that." She hugged Tobias possessively, in the way only a mother could. "And Fateh's not the only one who can see the chains, you know." She smiled faintly. "My parents could see all sorts of stuff. They used to call their kind the 'clear-eyed' ones, those who could see through the smoke."

"Yeah, but ... but Fateh doesn't have to joke around with them," Tobias tried, relaxing a little at having an explanation for what Fateh could see. He visibly faltered when Fateh's mother shook her head again.

"If he didn't go along and pretend like it was fine, then he would get in trouble. This ... one that follows Fateh around expects Fateh to act a certain way. He seems the type to get offended if you *didn't* piddle on the carpet." She gave her son a look. "And I bet he doesn't try and advertise the fact of what he can see. It just slipped out."

Meira snorted and held the door open a little wider. "I know someone like that," she said dryly. "Come in, I guess. We're just being cautious. Those who sell out themselves will sell their friends out, too. I'm old enough to take care of myself and I just don't want anyone telling me what I can and can't do."

"Oh, like I'd do that to you," Fateh snorted, relieved that she had relaxed enough to let them in, putting down her guard so he wouldn't be skewered because he had a literal Shadow, well ... shadowing him. He should be more scared, he guessed, but Tabor wasn't scary to *him*. He was mostly an annoyance, sometimes a help, but not as scary as the Shadows that plagued the rest of the people in his town.

"I want to know why you never said you could see the chains before." Tobias wasn't giving up that particular tidbit and Fateh sighed.

"With how you were acting?" Fateh snorted. "And I've seen what it did to my grandparents. Believe me, it's not a *good* thing to see crap like that." He shuddered at the mental image of the shimmering lines that connected humans to Shadows, with the humans unaware of how they were literally leashed and collared.

"Tobias ... just leave it for now." Meira dragged her brother backward. "I don't want to keep accusing friends. We don't have that many we can trust anymore and while Fateh's always been a little weird, he's not evil like those creatures are."

"I don't know whether to be relieved or insulted." Fateh had a faint smile on his face as he made himself comfortable next to his friends. He was a little disturbed at how much Meira's and Tobias's roles kept flipping. One day, Meira was reasonable, and then she would switch. At least it seemed like both of them had calmed down enough to keep from killing him.

"Look—we just have to be careful." Meira exchanged a quick look with her brother. "We didn't want to get you involved, but ..." She nudged Tobias. "Big mouth here pretty much already alerted you that we've been thinking about stuff that the Shadows wouldn't like."

"Such as threatening to come after your friends because you thought they sold out to the enemy?" Fateh asked dryly.

"Well, if you did, Fateh—" Meira's smile was teasing, but something about it disquieted him. "We'd have to keep away from you. State secrets and all, can't let them get out." She shrugged and stared down at her lap. "Besides, we've all seen what happens to the taken. Do you want to end up like Amanda?"

Fateh pretended to think it over as if Amanda hadn't died at the restaurant along with the Shadows she had served. "Not really. Skirts and aprons aren't my thing. Guess I can't sign a contract. They might even ask me to wear makeup or something."

"I'm being serious, Fateh!" Meira protested. "It's really serious, what they're doing now—leashing us like this. You've read history, nothing good comes out of all of this ..."

"Yeah, I've read history, Meira." Fateh sighed. "We have to fight back against our oppressors or else things will go to hell in a hand-basket." He caught Meira's triumphant look and held out a hand to cut off her next words before she said them. "But that was with humans fighting humans. In the fairy tales, it never ends well when you fight the fae." His tone was somewhat bleak while he leaned back on the couch, one arm over his eyes as he continued to talk. "Maybe the Shadows are like our predators or something, like it is in the animal kingdom. Something bigger and badder than humans had to come around to make us stronger."

Silence met his words and it stretched so long that Fateh sat up, uneasy at the looks everyone was giving him. Even his mother looked a little surprised. "What?" he asked. "It's logical," he protested.

"But not something we voice." His mother patted his arm. "I know you're more logical than I ever was," she laughed faintly, "but ... while it's a good thought, it's not a comfortable one." She shivered faintly. "I don't want to think of myself as a hunted animal."

"What about on the wrong end of a conquering force?" Fateh suggested. "We did it to whatever native population had been here before us and humans have done it in places all over the world. We didn't just pop out of nowhere. Something was here first. Who's to say that the Shadows really weren't here first and we took over their lands?"

As soon as the words were out of his mouth, Fateh realized that he probably wasn't painting himself as an 'enemy of the Shadows' at that point. "Look." His voice was cross. "I can't *help* being logical. It's just the way I view things, okay? It doesn't mean I like it, but it makes it easier to take the emotions away from it."

"You're really weird," Tobias pointed out, "but you always were bizarre. It just ... it sounds like you're siding with the enemy, Fateh."

"No, I'm not stupid enough to get tangled up in a mess that'll get me and my mom turned into lunchmeat," he pointed out. "Look—you guys do your thing and we'll continue doing ours. We're not enemies; we're all just trying to survive."

"You're either on our side or you're on the side of the Shadows and the contracted." Meira was gearing up for something and she faced Fateh with her hands on her hips. "Those who are Shadow-held are just as bad as the Shadows. I didn't think you were like them, Fateh, but you're really starting to worry me."

Sometimes their friendship seemed one-sided to Fateh, as if he hadn't been doing enough for Meira and Tobias lately. Bringing them food and milk didn't seem to balance out how they took care of him when he was in town.

"Meira, behave." His mother's voice sharpened. "Fateh's always seen it this way, even when they first appeared. You're not going to act like the world is against you because he's looking at this whole mess from a different angle. You're all friends. Try to remember that."

Fateh looked up at her in shock. He'd rarely heard her lose her temper like that. Whatever had gone on in the office today must have really upset her.

She continued, taking a deep breath. "Look, the Shadows aren't going to be leaving anytime soon, so let's just deal with them and not aggravate them. Throwing stones at the hornets' nest will only make you sorry, no matter what your original intent was."

"We're old enough," Meira mumbled under her breath, but she subsided when her brother smacked her lightly. "But the offer's appreciated. We're just too used to being here in town, I guess. I think I'd go crazy being so isolated, lack of arrogant Shadows or not."

Tobias nodded and sighed. "I know you mean well, but it's our way of dealing with it. Fateh bickers and acts tough and sure, fighting the changes is not the smartest thing to do. We should adapt easier, all of us, we shouldn't fight it so much—but laying down and letting them kick you while you're there isn't the way to go, either," Tobias tried to point out. "I mean ... just think about it. This is our home and if they weren't such jerks and looking down on us ... and they're *evil*, not-human ..."

"Are you saying they're evil because they're not human?" Fateh's mother raised an eyebrow. "All those cats you've adopted ... are you going back a few centuries and declaring them evil because they wander around at night and don't talk in a way that we can understand?" She tapped her fingers on her side. "You've seen the regular fae get harassed by the Shadows. Are they evil as well?"

"That's not even the same situation!" Meira protested, staring at her. "Are you defending them, too?" she demanded. Her face turned red. "Get out, then! We don't want you here if you're just going to defend the monsters that have destroyed us and taken over our homes and ..."

"And nothing. My parents were taken, Meira. I very well know what happens to people who *speak up*. I fight in my own way and shouting 'hit me' from the rooftop isn't the way to accomplish your goal and survive. It's already settled down some. Give it some more time and things will go back to something a little more normal."

Fateh paled at his mother's words. He knew his grandparents had gone 'underground,' but he hadn't realized they had been taken.

"No," Meira said. "As you said, we'll each do it our own way. Find some other place to think over your decision to sell out. We don't want you here." It was amazing how ugly Meira's expression could turn in such a short amount of time. "You and Fateh can go back and hide in the country. Pretend that everything is all fluffy and easy to deal with and that you don't have to worry about your neighbors being taken or locked up like animals."

"Well, I didn't want to come here anyway!" Fateh snapped, standing up quickly and grabbing at his mother's arm. "Not with people who are screaming their plans so loudly that the upper Shadows know what you're up to." He crossed the room quickly, his free hand on the door. "I'd start whispering your plans behind lots of locked doors if you want to keep all that freedom we all enjoy. Don't make it worse because you can't stand what we've been allowed to have."

The distrust in Meira's eyes was quickly shifting to something that looked an awful lot like hatred. Fateh sucked in a breath, trying to tear his eyes away from the expression he feared would come to mind whenever he thought of her from now on. The face that once held a smile so bright it outshone the sun was now twisted in small edges. He was losing her, and losing Tobias too, and maybe it was for forever. He'd brought this upon himself, not a *Shadow*. It was him, and he would have to live with it.

Chapter Fourteen

He was fuming by the time he dragged his mother outside. "How can they ... we're not the bad guys and ... they're planning all sorts of reckless things and they think that it hasn't been noticed and ..."

"My, you're saying a lot more than normal. Guess this has bothered you a lot more than you've let on, hm?" She stroked his hair and slowly, Fateh calmed down. "What they do is their choice, Fateh. We can't control them."

"Yeah, but if we're associated with them, they'll get us killed." His words were a mumble, barely discernible. "I'd rather not die because they were having a fit. Fighting with the Shadows ... getting upset because they've done all this—it's not going to solve anything. They're going to get themselves and all those around them *killed* because of it."

"I know, I know ..." She sighed. "Come on, let's find a place to stay for the night since we got kicked out of the apartment. We need to be in town for a few days like I said." She rummaged through her bag. "I just hope I have something to trade."

Fateh stared at her. "Why are we staying in town instead of going home?" he asked, worry in his eyes. "We've never stayed in town if it wasn't with Meira and Tobias."

"Because I have things to do," she said firmly. "Things that can't be done at home, items to buy that we can't grow."

Fateh looked around, a little sick inside. Being stuck in town without a safe haven was almost like having a sign around your neck that said "free food." "There's the hotel still running ..." he said absently. It was more of a joke than anything, something set up so that Shadows could collect favors and trick humans into bargains. Rarely did anyone have anything of value. The patrons, like in so many places in town, were mainly for the benefit of the Shadows.

"Let's go and see the price," Fateh continued as he hunched his shoulders. "Everything has one these days, even if it's not cash anymore." He knew it was mostly his big mouth that got them into this mess, kicked out of their safe space for the night. Going home in the dark was out of the question.

"It's not your fault," she murmured, startling him. "I said just as much as you did." Her smile turned rueful. "Maybe it's good that we didn't stay any longer. What else do you think we'd say?"

"Nothing good." He wrinkled his nose, eyeing the hotel and the patrons milling around it. The ones guarding the doors were ... well, he knew they weren't the smaller Shadows that haunted almost every crevice of the outdoors, but they weren't the high-ranking ones that were at the restaurant, either.

"Hmph—a pet is coming here?" The mocking laughter filled Fateh's ears and it rankled him all over again, to be called such a thing, to have to deal with it. But staying silent was the only way to get the safety they needed at the moment. He gripped his mother's hand harder, unaware of her wince.

"They're with me. They are tasty little things, aren't they?" Fateh wondered just *how* Tabor kept on showing up without any warning. He wasn't sure if he should be grateful or not in this situation. He didn't know how it was going to end up.

The doorwoman, if that was what she was, reached out a hand that was more bone than flesh, but Tabor slapped it away. "They are mine," he said. "I'll be taking them with me up to my room for the night."

"Whatever you want, Master Tabor." Fateh couldn't help but stare at the melodious voice coming from something that should hiss or rattle or something—not sound so ... nice. "We can play after you've taken care of the animals." Fateh tried not to wince away as a piece of decaying flesh dropped off her face and hit the ground with a sickening plopping sound, especially when she reached down casually to fix it back to her face.

"Not tonight. I think I'll be having plenty of fun with these two," he murmured, giving a little wave as he took hold of Fateh's arm and almost forcefully pulled him up the stairs.

"My, and here I thought you had *safe* quarters to stay in for the night. What sort of favors were you going to sell tonight, little Fateh?" Tabor asked him once they were behind closed doors. He smirked at his mother as she sat down heavily on the small bed in the room. Fateh was on edge; his mother had gone along with Tabor too easily.

"Fateh ..." Her voice was slightly dazed. "You really are this close with..." She looked up at the Shadow. She swallowed hard. "I mean ..." She rubbed her forehead. "I know he helped you out, but this isn't normal," she said weakly. "Just to come out—" She flushed and looked up at Tabor. "Not that it isn't nice to have a place inside."

"Oh, don't get all polite on me," Tabor snickered. "Your son rarely is." His smile was all sharp edges and mostly insincere. "It makes him such an amusing target when he comes into town."

"He was raised to be more polite than he is." Her voice was tense and on edge but Fateh could clearly see the fear in her expression, even as she tried to hide it. "I want to apologize since he doesn't have the sense to do it himself." She grabbed at Fateh, scowling at him. "Be quieter next time."

"Oh, I'd rather have him and his smart mouth around than some of the other humans who plot oh-so-secretly about taking back their town." Tabor raised an eyebrow. "I like him because he's not cringing in fear every time I come near him. He's amusing to talk to."

"Glad I can be of some source of entertainment for you," Fateh said dryly. "What do you want from us to help us?" he asked, expression gone from his face. "We didn't ask for your help and I'm *not* going to let you do anything to my mother."

"So defensive." Tabor laughed, leaning forward enough to brush Fateh's cheek, his smirk growing as Fateh jerked away. "What if I was simply being kind?" he asked.

"Yeah. Sure." Fateh's expression didn't change. "Everyone wants something in exchange for helping." He'd received his salt back, Tabor had dried him off in the rain, and now this room? It was a debt that Fateh didn't like the math of. It was dangerous to be owing so many favors to one of the fae.

"Should you be so cynical this young?" Tabor shook his head, tugging Fateh away from his mother. "You'd think that with such a loving mother taking care of you, you'd be a bit more bright and cheerful."

"Can't change his personality." Fateh looked back at his mother, who just shrugged and gave him a faint grin. "I've been trying to break him of that habit since he was a kid." She tugged Fateh back, who was starting to feel like they were fighting over him.

"That makes him so amusing, so interesting, that I want to keep him close." Tabor's voice was low and Fateh didn't miss how his mother tensed and wiped at her forehead, releasing his arm to do so. "If I said the payment required for you to stay with me? Debts always need to be repaid; it's true. Let us call it a loan. I'll know when to collect on it."

Fateh blanched at the idea of being in debt to a Shadow. That was worse than thanking them; it could screw you over. "No," he said sharply. "I won't be in debt to you." He shivered, scared of what clearing the debt now could cost, but it had to be better than having Tabor hang it over his head for an indeterminate amount of time.

"You're smarter than most of your kind." Tabor sighed and shook his head. "Not all of us are as bad as the others, you know, but if you are so insistent on clearing this right now, I'll take your bonded word that if you do fall to needing to sign a contract, you will sign one with me, no other."

Fateh stepped back, eyes wide. Of all the things ... "I ... what?" he demanded. "Why would you even want something like that? I don't even have any intention ..." It was too startling after his mother mentioned that if he had to do a contract, she would want him to do it with Tabor.

"Because," Tabor's expression didn't change, "you're smart enough to realize that it will happen eventually and I want it promised that you will chain yourself to me when it comes down to the crucial hour. I'm very patient, little Fateh. I can wait years if I need to for you to make a contract with me, but I know I don't have to wait that long." He smirked. "Tick tock, little Spark. You're almost at your majority."

"Good, because it would be years," Fateh snapped, off-balance from the suggestion, from the very possibility. "I'm still a teenager and we don't do contracts." He wrapped his arms around himself, backing up until his legs hit the edge of the bed.

"True, and you'll be so much more amusing to play with when you're older. but I want your word, little Fateh." Tabor held out a hand. "Do it now and consider any debts erased. You may not even have to ever fulfill it, but I want you to promise me that if it comes to it, you will uphold your end of the bargain."

Fateh saw the worry etched on his mother's face as she looked from him to Tabor. He wanted to ask her for help; it wasn't the time to act tough, to bluff his way out. Whatever he did or said would leave a permanent impact on his life. There wouldn't be any going back from this point on.

She seemed to understand his unspoken question. "It's your choice, Fateh," she murmured, hands tracing the spiral patterns on the comforter. "I think it's a good idea, though. You ..." She winced. "Having a debt hanging over your head is worse than a word of the bond. You know what we've already talked about concerning the contracts."

"I ... yeah." Fateh was feeling sick inside, his insides twisting into knots before he gave Tabor a defiant look. "Fine. I give my word that if I have to sign a contract—if my world gets that damn screwed up—I'll sign it with you. Happy?" he asked. "But I want to read the terms of my agreement before I sign anything. I'm not going to be your slave, your puppet, or your toy." He crossed his arms against his chest, trying to close in his feelings before they spilled out. "I've read the contracts that you people have written, and I'm going to choose my own. Do we have a deal?

"Yes," Tabor murmured, eyes meeting Fateh's. "I'm glad to know that I can trust your word, Fateh," he murmured. "We'll see what comes out of it, won't we?" He smirked at Fateh before stepping into the deep pile of shadows in the corner of the room, vanishing into them.

"Did you know that he could do that?" Fateh asked his mother, starting at the shadows and edging away from them. If the Shadows could leave by them, who was to say they couldn't just appear in them without warning? The visible sign of their ability to travel like that was more than a little unsettling. "I don't know if staying here's such a good idea anymore."

"We already got signed into something," she said, rubbing at her arms, trying to soothe away the fear. "Fateh ... he doesn't seem like a *bad* sort, but you've never been in debt to one of them, either. We've always been so careful ..."

"Yeah, I know." Fateh sat down hard on the bed, legs going weak. "I ... it'll work out," he said confidently. "I'm smart, I can work my way around any contract. Tabor's ..." Tabor had been his *friend*. It was all so *wrong*. "Tabor isn't the worst thing out there. I just have to be smarter than him."

"That sounds like a good idea." She smiled and patted his hand. Fateh could tell there was something she wasn't saying, but he didn't speak up about it. They'd get around to it in their own time. They were both more likely to keep it inside until they had everything sorted out.

Something in the way she was acting about the contracts, about pushing them and researching and practically insisting that Fateh promise he would take one, set off warning bells in his head. Still, his mother wouldn't make him do anything he didn't want to do, right? He shut off the lights until there were no patches of shadow, only regular darkness in the room. They'd worry about it all tomorrow.

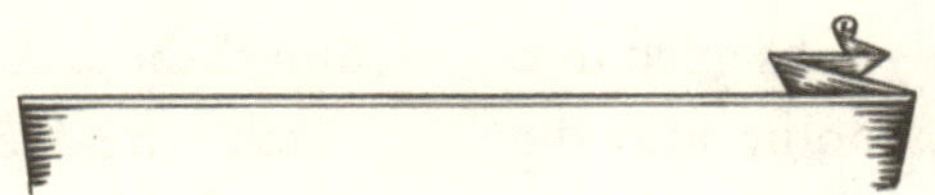

Chapter Fifteen

"So, I'll be going back to the office." Fateh nodded slowly as his mother brushed her hair away from her face, clearly more nervous than she was letting on. "There were some things they discussed yesterday and, well ..." She sighed and rubbed at her forehead. "I'm going to try and talk them out of it."

"What things?" Fateh asked suspiciously. "You're not taking what Tabor said seriously, are you?" he asked. "Mom ... we both know that it's going to come to pass, but why hurry it along?" he demanded. "Let's just go home and leave well enough alone."

They left the hotel with no further problems, the staff at the front seemingly not as interested in people leaving as they were in extracting payment from those coming in. *Of course, it could have to do with Tabor and his stupid 'mine' comment, too,* he thought sourly.

"We can't go home quite yet," she said with a sigh. "What that Shadow said—he hinted at a lot of things, Fateh, and I want you to be safe, especially with recent events." She didn't have to say Meira and Tobias's names or detail the recent incidents. "Although the idea of you being close to that Shadow worries me, he's probably the best option in this situation. He's really taken an interest in you, Fateh. If you were any older, I'd be worried about that deal going through."

"I wouldn't worry about it now." Fateh squeezed her hands reassuringly. "That's years away at the very least," he pointed out. "Look, as long as I'm underage, he can't claim me, right? You've still got the whole mother-to-son thing that they value and so I'll be just fine."

"Another thing, Fateh—" She looked away. "We may have to move into town. They want to monitor people more closely and I'm not sure how safe our house is now with the Shadows increasing out there. Being around other people might be safer. There are a lot of new rules, Fateh." She sighed. "One group makes it more difficult for everyone else."

"Even with *us* being as good as we are, they don't want their livestock wandering and going feral?"

"You put it in such charming terms, but yes." Her lips quirked up briefly. "It's either contract so we have one Shadow watching over us, or living in town and having a lot of Shadows watching over everyone. Either way ..."

"... We're trapped," he finished. "Great. It's not *fair* that we have to either be leashed or move." His expression darkened. "I don't want to give in. Can't we just ... move somewhere else?"

"And where are we going to find a place without Shadows?" she asked logically. "We don't even know what places outside of our town are really like, not accurately, anyway. We're not allowed to leave. The Shadows keep a close eye on us, and it's not like we have news anymore." She sighed. "Fateh ..."

"I know, I know ..." he muttered. "I still think it sucks. You'd be the one stuck signing the contract since I'm too young ... and you'll be the one to take the flack for whatever I say or do." Annoyed, he crossed his arms over his chest and faced the flow of people in town rather than looking at his mother. "I guess I'll have to watch my mouth if you decide to sign."

"I'm not signing my life away yet." She laughed, ruffling his hair. "I told you, we're in this together."

Fateh knew how much she loved their home, though. It had been her parents and grandparents and more generations going back before that. It was well-lived in and spacious and Fateh knew it'd kill his mother to leave it. He closed his eyes, breathing deeply as he made his choice. For better or for worse, it was going to affect them.

"You make the choice, Mom." He stared at the ground. "I'll stay by you, either way. You do what you want, not what I want, okay?"

He gave her a pleading look; he'd give up his freedom to make her happy and he'd give up his home to make sure she stayed safe.

"Fateh ... even if we'd have a Shadow living with us?" Her grip tightened and her hands trembled. "I know you don't want to do it."

"Might as well be comfortable if we're chained, right?" He shrugged, trying to make light of it, but he was trying not to tremble as well at the idea of being under someone's control, especially being under Tabor's control, chained to him so that he could never be free again. "I mean, come on—can you see one of the Shadows trying to garden?"

She laughed as well; neither of them mentioned the quiver in it. "Alright, then. If you're sure about this, Fateh, we'll do it." She rubbed at her arms. "We have to make the decision now and there's no going back so please, be absolutely sure that you want to do this."

Anything to make her happy, Fateh decided and he nodded, gripping her hands. "Yeah, Mom. I'm sure. Gotta keep my space as it is, right? Can you imagine us trying to fit all of our stuff into an apartment in town? We'd be having the yard sale of the year to cut down on all the stuff that we desperately need in our lives."

That made her smile a little more and she ruffled his hair as she moved back towards the office, speaking quietly to a guard at the door and handing over the sheaf of paperwork that she had so meticulously gone over. She was invited into a side door, giving Fateh a little wave as she vanished inside.

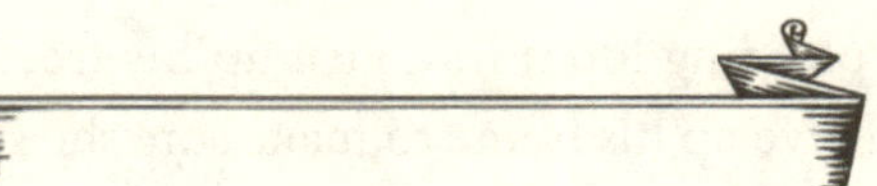

Chapter Sixteen

"And so it begins." Tabor's voice was clear, but Fateh couldn't see him and he scowled in the general direction of the voice.

"Why are you acting surprised?" Fateh demanded. "You dropped so many hints last night. You knew my mom would give in so I could be protected." He frowned deeply as Tabor stepped out of a darker piece of shadow and into the sunlight.

"You agreed to let your mother sign that lovely little contract, and you fall underneath the guidelines of it. Not chained to me yet, but there are only so many years that your mother's protection will extend to you. Less than two years. Delay it all you want, little one, but it's inevitable. How does being in a cage feel, I wonder?"

"I've been in a cage since your kind started treating us as animals," Fateh snapped. "Did you ever think of working nicely with us?"

"Humans would never think of it," Tabor said flatly. "Too stupid by half, always suspicious, and crying demon and monster. They aren't the kind that would play nicely with us. Your own mother kills the children for being children."

"Don't give me that," Fateh snapped, rolling his eyes at the over-dramatic tone that Tabor adopted. "Those so-called children tried to gnaw off my mother's ankle while she was weeding the garden. We're not all that damn helpless and you'd fight back as well if something attacked you. Humans have a survival instinct a mile wide, you know."

Tabor's smile was slow in coming, but Fateh didn't like the look of it. "Why do you think the Shadows are removing everything that you can fight back with, then?" he asked, voice low and amused. "Why do you think they're chaining so many of you up?"

"Because you're sadists?" Fateh suggested. He didn't want to think about why they did it; he knew very well why. To voice it out loud, though, would make the reality of the people around him so much sharper, so much more real. They didn't realize yet what was really going on, he knew. They couldn't see the chains he could.

Tabor shook his head. "You're a smart boy, for all that you act human. Why would we do such a thing, little creature? Why did the humans of the past do such a thing to their fellow humans?" He was leaning close again, but this time, no one around them paid attention. Such was the way of the changes already made. No one made a fuss if a Shadow was talking to a human. Most assumed that the Shadow and human were contracted.

Fateh couldn't back up anymore; he was pressed against a wall with Tabor's intense gaze boring into his own. "Damn, you don't give up. Jeez, get away and let me talk." Fateh huffed and shoved at Tabor, but it was like pushing the wall at his back. "What do you know about it?"

"Humans are always fighting, always trying to be better than one another," he said with a smirk. "Don't you know your own history?" he asked. "From even when we were here last, your kind was chaining those that you deemed lesser."

Fateh opened his mouth, wanting to argue and defend his race, but he couldn't. He'd always been the one saying how they weren't any better than what the Shadows were at times. No matter what country you pointed to, there was always one group of people who thought they were better than the other, always those that chained the ones less able to defend themselves, a minority that was an easy target. It irked him that Tabor could be so logical like that, to throw the mistakes of the past in the present's face, but even those living in the here and now weren't completely blameless.

"You know so much, then," Fateh huffed. "Why didn't you come back earlier to make sure we behaved ourselves, then?"

Tabor smirked. "Oh? You wanted your little babysitters around to make sure you all played nice together?" He was practically purring with amusement.

Fateh didn't share in the amusement and he growled low in his throat. "Look," he snapped, irritated. "We may have made mistakes, maybe we're still making them, but that doesn't give you the right to chain us."

"Here with us, at least you are free as you can be, just ... watched more carefully. Don't you agree, little Fateh, that humans could bear to be watched a little more closely? To have all those nasty toys they've done so much damage with be taken away?"

"That's not your decision to make," Fateh hissed, keeping his voice low to keep the attention away from the two of them. He pressed harder against the wall as if he could vanish into it and get away from Tabor. He made an undignified yelp when the wood underneath his hands suddenly gave way and he slipped and nearly sprawled on the ground. "Ow!" he yelled. "The hell?"

Tabor leaned around him to look at the building, eyebrows raised. "Well ... this is an interesting development." He brushed against the wall, ignoring the sputtering Fateh that was pressed up against him completely at this point. His face was too close, his breath too warm. It was a strangely pleasant scent and Fateh shook his head to clear it. As he yanked away, his hand came away with ashy wood. "Upset with me, were you?" His touch was careful as he took Fateh's hands, turning them over and humming under his breath. "And not a mark on you."

It took Fateh a moment to get over his shock enough to jerk his hands away. "What the hell are you talking about?" he demanded. He stared at the crumbling remains of charred wood that Tabor placed in his hands. "I didn't ..." His voice trailed off at Tabor's wide grin.

"That was all you." He ruffled Fateh's hair, lips against his ear. "Should I let your fellow humans know what a startling little bird they have in their nest?"

Fateh swallowed hard at the implication; Tobias hadn't taken him seeing the chains well and if he was told about this, it wouldn't end well. This was more than just the metal bothering him or him not being affected by Tabor's heat. This was serious. He could bluff and pretend. He *had* to do so that he could save himself. "I don't know what game you're playing at," he began, "but I couldn't have ... I don't ... you did something somehow."

"I wasn't even touching the wood at the time," Tabor pointed out smoothly. "You were the one so very angry with me when you were touching it. Now, you seem to be the logical sort, little one—what conclusion would you come to with those facts?"

"What about the fact that I'm human?" Fateh shot back. "Ever think about adding that to your little theories?" He didn't like the smirk on Tabor's face. He was human—completely. He'd just had a few things go wrong lately. That was all.

"Oh, but humans are so very quick to jump to conclusions—like your little friend. He thought of you as being contracted, but what if he thought of you as much of a monster as he sees my kind?" Tabor couldn't pull off a conciliatory expression very well. "Oh, wait—isn't that why he ran off so very quickly? I'd sleep with my eyes open, little creature. You never know who will creep up with salt in one hand and metal in the other to take care of pests."

"Like anything could get that close to you." Fateh rolled his eyes at how dramatic Tabor sounded.

"We weren't talking about me, Fateh." Tabor raised an eyebrow. "We were talking about you. How close are those little friends of yours?"

"What good is the contract, then?" Fateh snapped back. "Isn't that supposed to protect us?"

Tabor laughed and shook his head again, poking Fateh's cheek in an almost playful manner. "It's supposed to protect you from other Shadows, little one. Not from the harm that humans inflict on each other. What do we care if humans hurt their own kind?" There wasn't anything remotely human in his expression at the moment. "It only proves our point that humans are animals."

"So, what happens if a human that's contracted to a Shadow gets hurt?" Fateh asked, eyes narrowing. "You don't do anything to help your little pets?"

"Are you encouraging me to kill humans?" Tabor couldn't pull off wide-eyed innocence, either. "My ... that doesn't sound very nice. I thought you'd want to keep them around."

"Stop putting words in my mouth," Fateh hissed, his eyes narrowed and dark. "You don't know me or my kind, and all your kind does is skulk in the shadows and scare people. What does it say about your own self-worth that you have to put others down?"

"And you don't know *my* kind." Tabor shook his head, expression serious again. "You think we are all the same as well, little Fateh. Think before you open your mouth—think to ask or use your own senses. I'll give you a hint." He leaned close, mouth brushing the tip of Fateh's ear. "We're not all Shadows." He didn't raise his voice at all. "Not all of us are friends with them, either."

Fateh jerked away in shock at this bit of information, eyes wide as he focused on Tabor. The thought that there were others that weren't Shadows—that they had just lumped them all together without thinking ...

"And why would you be telling me this?" Fateh kept his own voice pitched low, not looking around so that he wouldn't attract attention.

"I think you need to know." Tabor shrugged and leaned back, all seriousness erased from his expression as if it had never been there. "Just think on that, little Fateh, and think of how it can help you when you need it." He tugged a strand of Fateh's hair loose, examining it as he twirled it between his fingers.

"Get help from you? Are you trying to trick me into more debt, more promises?" Fateh scoffed, but somehow ... in the way that Tabor was examining him, his words weren't as strong as before. Tabor had been a jerk every time Fateh came into town, but he'd never actually hurt him.

"You never know when you'll need it." Tabor smirked. "I promise I won't add any more debt to what you already promised to pay. Think of it as an added bonus. Promises carry weight, you know." He looked around and shook his head. "Now, go play nice with your friends—there are so many of them coming this way."

139

Chapter Seventeen

Fateh's head jerked around to stare at the ... he could say a mob and not be overly dramatic. "The hell?" he backed up, straight into the remains of the wall again, and shook his head. "Oh, this isn't funny at all." It especially wasn't funny when several of them—sporting weapons—slid into the contract house, where his mother was.

Meira was in the front of the group that came to face him and he stared at her wide-eyed as she brandished a sharp-edged weapon at him. It wasn't a knife, but it looked like a piece of metal she had sharpened and honed to a fine edge.

It was obvious that Meira knew how to play him and she proved it with her words. "Stop the contract now, Fateh. Kill that Shadow you're with or we'll make your mother pay."

It was obvious what she meant. She held out the weapon to him. Where had this come from and what the hell was going on? How long had they been planning this?

"Are you absolutely insane?" Fateh shouted. "Meira—"

Several people came out of the building, his mother gripped tightly between two of them, her eyes wide and terrified as she caught sight of Fateh. He only had to wonder what the rest were doing in there. He didn't want to know—not after what happened the last time. *No ... this isn't going to end well, this—it's all wrong. Why are they doing this?*

The Shadows were doing nothing, simply ... watching the whole thing, their eyes cold and uncaring. It was simply one more human drama. He ignored the weapon that Meira held out and ran forward, closer to his mother, but he was shoved back with something that burned his arm.

"You stay away unless you're prepared to join us, Fateh." Meira stood over him, eyes as cold as the Shadows surrounding them.

Fateh growled and tried to get up again, to move out of the way, but he froze when he saw the group surrounding his mother. He twisted to see Tabor was gone. "Tabor!" he shouted out. "Can't you do something?" It would be another debt owed, but ... he wanted to save his mother. He'd do anything to give her a chance.

A booted foot kicked him in the side. "You're not going to call for your stupid protector." Fateh didn't even recognize the kid glaring down at him. "You stupid idiots are all the same, traitors to your kind—teaming up with the demons that enslaved us. Do you lick their feet, too? Thanking them for the leashes they put on you?"

"Are you ... the hell?" he asked. "Have you all gone completely insane?"

"I would watch what I said, Fateh." Tobias lowered himself next to him, eyes intent and expression a little sad. "One wrong move and well, I don't think anyone will be too sad if we get rid of your mother. She gave in. She's no longer one of us."

"She's just ... she had to do it, idiots!" Fateh squirmed again, but whatever they were pressing into his arm to keep him down hurt like hell. He couldn't quite see what it was, but he just wanted it off of him. "We were going to lose our house—we would be trapped, anyway!"

"I'd rather die free than be chained like an animal," Meira sneered at his mother, who only held her head high, shaking just a little. She knew the paperwork and that she wouldn't be saved, even if she had managed to make the contact. It was humans who were attacking her, not a Shadow. She couldn't expect any help from anyone around her—there were so many already beaten in spirit and those who weren't were on the side that was threatening her.

"We're doing you a favor, Fateh." *There's no mercy, no sanity*, Fateh thought, *in her voice*. "You always said that you didn't want to be chained. Look at you now—your own mother being treated like a dog."

Fateh growled and managed to shove whoever was holding him down away long enough to get to his feet and make it a few steps closer to his mother. "You're all insane," he protested. "Leave us alone. We're going home, we're not going to bother you, and damn it, we had to do this to survive."

"You've tossed in your lot with the other side." Meira shrugged, barely acknowledging the smoke that curled out of the contracts office. "Look at you, Fateh—so full-on committed to them that you get burned by what hurts *them*. I should have seen it before. Completely Shadow-bound, Shadow-touched. You're not even human. We're helping to free you."

The scariest part was that she sounded almost sane; she *believed* in what she was saying.

"I ... no," he whispered, backing up as much as the crowd would let him, still trying to get close to his mother to protect her in any way he could. "You're really not thinking, guys ... c'mon." They were surrounded by this point, by both Shadows and humans, and none of them looked as if they wanted to help.

"Just relax, Fateh—it will all be over soon," Meira practically crooned. "Just sit still and accept it and it won't be as painful." Her expression saddened for a moment. "I didn't want it to come to this, you know," she murmured. "But we all have to do things we don't like if it's for a good cause."

Fateh opened his mouth to protest, especially when someone shoved the blunt end of a shovel into his mother's stomach, causing her to double over in pain. "Make sure she doesn't call on any help, either," Meira ordered as if this wasn't her friend's mother—someone who had not so very long ago brought her presents and taught her to cook and helped her through her first breakup.

Everything seemed to slow as one of the idiots holding his mother smirked, flipping his knife to the side and holding it to her throat.

"If I kill her now, would you be upset?" he asked. "Give in, Fateh, or else your mother will do it unwillingly."

"You ... you asshole!" Fateh jerked to go after him, but he was still held tight enough that he couldn't free himself.

His mother swallowed hard, trying to shake her head, but the knife was too close. "I'll be fine." Her voice was strained, but he heard it and wanted to tell her to not say anything at all. "You get out of here."

Her eyes warned him, pleaded with him, but he couldn't just ... just let her go. He didn't have a choice, though—she was dragged backward. The boy had one hand clamped around her middle and the other holding the knife to the delicate skin of her throat. He heaved her along, not noticing the scrap of wood behind him, making him topple backward. His hands immediately went out in a gesture to keep himself from falling and the knife slipped, spraying red over Fateh. The knife that was held to her neck—the knife that was only supposed to be a threat—had torn his mother's throat open.

His ears were filled with an almost painful sound as a gurgling noise choked his mother's gasp off and she fell forward, no longer needing to be held back as the life drained from her body.

He swallowed hard as all eyes turned toward him. It was only then that he did as she'd told him to do. He couldn't save her. He shoved past those holding him, barely hearing their cries of pain. He needed to get away—his mother had died because she tried to protect him and make him run away. His nose filled with the smell of smoke but he didn't stay; it encouraged him to run all the faster. The world seemed to spin around him, making his steps stagger as he tried to right himself in a world gone topsy-turvy.

Fateh heard the Shadows laughing, mocking, and teasing, and he shuddered. He wanted to get home, but ... it wasn't home anymore. All that his mother gave up was worthless now. She was gone; it wasn't right. His shoes smacked the cracked pavement as he bolted and his breath was loud in his ears. It cut at him and his entire world was focused on the task of getting away, hiding, and getting revenge for the ones who caused this. Houses blurred as he ran past them, people smearing into inconsequential shapes. His breath was ragged in his chest as he struggled to breathe around the pain of losing his mother, of running for his life, of just trying to survive. He scrambled to think of what he was going to do next, where he was going to go. Who could he trust?

He found himself at the remains of what had been the high school, almost completely collapsed in from the wild vines and trees that had overtaken it. The Shadows that lived here had wasted no time in destroying any vestiges of humanity. *Guess the school won't be reopening here,* he thought inanely.

He ignored the whispers, his eyes wide and trained on where he came from, heart pumping so hard that it hurt. As he tried to catch his breath, to hide in the greenery, it hit him what had happened. His mother was dead, his friends had killed her, and no one had done anything to try and stop it. He trembled, knees giving out as he sank to the ground.

What had his mother meant, that she was safe? She had to have known that she was going to ... that they ... or had she thought that the Shadow she was contracted to was going to save her somehow? He tried to concentrate on the memory of what just happened, to see if there was anything that he'd missed. The only thing he could think of was that strange light, the links of the chain fading into the dark. Had something come to take her soul? He growled at the thought; she was barely dead, and they were already going to manipulate her soul. The despair at what had happened and what lay before him twisted at his insides.

"We have him." The voice was calmer than Meira's had been. "Fateh, stay still and we will help you."

If anything, that was worse than before and he struggled to get up, but a firm hand closed around his wrist, pinning him in place. "Who are you?" He didn't recognize any of them and the town wasn't so big that there would be an overt amount of strangers.

"We're here to help you." The woman gave him what he was sure was meant to be a comforting pat. "We saw what happened—terrible, terrible." There wasn't any sympathy in her voice, though. "We're going to take you away to a safe place."

One of those homes, Fateh realized. His mother was gone and after what the town and his friends had done to him and how they saw him ... he was being taken away. The fact that they had found him—did they have spies in this place or something? That sent a chill down his back.

"Fateh, it's okay," another voice said—this one sounding a little more real with her kindness. "We know it's not your fault what happened here. We're going to do all that we can to protect you."

"Of course, it isn't my fault," Fateh snapped, rousing out of his shock for a moment. "I want to go home." He desperately wished what he'd seen had been a mistake. "I ..." He wanted his mother to be there, wanted everything to be normal.

"Shh—Mary—will you?" The person in front of him nodded and before Fateh could see or jerk away again, a syringe was pressed into his side and darkness overcame his senses.

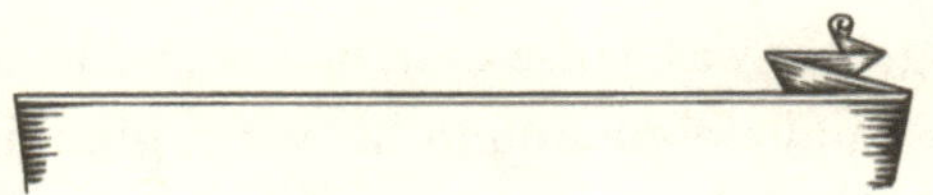

Chapter Eighteen

"**O**oh, he's awake."

"My head ..." Fateh whimpered and rolled over, closing his eyes against the blur of color and strong light.

"Yeah—guess they thought you'd be trouble and gave you the dose." Fateh didn't recognize the voice and forced his eyes open again, trying to focus this time. Yep, he definitely didn't know the person or where he was.

"They mentioned a safe place," he muttered, sitting up slowly. "Is that where ....?"

"Yep—and you got the metal bracelets and everything. Guess they thought whatever happened to your town was enough to warrant 'em. They don't give them to too many people. Metal's too hard to come by these days. Even that's not all the way pure, but ..."

"How would you know what it's like?" He stared at the thin metal circling his wrists, rubbing at where it chafed him. He was scared that it would burn his wrists as the metal had before, but it was just ... irritating.

"You're not the only one they've tagged." The boy—younger than he was—gave him a bitter smile and held out his arm, displaying the metal armbands there. "Anybody who was in close contact with the Shadows gets wrapped in metal in some way so they won't corrupt us." His eyes shifted to the side, where a woman was watching the proceedings calmly but not interfering. "Ms. Winger makes sure of it."

"They think I'm corrupted?" Fateh growled. "I didn't have a damn thing corrupting me—it was my friends who caused all of this—this—" His throat closed as he thought of his mother. "My friends and their stupid vigilantes killed my mom. It wasn't Shadows corrupting us."

"Yeah—but I bet they killed her because of the tylwyth teg, huh?" Fateh wanted to strike out at the nosy kid, age be damned. "What was your town like for that to happen?"

"We had contracts," Fateh said slowly. "If you chained yourself to a Shadow, then you were supposed to be safe." He snorted. "It didn't work all that way, obviously."

"No wonder your friends were pissed," a girl with cropped blonde hair snorted. "If they thought you were the enemy, then it's no wonder they attacked you. They were just defending themselves." She was free of any metal, Fateh noted.

"You don't know a damn thing," he started, standing up to face her. "They were my friends, *and* they knew we weren't Shadow-touched. Mom had been just weighing all her options. We weren't safe, none of us were, and we were trying to make the best of it." He barely noticed the small group gathering around him, just as there was a group around the blonde girl.

"A group of fae-touched torched my family's home, with my little sister in it, just to prove to their new masters that they had no connection to humanity anymore." Her eyes were cold and her voice flat as she regarded Fateh. "You planning to set off any fireworks like that, newbie?"

"Why would I do anything that the Shadow-touched do?" Fateh snapped. "I'm not one of them, no matter what anyone thinks. These stupid metal handcuffs aren't needed. I'm perfectly normal." He looked around desperately, hoping someone would believe him. Even those who were around him looked resigned as if they had heard this all before; they had probably even said it themselves.

He noticed that she didn't use the term *Shadow* when it came to those who invaded homes. She said fae. Maybe where she had been, the *fae* had been more of a problem.

"We have restrained you this way because of what several witnesses in your town have reported." The calm, clinical voice of Ms. Winger answered him instead of one of the kids. "There are witnesses who said you were burned by metal and a fae named," she consulted a folder, "Tabor, seemed to assist you in some way by causing a fire in the lower part of town."

"He ... " Fateh scowled at the mention of Tabor's name and how utterly useless he had been. "I never asked for his help. He was just always hanging around and being a nuisance. My mother was just doing what every person in town was going to have to do, eventually. Maybe it's different in this town here, but where I'm from, you had to contract to make sure you were going to be safe."

Ms. Winger put a hand on his shoulder and tried for a conciliatory tone. He had a feeling she'd done this before and was only reading from her own internal script. There was no genuine emotion in her voice. "Fateh—he influenced you, tricked you—as all their kind do. We'll protect you from him. He can't touch you as long as you wear those." She tapped the metal. "This is your home now, Fateh. You're safe here; no fae can touch you."

The room was furnished in an eclectic style, as if someone had gone to a rummage sale and picked up whatever was there. It wasn't cozy by any stretch of the imagination. It looked ... sad, almost. As if it had tried to be something more than it was. There were kids lounging in the chairs, but their posture was anything but casual. They were all staring avidly at Fateh and gauging his reactions.

The windows were tall and barred—not with metal, but with wood, Fateh noted. It would be too much to expect metal everywhere. The fact that he wore bracelets of it was more than a stretch. There was a slice of the outside visible from where he was standing and Fateh glimpsed a large pond. He shuddered and turned away from the sight. He hoped that he wouldn't be going anywhere near that.

Fateh had to wonder where they got the metal and even though he knew it wasn't pure, it was still enough that his wrists were more than a little cold from wearing the handcuffs. It scared him; nothing like that had really happened before. "This isn't my home," he said fiercely. "I've got a home, and it isn't this place." He glared at Ms. Winger. "I want to go home."

"Your mother is dead," she snapped, the caring tone going out of her voice. "Your father has never shown up. You are underage and there is no way that you can live alone. Do you want your mother's sacrifice to be in vain?" she asked him, trying to switch tones and instead sounding like something was stuck in her throat. "She died to protect you and if you go out on your own, you will die. You aren't protected."

"How do you know so much about me?" he demanded. "How long have you people been watching me?" He scowled harder at her, trying to hide his unease under the bravado. "Kinda creepy, if you ask me."

"We talked to several people in town about you," she said calmly, unaffected by the glare he was giving her. "A young lady named Meira was most forthcoming with information about you." Her smile turned sly. "It seems that she knows you quite well and was eager to have you in a safe place." She squeezed his shoulder tightly. "You can't go back to where there is no protection. You said it yourself. You would have to get chained to a fae to be safe and you don't want that, do you?"

"I know Meira," he growled. "She was supposed to be my friend, but instead she's the reason my mother got killed." He rubbed at his arms and choked back a sob. He had a hard time thinking through his grief. With everything that had happened, it didn't seem real yet that his mother was gone, nor that it was the fault of who he thought were his friends. Who was he supposed to go to for protection now?

I think Tabor is supposed to protect me ... he thought idly, but it wasn't a thought he enjoyed and it certainly wasn't one that he was going to share with the head of this establishment. Who knew what they'd do to him if they knew he was under a type of contract? He was promised *to* a Shadow, at least, even if he hadn't signed anything yet. *Even though any sign of protection is pretty piss poor at this point.*

But maybe Tabor isn't a Shadow but actually one of the tylwyth teg. That would change a lot of things. The tylwyth teg weren't all bad, not like the Shadows were. They got harassed just the same as humans did.

"Boy, way to roll out the welcome wagon, Ms. Winger," one boy snickered, interrupting whatever the woman was going to say next to Fateh's comment. "He'll really feel at home here now. Bring up his friends that betrayed him, not show any caring for his dead mother ..." He shook his head, his brown hair flying in his face. He ignored it and grinned through his hair. "It's no wonder he looks ready to break through the bars and take his chances outside."

"Hush, Michael." She frowned at the boy. "He needs to know the truth. There will be nothing good in sugarcoating it from him. That is how we all got into this mess in the first place." She straightened a little. "With constant vigilance, we can fight back."

"Ooh, yeah—'cause we really could fight the creepies," the girl spoke, the one who'd talked about the fae-touched killing her family. "Leave the new kid alone. We'll tell him how it is here." Her tone was syrupy-sweet and Fateh didn't trust her for a moment.

"Angela ..." Ms. Winger sighed and rubbed her temples. "Fine—you have been here long enough that I am sure that I can trust you to instruct him. He needs to know the rules, the dangers, and the consequences if he decides to go against what we do here."

"Sure thing, Ms. Winger." Angela smiled sweetly until the woman was gone, and then she turned to Fateh.

"Listen up—I don't care for your kind—halfway to fae-touched, you are. Just like the rest of those losers over there." She indicated the other ones wearing metal and Fateh noticed, with some uneasiness, that there was a definite separation in the group of kids around him. He was grateful that he wasn't alone, but nothing good came out of such a strong division. "Your kind ended my family's life and I'll be watching you to make sure you don't feel like doing the same to me."

Fateh was starting to get irritated at the accusations. His day had already been bad enough and he just wanted to sit in a corner, away from everyone else, and cry. "I don't plan on doing a damn thing to you," he snapped at her. "You leave me alone and I'll do the same to you. I don't want to stay in this dump, anyway."

"Even if it's a safe place for you?" Another girl spoke up, wispy hair red hair pulled back in a braid. He noticed she, too, was wearing the metal bracelets. "I know this isn't a nice place, but it is safe. You're safe and among friends. We know what it's like, Fateh." She gave Angela a quick look, then turned her gaze away, touching his hand gently. "We'll teach you."

"I don't want to be taught. I just ... I just want to go home." He thought of their barn, filled to the brim with junk that was collected over the years, of their house that had been in their family for generations. He didn't know what the Shadows would do to it and he felt sick; his imagination painted all too vivid a picture of them rifling through their belongings, of throwing away memories, or even worse—burning it all. He could never get it back, just like he'd never get his mother back.

"You can't." Her voice was quietly insistent. "Whatever happened to you, Fateh—it's changed your fate. I know it seems hard now, but we're well taken care of here. There are these stupid bracelets that sometimes burn." Her smile was more painful than anything else. "But other than that, it's not bad."

"Maybe he doesn't like being surrounded by all these humans," Angela sneered. "I hate the fae-touched. Losers. You teach him the rules then, runt. Since he's one of *you*." She shoved past Fateh, nearly knocking him into the girl who had been trying to reassure him.

The girl sighed and held out a hand. "I'm Randi," she said, giving him a more real smile. Most of the kids had followed Angela out; the only ones left were the ones wearing metal bracelets like he and Randi. There weren't that many of them. "We should really talk, Fateh."

"I ..." He wanted to be angry still, but she seemed to take the wind out of his sails with her genuine kindness and he relented, nodding once. He couldn't be angry at her—she was younger than he was, just a kid. "Fine."

"Good." She made herself comfortable on the couch, patting the seat next to her and sighing when Fateh continued to stand. "Fateh—I know this doesn't seem like the best option, but let me tell you a little of my story. Maybe then you can tell us what actually happened with yours. We stick together."

The other kids nodded in agreement, one keeping watch at the door for anyone to come in and surprise them. Fateh winced at all those eyes focused on him. There were only five of them, including Randi, but they seemed to multiply in his mind.

"I ... I guess it's different in different places." He swallowed hard. They didn't know what the rest of the world was like outside their town; no one traveled that much. He didn't imagine that the Shadows just stayed in one place. They had probably spread all over the world. "But there were a lot of the what we called the Shadows in my town. They took over the whole place, really."

"Ohh ... You had a nest where you were." Randi grimaced. "That makes it a lot harder. My place ... it was isolated, deep in the country. I got caught and taken." Her expression was haunted for a moment and the bile rose in Fateh's throat at what she was implying.

"Mama and I had gone for a walk to the observatory when I was attacked." She rubbed at her arms, expression distant. "I knew we shouldn't have walked at night, but ... we had been safe so far. No reports, no talk of anything ..."

"I was warned about walking at night, too," he said dryly, trying to ease the pain on her face. "Mom and I lived up in the woods and the only thing around there were the little Shadows. The worst stuff was in town and we hardly ever went there."

She nodded and twisted her hands together. "Walking in the daytime was just fine, but ... Mama had a telescope and there was this great observation point to see the constellations and the moon." She sighed in remembrance. "Daylight was safer, because all the trolls were stone."

Fateh blinked and stared at her, sure that he was hearing things incorrectly. "... Trolls?"

"Mmhm ...you didn't have them where you were?" She looked surprised and a girl next to her gave her a playful shove. "I thought they were everywhere."

"Not everyone had trolls in their backyard," the second girl teased, "posing as garden gnomes."

"Really *ugly* garden gnomes at that," another boy said with a grin.

Randi swatted at the both of them but it was playful, her mood lifting a little. "Well, yes—trolls. They were harmless in the sunlight; the sun turned them to stone. In the night, however ..." She grimaced. "If you went across their territory, they could do with you what they wanted." She brushed at her arms again. "My mom wasn't as lucky as I was." Her tone of voice indicated her mother might have gotten off better in the long run. "She didn't survive and I ..."

"Whatever they did to her," the girl who had teased Randi about garden gnome trolls said, "she's more sensitive to sunlight now. She can't go out in it that much."

"One of the trolls married me." She made a face. "Or whatever they call it. It changes you a bit, I was told. When Ms. Winger found me, she took me away from them, but I was already partially tied to them. It took a stronger fae to break my contract with them. That's what this house is all about. They've got super connections or something and it's really okay here." Her look turned far away. "The trolls and other fae can't cross the border of the grounds."

"And she's gotten a lot better now," the girl next to them pointed out. In a way, she reminded Fateh of Meira, but she was so pale that she was practically a ghost. "She can be out in the sunlight now without wincing. She just gets a little tired, but nothing like what it could have been."

Randi nodded seriously. "So, see?" she asked Fateh. "Whatever happened to you, whatever they did to you—it'll go away, eventually. You'll be better. They'll let you go when you're eighteen." Her look turned ironic. "They don't care what happens to you after you're eighteen. A lot of people decide to stay here, though. They work as teachers or counselors or something useful."

"How long has this place been open?" Fateh asked, startled. It sounded like it had been running for a long time, but the Shadows or fae or whatever they called themselves hadn't been in power for *that* long.

"Ever since the Shadows first came to the towns around this one." Randi shrugged. "This town is one of the few around here that don't have any of the tylwyth teg. I mean, this isn't the only safe house, it can't be ..." She shook her head. "But it's the one that's been running the longest, as far as I know. Nearly ten years."

"That's longer than the Shadows have been in my town," Fateh mused. *Maybe we got lucky in a way.* "No one ever thought about what was happening to the world outside our town. I guess we were sorta ... insular." The news hadn't reported anything on it; the Shadows came and then the fae appeared. It all happened so fast.

"Or the Shadows did something to your town to make you forget that the world outside your town existed," a boy pointed out. "They have tricky magic, stuff that we don't even know about or how it works."

"So, you see, Fateh— we know stuff here, and you can learn about the different kinds of tylwyth teg and what they can do. You're among people who *understand*." Her hand on his shoulder was gentle and caring, unlike Ms. Winger's earlier grip. "You can't be hurt here like you were back in your home."

He hadn't ever signed a contract; he hadn't been hurt by the Shadows, but that wouldn't change what had already happened to his mother. His expression changed abruptly and he looked away from the group, shrugging his arm away from Randi. "What, if I stay here long enough, my mother will come back?" Even Fateh was shocked at the bitterness that colored the edge of his voice.

"Do you mind telling us what happened, Fateh?" Randi asked quietly. "You know what happened to me. All we know is they rescued you from a town that was on fire and there was a lot of fae there."

He nodded, curling his hands together and taking a deep breath. "If people wanted to be safe, they forced contracts on them. Since my mother and I lived so far away, she decided that it would be the best option." It hurt to think about her going over the paperwork, so hopeful that it would keep them both safe as they could be. "My friends ... objected to it," he said shortly. *That* was the understatement of the year.

"There had to be something else," the youngest kid spoke up. "They wouldn't just interfere with contracts; we're practically under one here, the house, I mean. That's why we're all safe."

"I ... yeah." Fateh took a moment to collect his thoughts from that particular bit of information. An entire *house* full of people was under a contract? "There was a Sh—tylwyth teg named Tabor that kept on nagging me. My friends really hated that and accused me of being in league with him." He thought again of the fire, of how it didn't hurt, and went pale. *Had* Tabor already done something to him? "It's ridiculous, though. He's been nagging me since I was a kid." When he thought he had been a friend, before the Shadows had really taken over. "I didn't cause the fire. I bet he did and set me up." His tone was doubtful.

She interpreted his expression correctly. "See?" she asked gently. "This Tabor hurt you, and you didn't even know it. These bracelets that we wear help protect us. They can't work through us when we're wearing them. Tabor can never touch you again."

It had never seemed to Fateh that Tabor had actually hurt him. Annoyed him, yes—but he'd been ... friendly. It irked him to think that *now*, especially with what that friendliness had cost him, but he never actually *hurt* him.

"So, he was a fire tylwyth teg?" she asked, tilting her head. "That must have been frightening. I hear that they're made entirely of flame. He must have laid some sort of claim on you so that he didn't burn you when he stayed near you." She shook her head. "It's gone now, Fateh. It won't ever go away, not completely, but you'll see—we'll be a new family here for you."

Fateh wanted to protest. He didn't want to accept Randi's matter-of-fact tone, but he could already feel the walls closing in. He didn't want their so-called safety.

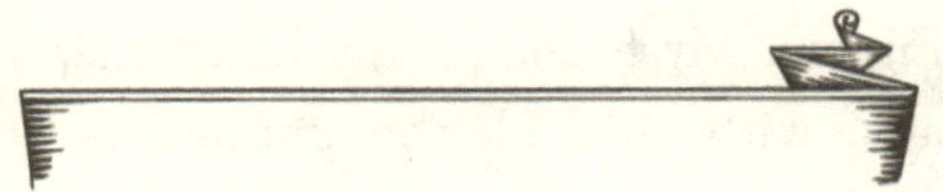

Chapter Nineteen

"So, Fateh, I'm Jonathan." It was the nosy kid, the one who'd talked about his friends betraying him. "You aren't the only one here that has to wear metal bracelets or that's been touched by the fae. Although where I came from, they didn't call themselves Shadows."

"That's what they called them in my town." Fateh frowned a little. "Why? What did they call themselves where you lived?" He was curious despite himself. He only knew them as Shadows and tylwyth teg because that's what they resembled. Hearing about Randi and the trolls was enough of a surprise.

"They're called *afon*," Jonathan said. "They stuck close to rivers and lakes; they had me living underwater with them." When Fateh stared at him, Jonathan shrugged. "They changed me so that I was able to breathe underwater. Even now, I can still breathe underwater, even with my armbands." Fateh looked surprised, but Jonathan just shrugged again. "They get their magic from the element they're in, which is why I can still access the magic in the water. Take them away from their element and they're not as strong." He considered his own words for a moment. "Of course, some can generate their own element, like the ones that deal in fire."

"How did you escape them?" Fateh asked despite himself. "It's not like Ms. Winger was dredging ponds looking for kids."

"She heard a rumor about the *afon* and came to investigate. She came away with me and Mokosh. We've been here for about five years now."

The other kids looked uneasy at the mention of Mokosh's name, but before he could ask who they were, the younger of the girls pushed Jonathan away. "You were a fish, we get it," she said. "At least you weren't a living doll, a *pet* for the fae."

"You got out before it got real bad," Jonathan protested. "At least they didn't change you. I can't be without water for long or else I dry out."

"They treated me no better than a mindless toy," she shot back at him, hands on her hips. "They raised me like I was their little doll. I couldn't do anything without them hovering. They fed me on the floor, dressed me—"

"At least you got out quickly, Mari," Jonathan pointed out. "You've been here almost as long as this school's been around. You're practically *normal*." He said it like it was a bad thing.

"Yeah, falling into shadows like they're pools of water is completely normal." She rolled her eyes. "I might not swim like a fish and be best friends with the *afon* that lives here, but I was changed, too. We all were, so don't think of yourself as special." She brushed at her hair, which was styled in perfect little curls. It was obvious she had tried to do something *to* the curls, but they were fluffy and perfect and all she needed was ribbons to wind around the strands of hair. She was pale with light pink spots on her cheeks and her lips were the perfect shade of rose. She looked vaguely unreal and it was slightly creepy how much she resembled a doll.

"Guys, let's not argue amongst ourselves," another kid protested. They were tall, with dark, ebony skin and tightly curled black hair. They were older than Fateh, but they couldn't be that much older, or else they wouldn't be here. "We save that for Angela's little gang," he continued, turning to Fateh. "I'm Sam." They flashed a grin. "Neither fish nor fowl, hence the nice neutral name." They fiddled with something in their hands and when Fateh gave it a closer look he saw that it was a bunch of weeds.

Fateh gave them an interested look. "And what's your story, Sam?" he asked. "Let me guess, you grew up in the wild and some plant fae found you."

"Very good." Sam grinned. "You're observant, aren't you? Was it the plants that gave it away?"

"Yeah, I didn't think anything grew here," Fateh snorted, gesturing to the bare walls. "This place seems a little devoid of life."

"Yeah, well, they weren't called Shadows where I was either. I think that's actually a specific kind of the fae. I lived on my own for a long time, ever since my parents abandoned me. I came across a group of what I thought were humans reclaiming the land. It was too late by the time I realized that they were doing much more than any human could have done." They sat down across from Fateh, handing him a single flower. "They called themselves the *gwyrddni*."

"I'm beginning to think that I came off lucky," Fateh muttered. "The Shadows didn't kidnap me or turn me into a fish or anything like that. They were just ..." he made a face. "They were *shadows,* mainly. There were other fae, but they were obviously not human." His expression hardened. "It was because of the Shadows that my mother was killed. If it wasn't for them, the people in my town never would have turned on us. There was only one that could be mistaken for human and I'm starting to doubt he was a Shadow at all."

"That was Tabor, right? I bet he *wasn't* a Shadow, but something different. Too bad you'll never have a chance to ask him." That came from the last girl. She was wearing layers of clothing; multiple skirts, a long-sleeved blouse, and knee-high boots. A scarf covered her hair so that only her face was visible.

She gave her a friendly smile, but something about her gaze was piercing, as if she could see deep within him. He gave her an uneasy look; he didn't know what she was seeing and didn't want to ask. "I'm Marisa," she said dreamily. "I like you. You're sparkly inside."

"Marisa is one of the few of us who wasn't taken by the fae. She has clear eyes. She can see what the fae try to hide, so she's here for her own safety." Randi's voice was quiet but filled with admiration for Marisa.

"My mother said I had clear eyes," Fateh said quietly. "What does that even mean?" He knew he could see things that others couldn't, like the chains that bound Shadows and humans.

"Marisa can see things," Randi explained. "Whenever she goes into one of her moods, the stuff she says comes true. The metal doesn't stop her visions. She can see the true nature of a fae just by looking at it, so they can't hide from her." Randi rocked back on her heels as she watched Fateh's reaction.

Fateh's skin crawled. He didn't want to be alone with Marisa. Who knew what she'd say about him? She'd said he was 'sparkly' inside; what did that even *mean?*

The metal was itchy to wear and he scrubbed at his wrists, trying to get some relief from it. He noticed the welts on the skin of the other kids. He knew that he shouldn't be relieved that it wasn't just him, but it brought him some weird sense of comfort to know he wasn't alone in this.

If he could act 'normal' and pretend like nothing was bothering him, maybe they'd take the stupid things off of him. He knew they wouldn't let him leave, not for another two years, but wearing something that made him look like a criminal hurt. It reminded him all too well that it was *his* fault that his mother had died.

"Well, we've dumped enough information on you," Randi said cheerfully. "I think it's time that we showed you your room so that you can get some rest or just have a space to be alone. I know how overwhelming it can be here the first time."

Fateh gave her a grateful look; it sounded like he would have a room of his own. It was a small blessing to have a space that was just his in this strange place. He needed time to sort out his thoughts, absorb what he'd learned about the other kids, and mainly just have a moment to grieve. He had a feeling that there wouldn't be many opportunities in the future.

"Fateh, how are you feeling today?" Ms. Winger tried to smile at him but as usual, it looked so strange on her face that he wondered why she even tried. "Are you getting along well with the others?"

He shrugged and slumped down in the chair as well as he could. "They're friendly," was all he said.

"And yourself? We haven't noticed anything odd about you lately." She gave him what was supposed to be an encouraging look. "Perhaps you were only barely touched by that fire demon."

"Seems like it." He raised his eyebrows at her. "Can we get rid of the really stupid fashion accessories now?" He didn't let on that they bothered him physically in any way. "I'm obviously not going to go up in smoke and metal's kinda rare to waste it on someone who doesn't need it." It was amazing that they could scavenge so much of the stuff; they must have a smelter or something like that on-site to be able to reform the metal into the bracelets and armbands that they wore here. The fact that it was *iron* was doubly amazing. Iron had seemingly vanished from the world—or at least it had for Fateh. Maybe iron was more common outside of his town.

"How thoughtful of you." She patted his hand. "But we have a supplier, don't you worry. We want to make sure you're safe, of course. We don't want any accidents. But since you've been so good, you get to come out with us tomorrow. Doesn't that sound like fun?"

Do I look like a dog or a preschooler? Still, he forced a smile on his face. "Getting outside would be nice," he agreed. "Thank you." Being cooped up inside wasn't enjoyable. He hated being closed up in four walls so much. He and his mom always had all that space ...

"Good—we'll make sure you're extra protected, Fateh." She patted his hand again. "We'll keep a good eye on you."

It came out as more of a threat than a reassurance, and Fateh had to wonder what she really thought about him.

————

When he was finally let outside, he gaped at the difference in the landscape. He didn't know where he was, but it certainly wasn't anything like his town or the woods he grew up with. He was grateful to be outdoors, though. He hadn't realized how cooped up he had felt until the breeze caressed his face without screens and bars to block it. It was wonderful to see the sunlight and feel the heat of it. For a moment, everything seemed right.

He was on his own. The others had all scattered. They had friends in town and Fateh didn't blame them for taking the chance to see them. He didn't mind being alone. It gave him time to take in the view.

The people in this town were used to the children, it seemed. Fateh scowled at their pitying stares. But mostly, people went about their business. Most people avoided him as if he was as bad as the Shadows.

Fateh was able to get a good look at the building where he was being kept. It seemed bigger on the outside, but that was probably because there were so many people crammed into the place and he hated such closed-in spaces to begin with. It was surrounded by greenery—almost like a park area, and he wondered if that was Sam's influence or if it had always been there.

He took a deep breath of the fresh air, trying to put everything out of his mind, pretending that he wasn't in a home full of kids as cursed as he was; that he just got 'sent away' for school. He liked that idea. It didn't hurt as much as thinking of the other reason why his mother wasn't there.

He could pretend for the moment. No one could ruin that.

"I can see inside of you."

He made a startled squawk as he turned towards the speaker. It was Marisa, and he winced. There was only one other person nearby, and it was an old guy sitting on the park bench. *So much for watching me like a hawk.*

Still—what could Marisa see about him? That he still missed his mother in ways he didn't tell any of the others here? That he hated this place and its stupid rules and stale air and metal bracelets? "So?" he asked her.

"You're strange inside," she whispered, eyes wide with that strange, unfocused look as she turned to him more fully. "You flicker ... it's very pretty." She leaned towards him, hands reaching out to touch him, and he instinctively backed away.

"I don't know what you mean," he huffed, expression wary as he looked at her. What if someone heard that and took it the wrong way? There might be spies. He gave the old man a suspicious look, but he didn't seem to even hear them.

Fateh didn't want to be at the school for any longer than he had to be, he didn't want to wear the stupid, itching, heavy metal bracelets ...

"You're all shiny inside." She leaned closer again, seemingly oblivious to his desire to keep his distance. "All flickering lights and warmth. It's so nice. I want to see more of it."

"I really don't know what you're talking about," he snapped, more scared than anything. It twisted him up inside, the fear—of what they could do to him if they listened to Marisa. They had told him that she spoke the truth and what she predicted came true. He didn't want any predictions. What she was saying was bad enough.

"I don't think it's bad." She pouted when he wouldn't let her near him. "I think it's very lovely—all sparkles and warmth and fire ..." Her gaze grew more dreamy than before. "It's exciting and relaxing all at the same time."

Now he was noticing others looking at him and he shivered. Maybe Tabor really had done something to him and Marisa noticed it, but it didn't mean that he had to agree with her. "You're crazy," he said flatly. "You don't see anything like that with me. I'm normal."

"It's not bad," she said again, looking confused. "I think it's marvelous. Interesting ... everyone else here is such dull colors." She sighed. "You're bright—red and gold and blue and white ..." She giggled, and it was off-edge. "Like sparklers on holidays or fireworks. Remember fireworks?" she asked wistfully. She sounded much younger than she looked and the crazy gleam was leaving her eyes.

"Yeah, I remember them," he agreed sadly. He, Meira, and Tobias would go from store to store trying to get the best set, but his mother always seemed to find the ones that would whistle the loudest, go the highest, and have the brightest colors or patterns. That had been a long time ago. No one that he knew put up fireworks anymore.

"So, you're not bad if you're like fireworks," she said seriously, eyes wide. "I won't tell," she whispered to him. "I don't want to share how pretty you are with anyone else."

"Um ... thanks." He coughed, brows drawing together in confusion.

She twirled around, giving him that dazed smile again, before chasing what looked like a puff of dandelion seeds, leaving him alone with the old man.

He took a deep breath, trying to understand what move to make next. Marisa seemed a little too flighty to be trusted with keeping his "shiny self" secret.

"Spark." Fateh turned around so quickly that he nearly sprained something. He *knew* that voice. He looked around for Tabor but saw no one that resembled him—just the old guy, reading a newspaper and feeding a flock of birds. *Who said that, seriously*?

The man scattered more seeds. "Got yourself in trouble, Spark," he teased, but something about his expression was serious and Fateh blanched at Tabor's voice coming from the old man. What did he do, possess him or something? "Need a hand? Some help to get free?"

Fateh scowled and made sure no one was listening closely. "Oh, sure—you were a big help before. That's why I got all weird and locked up and having to wear these things—" He gestured to the metal around his wrists and the man flinched.

"Glad I don't have to wear them." He made a face. Fateh tried to rewire his brain to accept that this was somehow Tabor. "Still, kid—I'm going to rescue you. Tried to before, before they came all out with the heavy metal," he snorted. "Not sure I can even take you now ... but I'll watch out for you and a chance to take you."

"Who says I want to be rescued?" Fateh raised an eyebrow.

"Who says you have a choice? You forget that we practically had an agreement." He smirked. "And face it, kid, you hate the place that they locked you up in. I can see it in your eyes."

Fateh frowned and shook his head. "It's not as bad as it could be," he muttered. "No one's trying to kill me and there aren't any Shadows."

"Ooh, so you want to stay then?" Tabor asked with a grin, getting up to leave, but Fateh's hand shot out and grabbed his wrist, stilling his movements. The grin only grew at that point and Fateh huffed in annoyance at his own reaction. "You don't fit in there and you know it. You're like a fish out of water."

Fateh snorted. "That's because of what you did to me," he hissed, looking around to make sure no one was listening in. "I've talked to some of the others here and ..."

"You have more in common with those kids than you think." Tabor raised his eyebrows. You should listen to their stories."

"What do you know about that?" Fateh demanded. "You aren't in the school."

"I listen to what the people in town say," Tabor said dryly. "Humans love to gossip, especially about people who they think are lesser than them."

"You're an insatiable gossip," Fateh snorted. "What do they say about me?"

"Nothing yet, because they don't know your story yet. I can't explain now, but try to get those stupid bracelets off." He turned abruptly, folding the paper under his hand and waving Fateh off. "They're going to do more harm than good soon enough."

"Are you threatening me?" he whispered, outraged that even now—even after all that had happened—Tabor would threaten to do even more harm. *What gives him the right to think that...*

"It's not a threat, little Spark. It's a warning. Be careful. This place is dangerous, especially for you." He walked away, not looking back at him. Only Fateh seemed to notice the surrounding shimmer, changing him from the old man to who Fateh knew him as.

What did Tabor mean? He tried to take enjoyment in the surrounding town but he couldn't concentrate, not after what Tabor had said. There was a lot that he didn't say, and Fateh wanted to see him again, just so that he could demand answers.

He tried to put it out of his mind as best as he could; thinking about what Tabor meant could only be bad and there were Marisa's comments, too. It was almost like they were related and that scared him more than just Tabor screwing around with him. It was almost expected that a Shadow would want to mess with his head, but when Marisa's 'insights' were added into the mix, it painted an unpleasant picture.

No one said anything to him about talking to the 'old man.' For all he knew, they never saw a thing or simply didn't suspect anything. And as he hadn't caused any 'trouble,' some of the others in the house were no longer as hostile to him.

He wasn't sure if that was a good thing or a bad thing. He didn't want to be their friend; he didn't want to attach himself to anyone or try and trust again anytime soon. He thought he knew his friends, those he had grown up with—and found out he hadn't known them as well as he thought he did. It wasn't that the group in the house weren't nice; it was because they were that he wanted to avoid them.

But they've been through the same things you have, he reminded himself. *They're not going to judge you as Meira and Tobias did. They've lost their families, too.* Tabor wanted him to learn more about them as well. Still, it went against his better judgment to become close to them. It was enough to talk to them, to pretend that he was normal and adjusting to life here. He appreciated having a safe place now, away from the Shadows that caused him such pain.

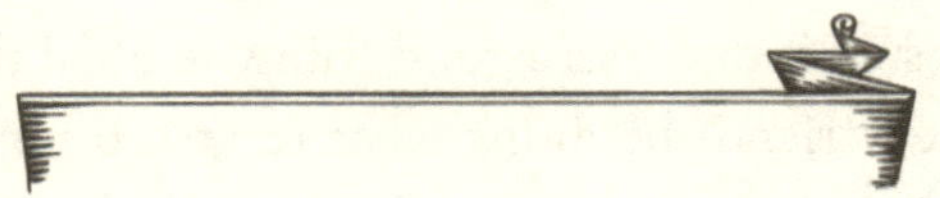

Chapter Twenty

Fateh was reading in the small library when Randi came in. It was a 'quiet day,' where most of the staff were in some sort of meeting, so the kids were free to do what they wanted inside. They were all scattered and some of them still didn't know what to make of him and he didn't encourage many questions. Randi was one of the few people he tolerated.

"You seem to be doing better," she observed, watching him as he turned the pages in a book. That was at least one good thing about here—he could read books that he hadn't before, so he wasn't going completely crazy from being bored.

"Do I?" he asked idly, looking up at her. He hoped that he was doing something right—that he'd be able to get rid of the stupid bracelets soon enough. "Maybe I'll get a reward for being such a good boy," he said dryly.

She giggled and sat next to him. "Maybe," she teased. She was looking better than when he had first seen her and she reminded him of what a little sister could be like, if he'd had one. Despite the promise to himself to not get attached to anyone, he still couldn't find it in himself to be entirely a jerk to her; she seemed almost too innocent for that, no matter what she had been through before. "Someone new is coming in, so Ms. Winger won't be staring at you as much anymore. She'll have new fodder." She made a face.

Well, there's something to be said for not being the new kid anymore, Fateh mused to himself.

"They're having the evaluations soon, too," Randi pointed out.

"Evaluations?" He stared at her, not understanding. He hadn't seen anyone being evaluated before.

"Oh—that's right." She grinned a little, rubbing the back of her head. "You seem like you fit in here so well now that you've been here awhile. Evaluations happen when new kids arrive and all the old ones are assessed to see how they're doing—if they've been ... fixed and can get the metal bracelets off." Her expression shadowed briefly. "The last new kid was you," she poked him, "so you were evaluated and didn't know it."

"They test you?" He didn't quite get it. How would they tell if they were fixed? Toss holy water at them and see if they burned?

"Yeah, they have all sorts of stuff they do to see if you're fixed. With me, they put me outside in the sun to see what happens." She grimaced. "Last time I was stuck there until the sun went down and they shut me in here again. The worst thing was knowing I was stuck and I was unable to move at all."

Fateh shuddered; he had been 'tainted' by a fire Shadow, by Tabor. What were they going to do, light him on fire and see if he burned? He didn't like the thought of that at all. The thought of *not* getting hurt was even more troublesome, though. He remembered Tabor's warning and wondered if he had anything to do with this at all.

"They won't try and hurt you." Randi caught his expression and lay a comforting hand on his shoulder; it took everything in him to not twitch away from her. "They do little tests—like with Jonathan? They take him to the pond we have here and just watch him swim, apparently."

Fateh held back his shudder at the idea of all that water. He had a feeling that talking about his dislike of it wouldn't help his case any. He had always disliked large amounts of water, though. That was nothing new. His mother had always talked about how she'd have to wrestle him into the tub as a baby ...

He pushed that memory away quickly.

"If you pass the tests," Randi gave him another serious look, "you'll be free of those bracelets. That's why Angela doesn't have them on anymore, even with what happened to her family." Her voice quieted, as if Angela was nearby and could hear them. "She proved she wasn't tainted and got to be free of them, even if she still has to live here."

"So, you really can't leave until you're eighteen?" He grimaced. The idea of being cooped up for another two years ...

"You'd be in your own home until you were at least eighteen," she pointed out. "And it's safer this way. Kids ... aren't as protected on their own. They can't make contracts without an intervention of some sort, like the homes." She sighed. "They just want us to be safe."

Neither of them mentioned it was too much like a prison at times. Any of them who wore the bracelets felt like that and it was a little too obvious of a thing to say out loud.

She patted his hand again. "I'll leave you to your book. It might be the last quiet day we get for a while." She smiled a little. "Or we might both be able to take showers without worrying about rusting." Her smile grew wider in response to Fateh's answering one.

"That would be a wonder." He shook his head and looked up at her. "Be careful, Randi."

"You too, Fateh," she snorted and gave him a slight hug, ignoring the way he tensed up. "You're too tricky and it's going to catch up with you."

He blinked at her, a little surprised that she had noticed, but she was already waving goodbye to him.

He'd have to be more careful. If she'd noticed, there was a chance that the staff could have noticed as well. He wasn't looking forward to the evaluation at all. He didn't know what to expect.

They were taken off, one by one, for their evaluations. Fateh didn't see any sign of the new kid; he supposed he would be shown to them after the divisions were once again made—those who passed for normal humans and those who didn't.

I wonder how many of us will be moving to the not-as-watched floor. He didn't even know how many other kids were here; he mainly just knew of those who were like him and a few others. There could be a plethora of kids here who found a safe spot, ones who hadn't been cursed at all.

He rubbed at his wrists, more as a nervous reaction than anything else, but winced a little as he rubbed over a raw spot on his skin under the metal. Well, it wasn't as if it would be a shock to see skin rubbed raw. They never took the stupid things off. He was just worried about the worst-case scenario because it was all too easy to imagine what they could do to him. Contrary to Randi's reassurances, he could still imagine all too well what they would do to 'test' him, and none of the scenarios were pleasant.

Randi came back in, eyes bright and happy, and she hugged him. "It worked!" She was bubbling over with happiness. "I'm really fixed and I can go back to being normal." She held up her wrists, unmarked, unadorned. She was at least semi-free—she still had to stay here, but she *wanted* to. She felt safe here and she was no longer going to be watched so carefully.

Will I feel that way, too? he wondered idly, giving her an awkward hug back. *If I pass their little tests?*

"You'll be just fine, too," she reassured him with a smile. "You're next."

Despite her easy words, he could see the worry in her eyes and he wondered again what she knew. What she saw or what she thought. He remembered she had lived with trolls and ... well, he didn't want to think beyond that point, but he swallowed hard. He didn't want to know what was going to happen to him.

Fateh didn't look up at Ms. Winger when she led him down the hallway and outside. His entire stomach was knotted up with worry and he tensed even further when he smelled the water. They weren't going to shove him in, were they?

"Now, Fateh." Ms. Winger had that creepy smile on again as she turned to him. "We know you had problems with fire in that town of yours and with that demon." When he gave a reluctant nod, the un-smile widened. "Well, it just so happens we have the perfect test for you."

Even if I fail, it's not like I'll be the only one, he reassured himself. *I'll just have to continue with the stupid bracelets and being watched and ...*

He wasn't expecting the form that was suddenly there, a fae woman perched on the water as easily as he was standing on the concrete area surrounding the pond. "Hello, little human. I've come to test you."

Fateh's eyes widened and he jerked away in real fear at seeing one of *them* again. "You said this place was safe from them!" he protested. "Why—what ... "

"Hmm ... the fear seems genuine." Ms. Wagner looked unconcerned, only mildly interested. "Now, Fateh—you already knew that we have a benefactor that helps to protect us. You said it yourself, that we couldn't get help without enlisting the demons." She patted his shoulder.

The woman standing on the water gave him a lazy, amused smile as she looked him over. "You can call me Mokosh." She seemed amused at her own name choice. "It fits well enough for you to use and for me to not be too terribly confused by."

So, this is the Mokosh that Jonathan came with? He didn't know she was a Shadow or *afon* or whatever she wanted to be called.

She was as shifting as any of the Shadows did, for all that she was more real—more *there*. It scared him again that she was so real. She wasn't wearing any clothing, but it wasn't as if she needed it. He could only guess that she was a female by her voice. Everything else shifted and moved around her, the water itself swirling around her form. He *hated* all that water and the thought of what it could do to him.

Fateh shivered and took a step back. Was this how others felt around the Shadows? He'd never gotten close to the powerful ones, except Tabor, and he found he didn't like this experience one bit. *Why did Tabor never affect me this way?*

"I'm not sure why they have *you* in those charming metal bracelets." Mokosh stepped closer to him, but never off the water, shifting forward in a way that twisted Fateh's stomach. Nothing should move that way. "You seem so very normal to me." Her eyes held nothing of truth in them, an odd blankness that Fateh wasn't sure how to react to. He wasn't sure how the others *trusted* this creature to protect them.

Ms. Winger frowned at the words, as if she'd expected something very different. "Fateh was found in a town that had many of your kind there, and not in a helpful capacity." She sounded miffed and almost scolding and Fateh had to hold back a laugh at how this woman thought she could hold something over the Shadows. "Are you sure he wasn't affected?"

"Oh, he was affected." Mokosh smirked, expression revealing nothing more than amusement at this whole exercise. "I could see the problems when he first came in, but I see nothing wrong with him now."

Somehow, instead of her words comforting Fateh, a slight chill ran down his back. The words were meant to be a good thing, he was certain—but something about them set off warning bells in his head. Nothing good could come out of the Shadows helping you. *Nothing.* They were self-serving and only saw humans as something amusing to play with. The way Mokosh was looking at Ms. Winger certainly indicated that.

"Well, if our expert sees nothing wrong with you, I see no reason why we can't continue with you here under more comfortable conditions. Their kind simply cannot tell lies." Ms. Winger looked far more self-satisfied than she had any right to be. "I've found it very useful in dealing with them." She smiled brightly at Mokosh. "Would you say that the metal has helped him?"

"Oh, there's no doubt that it helped to speed his recovery along." Mokosh reached forward and as she stroked his cheek, the blood drained from his face. He had a sudden urge to just sit, his legs not quite wanting to support him. "Such an interesting little addition to this safe house."

"Now, now—with those bracelets on still, Fateh won't deal well with your touches," Ms. Winger scolded. "Thank you, Mokosh."

You're not supposed to thank them. Fateh's eyes widened as he watched as Mokosh's smirk widened. *How could she not know?* He had a sudden feeling that even if the bracelets came off, things were going to get worse, not better.

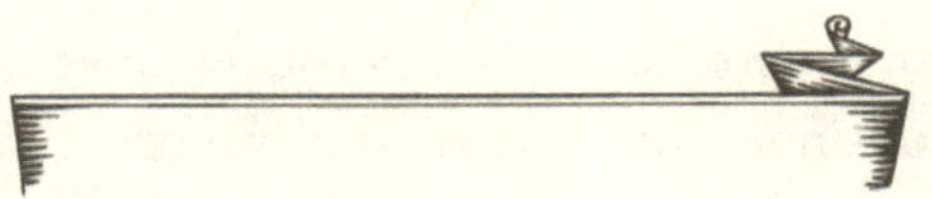

Chapter Twenty-One

Fateh was tackled by Randi as soon as he walked back into the room. "You passed, too." She beamed up at him.

There was only her and Fateh there who'd 'passed' the tests. Angela didn't seem happy that they were there. She made her feelings clear to Fateh.

"I still don't trust you," she snapped. "You were friends with that fire demon. No matter what you are now, you were friends with the enemy *then* and you should have killed yourself when your mother died."

Fateh's chest hurt and his eyes blurred. He wasn't sure how to respond and he was saved from it when a hand clasped his arm and a comforting presence filled his vision. "Don't listen to her," Marisa murmured. "She's all dusty and smoky and angry inside." She shivered. "All sharp edges to cut if you try and get close."

"No one asked you, freak," Angela snapped. "At least I was never Shadow-touched."

"Why didn't *you* kill yourself, Angela?" Jonathan glared at her. "If it's such a trial to be alive after tragedy hits?" His hair was still damp from his test. "I don't see you running toward the windows to end it all."

"I never associated with them!" Her voice was shrill. "They killed my family. I never asked for their help or got dragged into their little families."

"And we didn't ask for it either." Randi gave her a dark look. "You think that I wanted to get married to a troll?" she demanded. "I ... I ... you have no idea—" She stumbled over her words and her hands trembled. "Don't talk about what you don't know. So what if your family died? At least you weren't changed by *them*."

"You should have all just ... just ..." Angela's entire body trembled. "I hate you all!" she shouted. "You're all tainted and you're going to turn on us. None of you should be out of your little shackles. You can't be trusted."

"You're just like Meira," Fateh said quietly. "She wouldn't listen, either, and it got my mother and a bunch of other innocent people killed. People got so scared they attacked others who were just trying to make their families safe. What did your family do to piss off that faction so badly that they used them as an example?"

She stared at him, eyes wide and face going blank with shock for a moment. "What did you do to have a demon tagging after you like a pet?" she demanded. "You were the one who killed your mother and all those innocent people. It's your fault she's dead."

Fateh didn't even think as he reached out and pushed Angela, resisting the urge to fully shove her to the ground. "You just ... shut up," he said, voice quieter than before. "You don't know anything and you go blabbing off at the mouth, saying all sorts of things you don't know anything about and it's pissing me off." He crossed his arms over his chest, staring her down. "You're nothing but a coward and spiteful and I don't *like* you." He felt the heat building in his chest and his hands and he balled his hands into fists, resisting the urge to punch Angela. She didn't deserve that kind of violence.

He stalked away before the heat could come to the surface and he did something he'd regret, ignoring Randi pleading with him to come back, that Angela didn't mean it. He hated to disappoint Randi; she didn't deserve to be mixed up in all of this.

He didn't care. He just wanted to get out of here.

———

He wasn't going to let them see he was upset, that he was still shaking from his experience with Mokosh, or that he felt almost light-headed after his argument with Angela. He couldn't let anyone know; they might take it all the wrong way. Without the stupid metal bracelets on, he could escape more easily, couldn't he? Where would he go, where he wouldn't get in trouble again right away? He doubted, no matter what Tabor said, that he'd be safe with the fire Shadow.

Rubbing at the raw patches left on his skin, Fateh wondered why the bracelets had bothered him so badly. Other than how they made him feel like a prisoner, he had been safe with them on, or so they said. The Shadows couldn't touch the metal. But he had just seen the source of their so-called safety and he thought it was insane to trust your life in the hands of a Shadow, *especially* when you didn't know how to properly interact with it. He recalled the shifting form of Mokosh and shuddered again. Something about her very presence made his insides curl.

"Without the bracelets, she can hurt you." Fateh jumped at Jonathan's voice.

"What do you mean?" Fateh couldn't keep the suspicion out of his voice. "The tylwyth teg can hurt you, Mokosh can hurt you—" Jonathan shrugged. "There's a reason most of us choose to keep the bracelets on. We know that it'll keep us safe." He stroked along the line of his bracelets and watched Fateh carefully. "I don't like the ones who take theirs off. They're more susceptible to being used than those of us who wear the bracelets. It's a shame you and Randi both lost yours."

There was an odd note in his voice that made Fateh actually *look* at him. *He doesn't believe what he's saying. He's glad we don't have them and it's not just because they suck.* "Yeah, people are just lining up to have them," he said dryly. "That's why Angela barks so much. She's jealous."

"Maybe she is." Jonathan smirked and sat on the edge of Fateh's bed. "But she trusts Ms. Winger and has faith that Mokosh is so very harmless to all of us."

Fateh made a face. "I don't see how she can trust a Shadow so much," he muttered. "I mean, Angela alone is pissed off enough at all of them that I never thought she'd agree to be protected by them." It was a real mystery, now that he thought about it, and said as much.

"Oh, that's simple." Jonathan waved it off, unconcerned. "Ms. Winger has Mokosh's real name."

Fateh stopped breathing for a moment and had to jerk himself into completing the act again. He stared at Jonathan, not able to actually believe that. "How did she ...?"

"Oh, well—that part's the mystery." Jonathan shrugged. "None of us know how, but it's a real stroke of luck for all of us; to use the fae instead of having the fae use us." He tilted his head and watched Fateh carefully. "Isn't it great to be on the other side for once?"

"Well, if she's protecting us, then I don't have to worry about those stupid heavy bracelets, do I?" Fateh was still trying to recover from the shock of Ms. Winger's little 'secret.' "And as soon as I'm an adult, I'm going to leave."

"You say that—but where will you go? Back home? It's probably all gone now. If they were smart, they burned it all to remove any taint."

"No ..." Fateh's throat closed up. Not his house, with all those memories, good and bad. With any pictures of his mother and even the stupid, old, dusty stuff in the barn. He needed that to be there to stay sane, to have something to look forward to.

Jonathan could see that Fateh wasn't going to listen and shrugged. "Well, believe whatever you want to. I guess it'll keep you sane. There's nothing else really to keep you occupied here. Keep your dreams."

"Jeez, you're more cynical than me." Fateh laughed, unable to think how his mother would shake his head over such a pessimist.

"Stay here long enough and any happy thoughts and hope you had will go straight out the window, too." Jonathan gave that parting shot as he left Fateh alone again, leaving him with a lot to think about.

——

The next time Fateh was allowed outside, Randi stuck near him and Fateh couldn't help but notice how she flinched at the sunlight still, even if she didn't 'freeze' in it. *Maybe certain things will never go away,* he thought. It was a depressing line of thought to follow, that they'd never be completely cured from what the Shadows did to them.

"So where are we, exactly?" Fateh asked her. It wasn't like he hadn't wondered before, but he felt uneasy asking while in the house. For some reason, he didn't trust to not be overheard and wondered why he was so worried over a simple question.

"Caergybi." Randi tilted her head, confused. "You never knew ... oh, that's right. You got hauled in here unconscious. You weren't ever told and I guess the rest of us assumed you had been filled it at some point." She hesitated and reached out a hand. "Are you okay?" she asked softly. "You know Angela didn't mean what she said."

Fateh grimaced and waved that off. "I ... I know, but it still hurts, you know?" he asked. "No one deserves to be told that. No matter what happened to them." Fateh had never wished death on anyone; it seemed a step too far.

He blinked at the town name filtered through his brain and memories. *Caergybi is right next door. How did I never hear of this place before so close to where we lived?* It hurt all over again, to realize that home was so close by, yet inaccessible.

"Where are you from?" she asked curiously. "I mean, you said that your town was overtaken by the Shadows and stuff, but you never said the name ..."

Fateh shrugged and laced his fingers together. "Felinheli."

Randi's breath caught. "Oh ... you're so lucky to get out of there alive," she whispered. "We heard about that town. It was one of those places that was ... recommended to not go to. It was shut off." She winced.

"So, everyone just left us hanging?" he demanded. "They knew what was going on and they could have helped, but they left us to fend for ourselves because they thought it was too dangerous? If everyone helped ... if ... if they tried, then it might not have been so bad." His voice broke.

And it could have been worse, a little voice inside remarked. *The Shadows reacted badly to just the small-town rebellion. If more people had gotten involved ... how many more would have died?*

"Fateh." Randi put a hand on his arm. "We couldn't do anything. We lost all of our transportation like you did. We just ... had different problems. You had almost a complete takeover, and we thought Felinheli had been destroyed, actually." She looked sad. "Your town isn't the only one that had weird things in it. Trolls, remember?"

"And I'm starting to think there are a lot more bizarre things out there." Fateh made a face. "Fantasy stories aren't so silly anymore, are they?" He took a good look at what he could see of the town. "I mean, what's here for instance?"

There was another look of surprise. "Nothing, really—I mean, there's the little fae, but they're like ants or something; they're everywhere. Mokosh, though, she keeps most of the others out. It's to keep us safer."

"She must be really strong, then." Fateh was more worried than before. "To hold all that out ..."

"I don't know." Randi shrugged. "I just know that around a certain area, they don't come near here. Guess she warns them off somehow."

And if Tabor got in the little circle of protection, does that mean he's stronger than she is?

It was a troubling thought.

———

Time seemed to move more slowly now that he didn't have the bracelets on and was more 'free' to go places. The town wasn't that big, though, and they weren't allowed to stray far from the house.

"It's for our own good." Marisa twirled next to him, scarves knotting around her as the wind kicked up. It was a group of them—everyone in the town knew who they were and Fateh flushed at all the pitying looks directed their way.

He stared at her for a moment, and she understood the look. "Why we can't go far. Mokosh protects us," she sing-songed. "Let's us stay safe and sound—no bad guys around. " She twirled more, nearly running into Randi and Jonathan.

Fateh shuddered. "Mokosh creeps me out," he whispered. "I'd rather go free than have her watching over me. You can't trust them," he said fiercely. "No matter what, they'll stab you in the back in the end."

"Poor Fateh ..." Marisa wrapped her arms loosely around Fateh's shoulders, peering into his eyes, unsettling him more. It was so *strange* how she seemed to look all the way inside of a person. He wasn't sure he wanted her to see that deep inside of him. Some deep-seated, unexplainable fear wanted her far away from that avenue. "The sparkle is brighter," she whispered in his ear. "The water won't put it out. Be careful. I like the sparkle too much to see it gone."

Even when she was talking like she was crazy, Fateh heard the warning in her voice. "I ... I'm better now," he whispered. "They said I was."

"You are better." She took a step back and smiled at him, simple and sweet and somehow more unnerving than before. "Soon, you'll be better than you ever were. That's why you have to be careful."

Randi and Jonathan were giving him curious looks, both wondering, but not asking, what Marisa was talking about. Marisa was dancing around the two of them now and while Fateh felt slightly bad that they were now the target of her crazy talk, at least they were nicely distracted from what she was saying about him.

He backed away, and there was suddenly someone there who wasn't *really* there. "She's right, you know," a voice whispered in his ear. The shadows felt overly warm around him. "You're getting all better, Spark, and that will cause so many problems for you."

Fateh grimaced. He recognized Tabor's voice and tried to pretend like he wasn't hearing a thing; he couldn't be associated with the Shadows now. Not when he had just gained more freedom. "Go away," he hissed under his breath.

"Oh, little Spark—soon you'll be begging me to take you away from here. I have from some very reliable sources that things are going to be very uncomfortable here soon. You know why humans never thank us, don't you?"

With that parting bit of wisdom, the presence of Tabor faded away.

———

"So, what did Marisa say to you?" Randi's look held nothing but simple curiosity, but on top of Tabor's little comment, it made him tense up more than he would have. "She was singing songs about how easy stone sinks to the bottom bottom bottom." She winced. "It was creepier than her usual."

"She told me how the water wouldn't get rid of the sparkle." He shrugged. "It didn't make any sense, but it hardly ever does."

"Funny—she told Jonathan humans don't swim as well as fish." She looked nervous. "She talks really crazy sometimes, but she can tell the truth, too. All her songs to us were about water. What's going to happen, Fateh?"

Marisa's and Tabor's words chilled him as the warning settled down Fateh's spine. "I don't know ... but I don't think we're as safe here as everyone thinks." When she stared at him, he gave an uncomfortable shrug. "I lived in that town with Shadows almost taking over everything, remember?" he asked. "We learned things quickly, like when bad stuff was going to happen or what not to do." He grimaced. Tabor's warning made it all the more real. "Ms. Winger thanked Mokosh."

Randi's hand went to her mouth; it seemed that even where she had been, they knew better than to thank the fae. "That's not good," she whispered. She hugged herself as if she felt cold. "Our protection ... it's gone. Mokosh can do what she wants to us."

"How do you know that?" Fateh asked. "You said you didn't have contracts ... you had other problems."

She snorted and shook her head. "I'm not blind and I've been around them all my life. You forgot that I was married to one of them." At his horrified look, she hastened to reassure him. "It's another type of contract, after all. It was only marriage; I had to live with them and clean and cook for them. There wasn't ... wasn't sex," she whispered, face flaming red.

Fateh gave a sigh of relief at that. Randi seemed too young and too innocent to have gone through that; he would have had to hunt down some trolls if they had hurt her in that way.

"They talk, Fateh. They don't think of us as very intelligent. Even the trolls didn't." She gave him a weak smile. "They tried all sorts of tricks to get a thank you out of me, but I saw what they did to those that said the words." She shuddered.

Fateh didn't want to know—he could only imagine what trolls would do to someone they had completely under their power. "Remember the days," he asked almost wistfully, "when trolls and demons and fish-people like Mokosh were in video games and books?"

She shook her head. "I'm younger than you, Fateh. This—this is all I can remember."

Fateh winced. It wasn't a fate he'd wish on anybody, but he wondered, just a bit, if it was better to not have known anything else, because you'd adjust easier. "You're not that much younger than I am," he protested instead. "And the fae didn't show up that long ago!" At least not where he was; maybe in other places it *had* been worse.

She shrugged. "Young enough, Fateh. Maybe I don't want to remember what happened before, okay?" she asked, temper rising a little. "Drop it." The normally calm voice sharpened as she looked directly at him. "Not everyone wants to cling to the past."

Thinking about what happened in the not-so-distant past, Fateh couldn't help but nod. "Yeah, I think I can see where you're coming from."

Randi smiled at him again, earlier irritation seemingly gone. "We have to tell the others, you know," she pointed out. "They can't be left in the dark about this ..."

"Unless Marisa is doing her fortune-telling to everyone who can listen," Fateh muttered.

"That might not be a bad idea." Randi grinned, watching her flit from person to person; the reactions were varied. Shock, disgust, outright fear, and disbelief were among the chief emotions. "She'll get the message across, that's for certain. Whether they believe her or not ..."

"They'll believe her." Fateh looked off in the distance. "She can see stuff—or else she wouldn't be here and she wouldn't say the stuff she does. She's a little nutty, but she'll tell you the truth."

"Then what did she mean about the sparkle you had?" Randi looked up at him.

"I was brought in because of the fire, remember?" Fateh shoved his hands in his pockets. "Maybe she's saying it'll come back or something." He shuddered at the thought. He didn't want that sort of thing anymore; he wanted everything back to normal. But as Randi had pointed out, wallowing in the past wasn't going to help a thing. You couldn't change it.

"Well, fire and water don't mix." Randi shrugged it off. "If you go up in sparkles like Marisa thinks you will, Mokosh'll cool you off quick enough." She grinned a little, almost seeming to forget that Mokosh wasn't to be trusted.

"If she doesn't drown me first," Fateh reminded her sourly.

Randi gave him an awkward hug. "Let's go inside, Fateh—find who hasn't been introduced to Marisa's little songs and try and figure out what we can do." Determination settled over her features. "If all of us work together, we'll get out of this together." She caught the look on his face and smiled faintly. "All of us know what it's like to be hurt by those around us."

Fateh rubbed at his arms and nodded slowly. Everyone in his town had been hurt by the fae—and they turned on each other as they tried to be as safe as they could. He only hoped that the same thing wouldn't happen here. He almost liked the kids he had been stuck with. He understood the ones who had been tricked and changed like he had been. He definitely understood the ones who lost their entire families to what the fae had done.

He also knew what people would do when pushed to it.

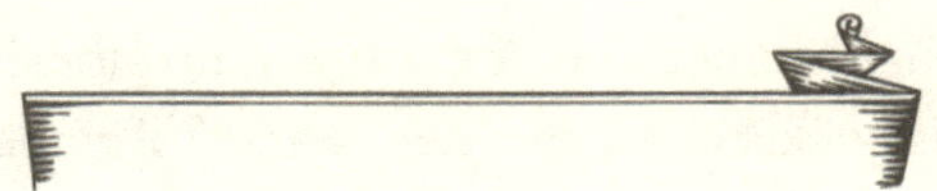

Chapter Twenty-Two

Even though he had the 'warning' from Marisa, Fateh wasn't expecting the water that was almost everywhere after that. Little trickles, damp floors—all of it smelling of the mossy water from Mokosh's pond. Part of him was almost gratified to see Ms. Winger having a meltdown over it and trying to hide it, but the other part knew how bad this was.

Everything was damp in some way—their clothes, the food, the bedding.

"This is disgusting," Randi cringed, tugging at her shirt. It wasn't even able to be wrung out; it was just a nasty sort of damp. "We need to get out of here." She looked toward Ms. Winger, but it didn't seem as if the comment was going to be processed by her anytime soon. All they could hear from the director was the squishy sound her shoes made as paced back and forth. "Ms. Winger ..."

"She's not going to listen to you." Angela smirked. "As far as we're all concerned, you and your little fae-taints brought this on us. Make friends with Mokosh, did you?" Her face twisted in hate. "Do you hate us all so much that you'd make a deal with her to destroy us?" She seemed to have taken Fateh's words of *I don't like you* to heart and was returning the favor.

Fateh scowled. "We didn't make any deals with her!" he snapped. "Ms. Winger was the one who decided to strike a deal with demons." He rolled his eyes, muttering under his breath, "And screwed it up, too."

More arguments broke out, the two factions clearly against each other. Even with him and Randi no longer wearing the bracelets 'for their protection,' they were still on the side of the kids who did.

"She was just trying to protect us. You," she glared at Fateh, "after you came in, it got worse. What do you do? How tainted were you? Are you still diseased from them?" She reached forward, clearly intent on doing some damage to him. It was like with his mother all over again.

Fateh opened his mouth, trying to duck out of the way and praying that the fire wouldn't show up again. Luckily, Tabor wasn't around and there was no fire, just anger that simmered under the surface like something ready to explode. "I don't want to deal with you," he hissed. "You're not worth my time."

"I'll make it worth your time," Angela threatened, but Fateh put his hands up and turned his back in clear dismissal of her, even though his skin crawled at exposing himself to whatever she had planned for him. A shove against his back sent him stumbling, but nothing followed and Fateh walked off, wishing that the coming year would be better than the last.

When Fateh woke up in the morning, he stared up at the ceiling, feeling numb. He was seventeen today and he was trapped in a prison instead of being with his mother. They'd always had fun on his birthday. Mom would make his favorite foods and cake and then they'd go into town to see Meira and Tobias. It had been more fun before the Shadows had come, of course, but they still managed to make it enjoyable even after things had collapsed all around him.

Now, though—it was just a reminder that he was stuck in this place for at least another year. His former friends were only a town away, but they only served as a painful reminder of what he'd lost. He couldn't go back home and he didn't know what remained after all this time. The animals were probably dead, unless someone had stolen them, and the garden would be choked with weeds.

He got up slowly, not wanting to start the day and not wanting to face anybody. They wouldn't know it was his birthday and he didn't think he'd accept any well-wishes even if they did. He paused when his feet splashed in water and he glanced down at the floor, slightly shocked. This was going beyond the dampness in the air. This was getting dangerous. Fateh picked up his shoes out of the puddle and wrinkled his nose; at least only the soles were wet.

He had a feeling though that things were only going to get worse, not better, as the day went on. Sloshing through the water and out the door, he mentally prepared himself for another boring day, trapped in a hell that he couldn't escape. Rubbing absently at the scars that the metal bracelets had left, he could at least be thankful that he wasn't shackled any longer. No matter what Jonathan had said, he was grateful that he wasn't wearing the metal any longer. Tabor's lingering influence on him had made it uncomfortable.

Randi met him outside his door, splashing through the water that was even in the hallways of the house. "Fateh! I didn't think you'd come out of your room today," she teased. "Is it as wet in your room as it is everywhere else?"

Fateh made a face and nodded. "I don't like it," he said slowly. "The water has to be coming from somewhere and the only place with so much water is Mokosh's pond."

"And we definitely don't want that inside." She shivered, then elbowed him gently. "Especially you," she said lightly. "You always turn green at the mention of all that water." Her look turned more concerned. "*Are* you doing okay?" she asked. "I know all that time with the fire tylwyth teg made it hard for you to deal with water."

"I don't like it, but I'm not melting away at it or anything," he laughed. "It's definitely uncomfortable, though."

As they walked into the main room, he kept a lookout for the others, especially Angela. He didn't want to deal with her today. She would probably blame the rising water on him again. If she knew anything, this place would be as dry as a bone, no Mokosh at all.

Sam was eating in the corner, a plate balanced on their lap as they talked with Marisa. Whatever the conversation was, it looked to be serious. Sam looked around cautiously, eyes lighting on Fateh and Randi, and they waved them over.

"Marisa has lots of things to say about the water," Sam said softly, keeping their voice quiet. "None of us like it, but Marisa says that we have to get out before it's too late."

"She was that clear about it, was she?" Randi asked, her hands on her hips. "She is never that clear to us about warnings. Last time, she talked in riddles."

"Sometimes warnings have to be clear," Marisa protested, her eyes wide beneath her scarf. "Right now, it's too dire to speak in riddles."

"So, your warning is to 'get out?'" Fateh asked.

"Especially you, Fateh," Marisa said solemnly. "You don't want to drown on your birthday. It's no way to celebrate."

Fateh grimaced faintly at the mention of his birthday. The last time he had discussed it with anyone had been with his friends and they'd talked about what they planned to do when Fateh was that much closer to being an adult. Of course, they had warned him against making deals with the Shadows; seventeen was still too young and eighteen was the danger zone. Other than that, they talked about the food they were going to eat and the games they were going to play ... it all seemed so long ago. Now he was in a prison for kids like him and there wasn't going to be any escape—if he even wanted to by then—until his eighteenth birthday.

Randi turned to him in surprise. "It's your birthday?" she asked. "Sorry that you have to spend it *here*." She gestured to the general area, eyebrows rising. "At least you're among people who under-stand?"

Others had gathered by that point, including Jonathan walking with Ms. Winger and talking rapidly to her, gesturing widely with his hands. She, in turn, was dismissive of him, waving away his obvious concerns with a wave of her hand.

"Jonathan knows it's dangerous, too." Marisa shook her head. "Ms. Winger should listen to someone who knows the water as well as Jonathan does."

If Maria was talking so much sense, Fateh knew he should be worried. If Jonathan was warning Ms. Winger, Fateh was ready to bolt out that door, permission or not. He was about to suggest to all of them to take a trip into town when he stopped dead.

The water had risen rapidly, curling around their ankles without notice and rising higher. There was silence for all of a moment, and then the mad dash for the exit started.

"Mokosh!" Ms. Winger shouted, still in place, seemingly not paying attention to the water that was creeping up to her knees. "You can't do this! I have your name!"

Randi tugged on her arm, trying to drag her to safety. "You thanked her! We have to get out now," she pleaded. It was one thing to hate the woman who made life so difficult. It was quite another to just abandon her to an indoor flood created by a malicious demon.

Fateh tried to help Randi but Ms. Winger was swatting them away, face red as she screamed even louder that she had to be obeyed. Fateh finally grasped Randi's arm, dragging her towards the door, struggling to get through the water that seemed to rapidly drain his strength. "She doesn't want to come," he said firmly. "We have to get out."

The water was up to his waist and he had just gotten Randi out the door (and into more water, he was sure) when Mokosh appeared from nowhere, smirking at him as she stroked the water that was all around them now. "My, my—a little Spark, struggling to go on, but most certainly about to go out soon."

Fateh struggled to get past her, to get somewhere safe. "You can't do this to me," he snapped. "I did nothing to you."

"Whether you are unaware of it, child, or not, you are my enemy and it's so very delightful to see you struggle so. To see the glimmers of fire spurt and die, to watch your soul be submerged under layers of water, watching you give up—"

Rather than making him despair, Fateh only got angrier—and somehow found the energy to move further to safety. "Who said I'm giving up?" Maybe now *was* the time for the fire to show up, to call on whatever Tabor had left in him. It didn't make him bad if he was using it so that he wouldn't *drown*, right? He just had to use enough so that he could make it through this alive.

"It won't work." She snickered and reached for him, but suddenly recoiled. "How very interesting," she murmured. "You're already promised to another, aren't you—what words did you give to the aodhamair?"

Fateh tried to keep the confusion from his face. He'd never heard that term before, but he had promised Tabor that he would sign a contract with him if things turned sour. Was that what she meant? Was that what Tabor really was? "What's it to you?" he demanded. "Let me out of here. The only one who screwed up here is Ms. Winger."

"How heartless of you, to sacrifice another to save yourself." She snickered, leaning forward again. The water drained around Fateh slightly, enough for him to move closer to the exit. "How very human of an act."

Fateh snorted. "She's not trying to save herself and not letting us save her. She put us all in danger," he pointed out, trying not to think of how it sounded, that he really was that uncaring of the caretaker.

"Silly child." Mokosh sighed and moved away from him. "You are correct in saying that she is the first who has to pay for the crime of trying to chain me to her will—but you best run as fast as you can, fire-child. You were all under my protection once. How many can you save before I destroy my prison?"

Fateh didn't look back to see what happened to Ms. Winger. The water was up to his chin by this point and he struggled to make his way through it. His limbs felt weighed down and with each push through the water, he felt more of his strength go. Finally, he just let go and sank into the water.

Fateh noticed Randi floating next to him, her eyes shut as she sank down into the water. There were other students there as well, some of them treading water, some swimming easily, but others were just as tired as he was and slowly sank to the bottom of the lake that was gradually taking over the house. He noticed Mokosh, but she was ignoring him, which he was grateful for, even as he felt some worry for the students who were in her grasp. He finally closed his eyes and let the water take over.

His last thought before he succumbed to darkness was that this was his worst birthday ever.

———

"Fateh—Fateh—are you okay?" Someone was shaking his shoulder and he opened too-heavy eyes to try and focus on the speaker. He could see a blurry outline of Randi and he winced. "You got out okay," he croaked.

"Nearly didn't," she confided. "I did start to sink—really fast. Guess I'm not all better," she murmured softly. "Jonathan saved me and you." She rubbed at her face, trying unsuccessfully to dry it. "Marisa, Mari, and Sam got out before the flooding got too bad, but Jonathan stayed in the water." Her expression was unreadable. "All the fae-touched children got out, Fateh, but none of the others or Ms. Winger."

"Didn't get ... out?" he asked slowly, still feeling drained, eyes closing again. He thought about Angela and her caustic nature, so traumatized by what the fae had done to her that she took it out on everyone around her. She didn't deserve to be drowned by Mokosh.

"Fateh—didn't you see what we're next to?" she demanded, voice rising with a hint of hysteria. "You have no idea how lucky we are."

Fateh forced himself to open his eyes again, to see what was upsetting Randi so much. He didn't think he'd be able to look away as soon as he saw what it was. Where the house had been was nothing but a lake. A small lake—but it wasn't exactly Mokosh's little pond anymore, either.

"What happened to the house?" he demanded, but his voice was ragged and broke at the end of his question.

"It's all underwater, Fateh." She swallowed hard. "All of it." She shivered in the wind, clothing sticking to her skin. "When we were trying to escape, the house was already sinking into the ground. That's why the water filled up so quickly. If it hadn't been for Jonathan—"

"What do you mean? How was Jonathan able to save us?" He remembered how friendly Jonathan seemed with Mokosh and shuddered. "Never mind. I don't think I want to know. So ... he's still in there?"

"Yeah." Randi's voice was subdued. "He wanted to be in there." They both remembered Marisa's words and warnings and stared out at the lake. He had nearly drowned, but Jonathan had saved him from dying in the water.

Fateh had to look away, had to try and gain some semblance of normality. "So—where is everyone else?" he asked quickly. "I notice we're alone."

"Everyone else scattered," she said. "Marisa said that you'd be taken care of and said to tell you to not let your sparkle dim any more than it has been." She shrugged. "She said you'd be taken care of, but to not forget us."

"Not let my sparkle dim?" Fateh shook his head. "I was almost snuffed out. I don't think I want anything to dim any more than it already has." He stared at the lake, imagining all those people under the water. "So, Marisa left after her warning. What about the others?"

"Sam left for the woods; not sure what they're going to do there, but they said that it's hard to get away from your roots and said they'd figure something out." Her lips turned reluctantly upward at the unintended pun. "Mari knows someone in town. I'm going to meet up with her, but I wanted to make sure that you were okay first."

Fateh stared at her, astonished that she stayed around, that she didn't run for safety as fast as she could.

She caught his look and snorted. "Fateh, it wasn't as if I could leave you alone. You're a friend, aren't you?" She gave him a half-hearted poke. "As weird as you are sometimes, we're still friends."

"I ..." He blinked at her, slowly warming up and regaining his sluggish thought process. "Thanks."

"Well—now that you're awake, do you feel like going home?" she asked. "You said your place was just a town or so over, right?" She had a wistful look on her face. "Your town is just next door and you're already aware of the dangers there." She held out a hand. "Or you could come with me and Mari and live in town here." Her look turned sour. "At least until another warden finds us and puts us back into another prison."

Fateh froze, eyes widening. Home *was* close, but it wasn't a place that he wanted to return to, not after what happened. He had managed to block most of it out over the last year, but it hadn't been forgotten by any means. He didn't even have to close his eyes to remember what happened to his mother, what his friends did, or what happened to neighbors and everything he had cared about.

"He can't go home, little bride." Fateh nearly jumped out of his skin at Tabor's voice. "Hasn't he told you of his problems there?"

Randi blinked and stared up at Tabor, eyes widening as the very air around them warmed, drying their hair and clothes. The same fright that had been in Randi's eyes for Mokosh was there for Tabor as well, but Fateh couldn't help but feel something like relief.

What the hell is wrong with me? he demanded of himself. *I was just pulled out of a lake that was a house an hour ago and I'm relieved to see another one of the fae?* It was because Tabor was familiar; because Tabor had never actually hurt him and actually *helped* on occasion. That had to be it. He was a weird, twisted connection to home.

Fateh rolled his eyes. "They all knew I got kicked out of town because of what happened," he snapped. "I know I can't go back, but I can at least go back to my *house*. No one ever went up to my house. They were too scared to leave town."

"Do you really think they left that, Spark?" Tabor asked dryly, not reacting to his tone—not that he ever did. His voice turned almost mocking. "You were a monster, and don't humans kill all the monsters and destroy everything connected to them?"

Randi stared at Fateh now. "Fateh ..." she whispered. She knew what Tabor was implying, what he wasn't quite saying.

Tabor turned his attention to her again. "Little bride—you do remember, don't you?" he asked softly. "All of what you didn't tell the others of what happened to you." He sat down next to them as if it were perfectly ordinary; as if it were a normal day and they were just having a conversation.

"My name is Randi," she whispered. "Not 'little bride.'" She leaned against Fateh, trying to hide behind him. "And we all had bad things happen to us; he knew trolls took me."

"But you know that you can never go back; often there isn't anything to go back to." Tabor looked almost sympathetic.

Fateh scowled. "Maybe her friends are worried about her. She got rescued, while I got tossed to the wolves by my so-called friends."

"No, Fateh—he's right. I was with the trolls for long enough." She shrugged uneasily. "They weren't very good to those around them."

"Trolls eat humans," Tabor clarified. "Was there anyone left in your town, Randi?" he asked, seemingly unconcerned at the way she blanched at the question. "You can't have eaten any of your people; that leaves more of a mark than can be easily erased by metal bracelets and watery walls."

"No, I didn't eat anyone," Randi snapped, almost forgetting who was asking, then looked up at Tabor's amused expression, voice quieting. "I mean—I wasn't a monster. I ... I was trapped. I could hear the s-screams."

Fateh winced; what he had gone through wasn't anything near to what Randi had. At least the Shadows back home didn't *eat* anyone. Tortured and tricked and killed, yes—but they never had a taste for human flesh.

"I don't want to go back, either," she whispered. "I don't think there is anyone left."

"Except the trolls." Tabor rolled his eyes. "Never liked dealing with them. They were always so ... crude." He smirked faintly. "A word of advice, though." He focused all of his attention on Randi. "You know enough to go during the day. Smash the statue of the troll leader and the rest of the factions will tear themselves apart to be at the top. It won't bring anyone back, but it will keep them from expanding their homes and provide you with a nice piece of revenge in the bargain."

"Why don't you do it, then—if you're so keen on trying to use me to get rid of them?" she demanded. "They have traps and guards set up during the day to protect them from people doing what you want me to do."

"Not my territory, not my problem." Tabor held up his hands, trying to look innocent. "Rebelling against those that have come before is a sure way to get yourself killed." His gaze met hers. "But *you* know the traps and tricks to get around them. Daylight is best, but be careful if you try anything. I'm only here because Spark and I have some unfinished business to attend to." He grinned at Fateh. "Aren't you glad that you know me now?" he asked. "I got you out of a watery grave."

"You said we shouldn't rebel," Fateh pointed out. "You said over and again how bad it was that Meira and Tobias were plotting against the Shadows."

"That was because I didn't want you caught up in it," Tabor said honestly. "I was looking after your best interests." He raised an eyebrow at Randi. "It all depends on what you think the cost would be if you decided to fight back."

"You don't know," Randi whispered, but there was a bit of a spark in her eyes as she thought about what she could do. It wouldn't make anyone come back, as Tabor has pointed out, but it could save others.

"You didn't exactly get me out," Fateh pointed out. "That was Jonathan hauling me out."

"Mm ... you forgot about your conversation with Mokosh already?" Tabor 'tsk'd' sadly. "It was because of your connection with me that Mokosh didn't drown you, little Spark."

"It was also because of your connection with me that Mokosh called me an enemy," Fateh snapped back. "And how did you know Mokosh had a conversation with me? I know you weren't listening in. There was too much water for you to be anywhere near there."

"Because I know of her and I know you," Tabor said easily. "She wouldn't be able to resist taunting you." Tabor waved that away. "Face it, Fateh." His eyes narrowed. "You were saved because of a promise you made to me. You haven't forgotten that promise, have you?"

"Fateh?" Randi looked nervous. "You made a promise to one of the tylwyth teg?" She stood up nervously, putting a little distance between herself and Fateh. "You always said it was a bad thing and you went and ..."

Grimacing, Fateh faced Randi. "You didn't know our town. I don't know yours and how it was. But things were really bad. If you were caught alone at night, with no protection, the Shadows could claim you. Tabor gave us safety, and he demanded the promise that if things got to rock bottom, he'd have my name as a promise to a contract to him." He glared at Tabor. "Things aren't quite rock bottom, are they? I'm also still underage," he pointed out to Tabor. "I can't make a contract with you."

"With the town about to investigate how their piece of historic land went underwater?" Tabor examined his hand, watching him. "With only two witnesses remaining and one of them," he gave Randi a sly look, "already scared of what you might represent?"

Fateh's expression closed off, especially when Randi looked away.

"Come on, little Spark. Don't be so heartbroken." Tabor was too close and Fateh scowled up at him, but Tabor continued speaking directly to him. "Can you really trust someone you've known for only a year when the friends you've known since birth betrayed you?"

Fateh took a step back as that day flashed through his head again. What if it happened again? What if worse happened? He knew, logically, there *was* no one left for him to be hurt by, but he was young and scared. Fateh made the hardest choice in his life.

"I'll keep my promise, Tabor," he said resolutely. He knew Randi would be safe; she said that she had a place to stay in town. She might or might not take care of the trolls, but that was up to her. For her sake and to get closure, he hoped that she would.

"Maybe I'll see you again," he said to her. "Marisa said to not forget you guys and I won't. Stay safe."

"You too, Fateh," she said solemnly, already backing away from him and Tabor. "Don't let that sparkle dim." She tried for a smile and Fateh's lips tugged upward.

"I'm probably going to have more sparkle than I want to deal with soon enough." Fateh made a face and held out a hand to Tabor. "Let's go."

"I thought you'd never agree, Spark." Tabor smirked and didn't hesitate, dragging Fateh into the shadows. It was intensely cold and painful, as if knives were dragging along his skin. It hurt worse than the metal that had burned his wrists. Finally, the pain became too much and he passed out.

205

Chapter Twenty-Three

"Fateh ... wake up, little creature." Tabor's voice was grating and Fateh moaned and tried to cover his ears, scrunching up in a ball. "You can't laze about, so open those eyes of yours."

"You... what the hell did you do to me?" Fateh's voice sounded ragged to his own ears and he struggled to open his eyes. "If that's how you travel, I'd rather walk." He could still feel the weird, slicing darkness on his skin and he shuddered.

"It's harder if you're not invited." Tabor's voice held a mocking tone. "I've gotten permission, and we'll obtain that for you later, little Fateh. First, we need to talk about our contract. We didn't get to finalize it all now, did we?" His grip was almost painful. "You really do not want to go back on your word. I warn you, little creature—it would be a terrible mistake to do so."

Fateh swallowed hard at the implication, but it still irritated him that Tabor thought he would go back on his word. "I said I'd do it, didn't I?" he snapped. "I'm not the type of person to go back on my word." He crossed his arms against his chest. "Even if I'm just *seventeen*. Don't you have to wait until I'm eighteen to make a contract?"

"That's your town's rules, not mine. We're in a totally different situation and if you notice, there isn't a contract office around us. I say that you can make a contract now, so we can." He gave Fateh a thoughtful look. "And it's so *novel*, having a human keep *their* word. You're worse than the Shadows when it comes to twisting promises."

"Don't judge us all the same," Fateh mocked. "If I'm not allowed to judge your kind all the same, don't do it to mine. I said I'd do it." He raised his eyebrows at Tabor. "Did you plan for this to happen?

For me to be put in a situation where you would have to rescue me?" He shuddered at the memory of all that water surrounding him.

"As much as you would like to think otherwise, I have no more love for that little lake than you do," Tabor snorted. "It just pays to be prepared." He laughed and poked at Fateh. "If I hadn't been so eager to have you by my side," his voice was dry, "then chances are, Mokosh would have had you in her arms, drowned in the lake that she created." Tabor out his hand, smirking. "Won't I make a great partner?"

"Partner?" Fateh's head jerked up to stare at Tabor. "Don't joke about crap like that. We won't be partners. You're going to own me and there's nothing equal about that."

"You already know *my* type of contract?" Tabor raised his eyebrow, smirking. "Funny, since you seem to know nothing about this at all. The Shadows never use this contract, little Fateh." He leaned forward. "This one will make us, more or less, partners. I'm just the older, more experienced partner."

"My mom read out all the contracts to me and we went over them, in case this sort of situation would ever happen." Fateh sighed. "We just didn't expect it to happen so soon." His gaze went around to the large trees surrounding them and he shifted a little to get a more comfortable position on the moss he had been resting on. It almost reminded him of home, but he half expected to see Sam in the trees. "We didn't see any that mentioned *partnership.*"

"Aren't you the clever one?" Tabor smirked at him. "Such foresight—I can't imagine many who would meticulously go over paperwork that they feared and didn't believe in anyway." He shook his head. "Still, there are certain types of contracts that I would rather deal with if I had to make one. I don't agree with those that bind you to a Shadow with no give in return." His mouth tightened with some remembered pain, but nothing showed in his voice.

Fateh was taken back momentarily, a little surprised that a fae wanted something that was more or less equal. He was still suspicious, though. *Everyone* had some sort of ulterior motive; Tabor helping him before was just so that he could trick Fateh into doing this very contract.

"That is not what we need to worry about now, though. I will have my contract with you sealed before something happens that prevents it." Tabor's tone was firm and his stance unyielding.

"Whatever," Fateh muttered, not looking at Tabor as he held out his hand. "Let me just see the damn thing so we can get it over with."

"So eager." Tabor's voice was dry enough to catch Fateh's attention. "Don't rush to the chance to be protected now. But what do you expect to see?" he asked with a smile curling up the corner of his mouth. "Something that you actually sign?" He shook his head. "That's just window dressing, little Spark, misdirection ..." He shrugged at Fateh's growing look of anger. "Or simply some sort of comfort needed for the humans and the power that lesser creatures need to hold sway over those humans."

"Don't strain yourself trying to be comforting," Fateh snorted. "What exactly are you talking about?" he asked, watching him, arms crossed over his chest in a futile effort to protect himself. "If not signing a paper, then what am I going to do to prove my ... connection to you?"

"Words should be enough." His eyes were dark. "But perhaps a little incentive will help matters along. I need your soul to seal it completely. You break a soul bond, little Spark, and you'll wish you'd have only my anger to deal with." He gave him a rueful smile. "As I would regret my breaking my word to you; it would go deeper than that. We'd be soul-bound."

"Soul-bound?" Fateh demanded. "I don't want to be tied to ... how does that even work? Do you even *have* a soul?" he asked. "I'm human, in case you've forgotten. Can we even connect that way?"

Tabor rolled his eyes. "Yes, I have a soul, even if it is different from a human's."

Fateh rubbed at his forehead. "Okay ... so, it's sorta like that normal contract stuff, you protect me, I work for you, and when I die, you get my soul, and that fun stuff if I've screwed up in any way." He looked at Tabor. "If I don't screw up," his tone made it clear how unlikely that scenario was, "then you lose out on my soul and I go to whatever afterlife there is?"

"Mmhm, you still know nothing. I told you, it's not like the contracts that you've read about. We'd be soul-bound, sharing power equally between us. I just happen to have more power than you, but you have your own power that you can contribute to our bond." There was something else he wasn't saying, but Fateh just cared about the part where he'd still keep his soul when he died if he followed the rules.

Fateh frowned. "What the hell use is a human to one of the ..." He raised an eyebrow. "You said you weren't a Shadow. To a whatever you are."

"You aren't quite an ordinary human." Tabor leaned forward, expression intense. "I haven't figured it all out yet, but we will have all the time in the world to understand it. Still, the sooner the better, and I won't have you unprotected. You are going to be quite valuable to me once I have you under my control."

He still didn't want to do it, but ... there wasn't any other choice, not really. He couldn't go back home, he couldn't go to town and get help, and he couldn't hide. *The only way*, he thought bitterly, *is to sign over my soul so that I can be safe.*

"I'm almost always upfront." Tabor smirked at Fateh. "Limited way of thinking does tend to get in the way of honesty."

"And your kind is so trustworthy," Fateh said in a low voice, even though they were upfront with their treachery. Tabor had only hidden what he was, but had he really? It wasn't like it had needed to be announced at the start of it all—but when everything came pouring in at once, Tabor hadn't hidden his own nature any longer.

"I've been nothing but honest," Tabor pointed out. "The Shadows never tried to hide the fact that they wanted to chain humans, that they thought you were lesser, and that their kind was going to take back something they'd lost long ago."

Fateh made a face, but he really couldn't argue with that part of it. Still, what did Tabor mean when he said the Shadows were taking back something they'd lost long ago? He eyed him. "So, if there is no paper involved, what are we going to do to seal the rest of the deal?"

"Names have power. Remember that always." Tabor's expression was deadly serious. "If I have your name and you have mine ... well, that's just the start of things. It's different with humans—but if you have mine, that is one measure of control that you can hold over me." He looked thoughtful for a moment, then leaned closer and pressed his lips to Fateh's ear so nothing else could pick up the name. "Tabor'aelos."

Fateh blinked up at him, staring when Tabor pulled away. "Well, that isn't all that different," he snorted, but he knew there had to be something more.

"Now give me your full name." Tabor stared at him. "I gave you mine. Just calling you Fateh won't cut it. You have to give it freely."

"Any fae that can access a public record can get my full name." Fateh's tone was sour. "It's on my ID, you know."

"Getting it from a little card or paperwork doesn't work. You have to offer it," Tabor said firmly. "You're giving it up for the sake of the contract."

Fateh considered that and then nodded. "It makes sense," he admitted before squaring his shoulders. "Alwyn Fateh Davies," Fateh whispered as if someone besides Tabor were here and would hear him.

"Alwyn?" Tabor snorted with amusement. "How ironic, Spark." He shook his head. "I know your mother had clear eyes, but did she ever think about that name?"

"Look, there's a reason I go by Fateh." He shrugged and felt his cheeks heat with embarrassment. "My grandparents weren't keen on the name; they said it was bad luck."

"Well, hopefully, it will be good luck for you. Now it's time for our contract." He stepped close to Fateh.

Fateh jerked back instinctively, but Tabor's grip on his chin was tight, not letting him leave. "This is the important part, little Spark. You're going to have to deal with it, no matter how strange it will seem to you or how much you think it will hurt."

Tabor moved back enough to grip Fateh's hand. "There won't be any marks to show it, but you will always feel it. Close your eyes, Alwyn Fateh Davies."

Fateh didn't want to. The idea made him sick and he shuddered when he closed his eyes involuntarily. His skin crawled; he knew Tabor was close and the fact that he couldn't see him made him nervous. Without any warning, Fateh felt warm lips on his and he jerked backward at the unexpected and unwanted touch. He held his hands over his mouth to prevent Tabor from kissing him again. There was a flare of pain and Fateh held his hands over his stomach instead of his mouth. It was like someone yanked at his insides, jerking him inside out. Stripes of color flashed behind his closed eyes and he tried to bite back the whimper.

"Alwyn Fateh Davies, you are to be contracted to Tabor'aelos. Your soul and mine will be intertwined and you shall not raise a hand against me or abandon me, and I shall stay by your side and protect you. We will be bound together for as long as we both shall live." The words were whispered in Fateh's ear so that no one else could hear them. It was barely loud enough for Fateh to make out the words.

"What is this, a wedding vow?" Fateh managed to be snarky, even through the pain of his soul being seared by fire. "I thought I was going to be your pet, not ..." He doubled over and nearly fell to the ground as his entire body lit up with pain.

"Almost over, little Fateh." Tabor's voice was too sharp, too loud in his ears. "Then the pain will go away and it will be like nothing ever happened—except you'll know. You'll see it won't you?" There was a grin in his voice as he patted Fateh's head. "And what is marriage but a contract?" he teased.

Fateh grimaced and forced his eyes open enough to glare at Tabor. He remembered what Randi had said about marriage and contracts. "I'm not going to be *married* to you," he spat. He could already see the chain, but it was different from what he had seen between the others; it was almost like a rope of fire, twisting and shimmering with different colors. He stared, entranced and unaware of how intently he did so.

"You'll break my heart with how you treat me," Tabor teased, then abruptly shifted gears. "Have you always been interested in fire?" Fateh jerked away at the sound of his voice. "You looked almost innocent there, Fateh. Does fire bring out your better nature?"

"Idiot," Fateh muttered, wrapping his arms around himself. "I was just ..." The pain had vanished as if it had never been there.

"Distracted by the chain," Tabor supplied the words Fateh refused to say out loud. "It's only natural, really." He eyed Fateh, sitting back far enough to watch his acquisition. "If humans could see their chains, they'd be a lot more entranced." Tabor sighed and rubbed his head. "Ever have a problem with fire as a kid?" he asked.

Fateh stared at him, frowning a little. "I know what you're asking; you didn't have to set things up so that my friends ... my ..." he faltered. "So what you thought happened; it didn't happen because of me. You're the one who did something."

"And that burn on your arm?" Tabor didn't even give Fateh a chance to protest as he pushed his sleeve up. "Hmm ... you've got quite a nasty burn there, little Fateh—and not one that was done by fire." His hand soothed over the burn and Fateh winced, staring at it.

It was different from the scars from the metal bracelets; this had been done when he was still in town.

"You ... you really didn't do anything to cause that?" Fateh looked up at him, trying to make sure of it; he didn't want to know the truth of it—not this time. Lies were almost preferable to the possibility of truth. That something was wrong with him.

"No, little Spark. I told you, you're a strange little bird to be in the nest of those humans." He looked around, head tilted to the side. "It wasn't my fault that the metal hurt you. That was all you."

"I wasn't the only one hurt by the metal," Fateh pointed out. "Those of us who were hurt by the fae were hurt by the metal. They said it was the fae's influence on us."

"You're half right." Tabor looked amused. "There's a lot more that they didn't tell you, but before we get into that, we should get moving to more neutral territory."

"What's wrong with where we are now?" Fateh demanded. He felt unsettled and raw inside and wasn't looking forward to another shadow travel anytime soon.

"We can no longer stay in this particular nest. We're not so far from Mokosh's territory that we can linger, even away from the lakeside view." He tugged Fateh to a darker patch of shadow, but Fateh balked.

"You said you weren't a Shadow, but you're using shadows to travel," he accused. There was too much that wasn't adding up. What was Tabor's real deal—and what sort of devil had he tied himself to?

Tabor rolled his eyes. "That's because of who I know and the deals I've made. There are limits and, as I said, now is not the time." He made a frustrated sound and yanked on the fiery rope so hard that Fateh went tumbling into him. "I'll tell you when we're not here. I don't want to have to deal with Mokosh spreading her territory any further."

"You ..." The protest was cut off as Tabor dragged them into the cold, dark shadows again.

Chapter Twenty-Four

This time, Fateh landed on his knees as he was sick for several moments, face pale and strained as he shook out the last of his tremors. "I ... don't like that way of traveling." He grimaced as he wiped at his mouth, looking around for where they were. He didn't recognize the area at all—they weren't far outside of a large city. His town could fit into the corners of this place.

"So polite." Tabor snickered and hunched down next to him. "I swore six ways sideways the first time I went through, but I had an aversion to Shadows. You're at least used to them from living around them for so long." He eyed him. "Still, to make travel easier for you, we have to get permission from someone who holds control of these particular pathways. You being my tagalong just makes sure that you don't die; it doesn't promise comfort."

"Oh, but that doesn't take too long." Both of them turned at the sound of the unexpected voice. Fateh looked up a moment later and spotted something in the trees above their head. "Ooh, you're smart to look up. Not many humans think of that."

The figure became clearer when it landed lightly on its feet in front of them. He looked around Fateh's age and seemed somewhat normal—if it wasn't for the number of piercings on his face, in his ears, and lingering on the backs of his hands—Fateh was sickened at all that metal and he wondered if he was feeling the side effects from those stupid shackles he'd had to wear or if it was something more. He refused to believe it was because something was wrong with him.

He tensed and got ready to run again, but Tabor shook his head. "No, he's the one we have to see and he's normally a friend—you are a friend today, aren't you, Etana?" he asked dryly.

The stranger—Etana—nodded and gave Fateh an impish smile and a half-bow. "Friend today, so no worries, Tabor. You can relax; I'm not going to report to anyone, now that I know who it is. I just came to see who was using the pathways so quickly and from such ... interesting ... places."

Tabor nodded and yanked Fateh to the ground. "Sit down. See? He's a friend, however temporary that might be." He seemed entirely comfortable and relaxed now. "Yes, yes—that was me and the little Spark here."

Even Tabor needs allies, Fateh mused, but still ... "Today?" he asked. "You're a friend today, but you might not be one tomorrow?"

"Exactly!" Etana beamed down at him. "You catch on quick, don't you?" He wasted no time in making himself comfortable on the ground in front of the two of them, but Fateh couldn't help but notice Tabor keeping his distance from Etana and his metal piercings.

Fateh huffed and kept ready to run if he needed to. It had been one hell of a day; scratch that, one hell of a *year* and he didn't want any more surprises. *Although I wonder if I can run,* he thought sourly, his stomach giving another lurch to let him know how twisted up inside he still was.

"The little one doesn't entirely trust me." Etana leaned on one hand, smirking. The sunlight caught along the silver chain, running from his eyebrow to his lip. "It's a good idea, little hu ..." he paused and stared at Fateh, eyebrows raising—more piercings in those, of course. "Tabor, what is *that*?"

"*That* has a name," Fateh snapped. "And it's Fateh." He gave Etana a once-over. "But if we're trading insults on the first meeting, *what* are you?"

Tabor snickered and ruffled Fateh's hair. "Well, he's certainly more interesting than the average human. There's something about him ..." He smirked a little. "Why, do you see something a bit deeper?" He was watching Etana carefully. Sometimes Etana's age was really an asset; it allowed him to see deeper below the surface than Tabor could yet.

"Hey, *I'm* a normal *miotal*," Etana huffed. "Metal elemental to you, and *you* shouldn't exist." He pressed close to Fateh, strong hands gripping Fateh's arm to peer into his eyes. "Really—what the hell happened to you to ... to be like *this*? Tabor, what the hell did you get into?" he asked with an exasperated sigh, finally pulling back.

"Exactly what I wanted to get into," Tabor said dryly. "I knew it as soon as I met him, but of course, everything was still so ... hush hush then. Couldn't make my move until those idiots started contracting humans; they're not able to learn from the mistakes of their past, it seems."

"What are you two talking about?" Fateh demanded. "The Shadows repeating their mistakes?" He looked between the two of them. "And what's so strange about me?" He shot Tabor a look. Was their contract not allowed?

"You're a little more than what people expect you to be, that's all." Tabor tried to soothe him, reaching out and sighing when Fateh flinched away from him. "No matter what this idiot says, you're nothing more than what you've always been."

"Yes, but what has it always been, Tabor?" Etana interjected dryly. "That sort of thing doesn't happen overnight." He shook his head.

"I am *not* an it," he snapped, eyes narrowed with anger. "I've always been myself, always been human." He crossed his arms against his chest. "You're not acting very friendly, you know." He shuffled nervously at the bland stare that Etana and Tabor were both giving him. "What?"

"Well, I'd admit that Spark is a bit unusual," Tabor agreed easily, mischief on his face. "It's not like it's something that happens all that often, but Fateh was in a school full of them." He shook his head. "The regular humans died, but Fateh's little posse of fae-touched all survived."

Fateh blinked at that; it was strange that the only people who survived had been the ones who'd worn the metal bracelets. "They weren't my posse," he protested. "We just had a lot in common."

Etana rolled his eyes. "You should just kill him and get it over with, Tabor. He's going to be a danger to you and to all those around him."

"I'm going to protect him." Tabor's voice went low as he moved closer to Fateh, his stance protective. "You say you're a friend today, Etana. Don't let your words make me think that you're not." He frowned. "The *scáthach* were close to getting him."

"Ahh ... I see." Etana's lips curved up into a knowing smile. "That's your reason, is it? Something so fragile, innocent, and new to his power—you don't want him falling into the same hands that ..."

"None of that." Tabor gestured for Etana to be quiet. "You don't know what you're talking about. I'm just taking care of him, that's all you need to know."

"Mind telling me what's going on?" Fateh asked, frowning deeply as he realized how easily they left him out of the conversation. "Since you're obviously talking about me, *partner*, I would like to know what part I'm playing in this little drama you're performing."

Tabor looked faintly uneasy. "Just wait on that, Fateh. There will be time for explanations enough; right now, I have to talk to Etana. There is ... a lot that we have to catch up on."

"Yes." Etana waved him away. "You're just a kid; let the adults speak, would you? Children don't need to be part of this conversation." He smirked. "And if I'm right ..." He let his voice trail off, eyeing Tabor, who managed to look even more uncomfortable.

"I am *not* a child!" Fateh shouted, standing up and feeling heat creep up his face. "You can't treat me like one and I want some answers, damn it. Like how you said that I'm different and all those problems with Mokosh and now all this cryptic crap—"

Etana's brows rose at the mention of Mokosh. "I heard she had contracted herself to a human—but your little firebird was taken in by her?"

Tabor grimaced. "Those idiots in the town he lived in—they thought they knew best and sold him to that children's home that Mokosh had landed in. His so-called friends made the deal and paid the money to get Fateh there. The human in charge of the home didn't know how to bargain properly and the whole place went underwater." He shuddered at the mention of all that water. "Nearly lost Spark."

The blood drained from Fateh's cheeks at that too-recent memory. He'd nearly drowned when the building turned into a lake. A very deep lake that had managed to take more than a few unwilling participants into its depths. "It's not like Tabor did more than dry me off and get me away from the lake."

Etana looked even more curious at that and shook his head. "Our Tabor is quite the ... helpful sort if he gets what he wants in the end." He smirked at Fateh. "Has he told you the truth about yourself yet?"

Tabor frowned at Etana, trying to quiet him. "He knows he's contracted to me and that it's more of an even partnership." He grinned over at the clearly frustrated boy. "Might even come with a few perks that he'll learn along the way."

Narrowing his eyes, Fateh turned to Tabor. "You're going to turn me into one of the monsters, aren't you?" he demanded. "My friends killed my mother for trying to save me. My friends already thought I was a monster ..."

"Exactly," Tabor said, voice bland. "Your friends already thought you were a monster, so why not give you the means to protect yourself if they try something like that again?" He leaned back, looking pleased with himself. "You get your revenge and they won't bother you again."

Fateh's breath came out in a frustrated huff. "It'd be nicer to be able to dry off on command more than toast my friends."

"Why don't you try and dry yourself off?" Etana raised an eyebrow. "I'm sure it won't take that much effort to do so."

"Because I'm not Tabor and can't summon fire?" Fateh rolled his eyes. "I don't care what he did to me. That all went away over the last year."

"Leave the kid alone, Etana," Tabor said sharply. "You want him to set the forest on fire instead of a little heat? He doesn't know jack about what possibilities have opened up for him. Knowing his temper, he'd set an inferno off." He reached over to Fateh, sending a gentle heat through him until he was completely dry and warm.

"Like you couldn't contain whatever small fry started." Etana yawned. "I think that spending all that time with the humans has softened your fun side." He grinned over at Fateh, his mood switching rapidly. "You should thank us for being so welcoming to you."

"Yeah, sure ... I'd love to thank the guy who started this whole downhill mess of my friends trying to kill me and succeeding in killing my mother. And thank *you* for... insulting me? Even if I didn't know that thanking was an absolutely *stupid* thing to do to a Shadow," he crossed his arms over his chest, "I'd hate to see what being in debt to you would be like. I'm already chained to Tabor."

"That's true." Etana grinned. "You are smarter than you look, but not all are as nice as me and Tabor. Some would kill you for such words. You have to learn how to screw with your phrasing so that no one gets insulted and you're not in debt." His grin dropped away a little. "And we're not Shadows. I told you that I was a *miotal*."

Fateh eyed Etana, a little uncertain about him still. He'd thought Etana was a Shadow, but he'd never seen one even touch metal, much less cover themselves in it. "What are you?" he demanded, his curiosity getting the better of him. "All the fae I've met, even Tabor, shy away from metal. But you're covered in it like some sort of freak trying to prove a point. I've never heard of a ... *miotal*." He wouldn't talk about his own growing aversion to the stuff. No need to shout his weakness.

"You're glad that I know you're a runt who doesn't know anything at all." Etana snickered and patted Fateh on the head, who cringed away from all that metal touching him. "Word to the wise, little cousin; not all of us are affected by metal. Most of our kind is," he traced the burn on Fateh's arm, "but there are a few that can shape it, hold it, and use it against our enemies."

Fateh squirmed away from that metal-covered hand, trying to hide his wince. The metal hadn't touched him, but it was uncomfortably close to his skin.

Etana just laughed as he pulled away from Fateh to stroke along the metal on his arm, the metal bleeding out and forming a shape before it shifted back to the piercings threaded through his skin. "You will see much more of my kind, little cousin. We can deal with the mess humans have created."

Fateh scowled at the 'little cousin' part. He was a contract of Tabor's, but that didn't mean that he was a Shadow or related to Etana and he wanted to keep it that way.

Tabor shrugged. "Hey, most of us don't like getting cuddly with your clan, but even we have to admit it's useful to have you around to get rid of some of the more dangerous elements for us. You're the only thing in the Otherworld that isn't burned by metal." He shuddered briefly. "I still don't get how you can wear more metal than cloth."

Fateh blinked up at him, curiosity overcoming frustration for the moment. "Are you talking about the Shadows?"

"The Shadows are only one faction, Fateh." Etana shook his head. "We're all different kinds, even you—although all from the same *happy* family."

"Hey, don't lump me in with you," Fateh snapped "I am *human*. I don't know how many times I've got to say it."

"And I don't know how many times you have to be told that you're not a normal human," Etana shot back. "Normal humans don't flinch away from metal." He looked over at Tabor. "He chooses to oppose the Shadows because of his past with them. I don't choose a side for good; it might be something you should consider, Tabor."

Tabor shook his head. "I don't think that's a possibility yet. Our little bird here showed the wrong plumage to the sparrows in the nest and got hauled off to one of those fae-touched prisons for his trouble. Was shackled to metal for almost a year. Have some pity on the kid and don't force his hand."

"Is that what happened?" Etana shook his head. "Tabor, I tell you this as a friend today: there have been all sorts of talk with the Shadows. You're acting as if you're their enemy most of the time, instead of only part of the time like before."

"Well, that's their fault, isn't it?" Tabor snapped. "They made their choice long ago, and I'm making mine." He crossed his arms across his chest, looking like a petulant child. "And who says that I'm keeping them as enemies?" His smile was sly. "I tell you this, knowing that friendship only lasts a short while. We were very friendly in town. Quite remarkable how we worked together at times."

"I'm sure," Etana snorted. "You play their game very well—but then, you have been playing it for a long time."

Fateh's brows rose at that particular statement, but it could mean anything at all. Still ... "You don't look that old," he said bluntly.

"I am much older than I look. We do not age like humans," Tabor said softly, as if trying to gauge Fateh's reaction. "I've looked this way for the last ... hm ... fifty years."

Fateh gaped at him and then at Etana, who only nodded. "Tabor's pretty young, which is why he's reckless and stupid and friends with me." He grinned. "I'm the older, more mature one." He raised an eyebrow at Fateh. "Much older than you, and a few hundred years older than Tabor."

"You look like you're my age." Fateh made a face. "Is that a personal preference, or do you really age that slowly?"

"We can change our age after a certain amount of time." Etana shrugged it off. "I like this age. It makes people *so* confused when I refer to things that happened in their grandparents' times."

"You're so weird," Fateh snorted. "No one my age *wants* to be my age. We're not able to live on our own. No one listens to us and when the shit goes downhill, we're locked away in prison for our own good."

"You're lucky Tabor saw the potential in you, kid—and offered the type of contract he did." Etana's look turned serious at Fateh's scoff. "He did it so that you wouldn't fall into the same trap that he fell into when he was your age." Etana rolled his eyes. "With him as your protector, it won't happen now, but still ... " He shrugged. "He should just sell his side as my clan does. It doesn't hurt anyone and can be rather ... beneficial. Well, except for humans, but most of them are rather worthless."

Fateh growled lowly. "We are not worthless," he snapped. "We were doing just fine before you all came and decided to ruin the lives we built for ourselves." He started to get to his feet again, but Tabor slammed him down again. "You ... you don't ..."

Etana yawned. "Loyalty is fine, but you can't really trust anyone unless you've confirmed that they won't hurt you—either by magic or money."

"Etana, enough," Tabor sighed. "Spark was very attached to his mother and his mother was quite human. He didn't think of her as worthless and as far as humans go, she wasn't bad."

Fateh blinked up at Tabor, bewildered at the unexpected understanding but not wanting to ruin the moment. He didn't want to think of Tabor being kind, or trying to help him out. He was the enemy, right?

"Still, why do you think I snatched him up?" Tabor snorted. "He would have caused problems sooner or later. Questions were going to be asked ... that, and I wasn't going to let them dick him around like they do the rest of us."

"So, you're going to do it instead?" Etana snorted with amusement. "Speaking of dicking him around. How many times has he slept with you? You did mention you spotted him in town before grabbing him as a contract ..."

"Not at all." Tabor sighed and grimaced. "For some reason when I try, the kid doesn't even blink at me. It's really kind of depressing." He stroked a hand down his chest. "Think I'm losing my touch, Etana?" He leered and leaned closer to Etana, who swallowed hard.

"Around the kid?" Etana blinked and looked at Fateh, who shrugged.

"I'd tell you to get a room, but he's got me leashed, so it's up to you." Fateh raised his eyebrows at him. "It's not like I'm going to join in. I don't do sex; I'm asexual."

"No sex at all?" Etana looked vaguely scandalized at the idea. "You're *really* unusual for your kind, human and other, you know. You could have anyone and you just don't want to do it?" He gave Tabor a hopeful look. "Well, if the kid doesn't mind, I know a nice spot ..."

"No." Tabor actually sounded regretful. "I have to get Fateh sorted out first and I don't want him to burn down the woods if he gets bothered by what we do." He sighed. "Hopefully next time we meet up, we'll still be friends. Alliances switch so easily these days, you know."

"Mm ... but it's always more exciting when we're on opposite sides," Etana snickered. "Well, come with me. I promise that my alliances will be with you for at least a week. We'll work out payment later, Tabor. You and the kid need a safe spot and he's about dead on his feet. You can tell me all about your side of what's going on in a more comfortable setting."

Tabor nodded and lifted Fateh up as easily as one would a sack of laundry, tucking him under his arm in the same way. "Lead the way. Just make sure that you recognize the kid so he doesn't puke over whatever place you're squirreling away in this time."

"Do I want to be recognized?" Fateh muttered, squirming at being held in such an undignified position, but he was getting to the point of not caring; he was too tired, too hurt, and too confused as his entire world was being spun around.

"It means that he'll recognize you as being connected to me," Tabor murmured. "You can travel the same paths—and you'll be safer than before. The scáthach won't bother you as much if the *miotal* recognizes you as an ally."

"I'll officially be your partner?" Fateh stared at the grass below his face, feeling sick. It was one thing to admit it in his head, to talk about it ... but to officially put away anything that linked him to his old life was hard.

"As far as the Otherworld is concerned?" Tabor nodded. "You'll be contracted, looked after by me. Same as those little contracts in town, Spark. Those who wish to hurt you will have to go through me first." His smile held a nasty edge. "I have many reasons to make sure they don't touch you."

"Fine, do it," Fateh mumbled. "If you recognize me, do I still have to keep the awesome chain you have on me?"

Tabor snickered. "Oh, you'll still be chained. That's unbreakable, little Spark. We're bound for all and ever." He turned back to Etana. "You heard him. He agrees."

"I think I caught that part." Etana's voice was dry. "Well, I recognize him and I can speak for my clan. He's safe to go through without throwing his guts up." He peered into Fateh's sleep-glazed eyes. "You're going to awaken a lot faster now." As if he hadn't said anything, he spun around to go deeper into the woods, where the Shadows were in dark, wide patches. "Let's go get some food and rest. I'm beat. This day sucked."

"You're telling me." Fateh closed his eyes as the ground moved underneath him at a rapid pace as Tabor walked quickly to follow Etana. As he let himself go limp, he drifted into sleep. He didn't even feel the coldness of the shadows enveloping them this time, taking them further than before.

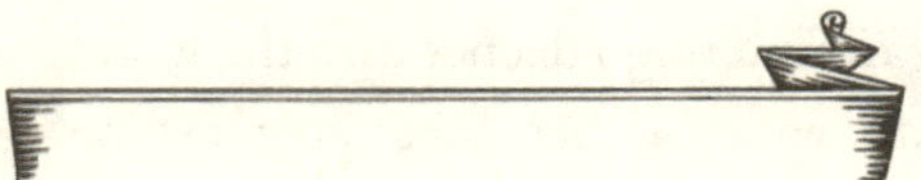

Chapter Twenty-Five

He wasn't sick this time coming through the shadows—only a little dizzy as the light in the room they ended up in made him blink at the brightness. "The hell?" He rubbed at his eyes, wincing a little.

"Etana keeps it bright here so that he has a constant shadow in this spot." Tabor put him down carefully, keeping him steady with one hand. "For when he's away and needs to get to his place rather quickly."

"Mm ... you'd do the same if you had your own nest again." Etana shrugged, flicking off the strong light. "Sucks that you had to lose whatever digs you were staying in because of what you picked up." The pointed stare at Fateh was obvious.

Fateh bristled at the implication. "It's not like I told him to pick me up," he snapped.

"And why should I give the place up?" Tabor asked. "It's not like we're running from anything. I have my partner, all nice and legal. No matter what Fateh is, he's safe. The humans may give us a bit of trouble, but ..."

"I don't want to go back to Felinheli." Fateh backed away as if that would keep him from returning to that town that had killed his mother, that had hunted him down as if he were an animal. The thought hurt, and he knew the town was worse than the lake where he had last resided. He hated the scared edge to his voice; it made him sound like a child. "No."

"Kid, they're not going to hurt you if you've got a protector ..." Etana's voice trailed off at the bitter edge of Fateh's laugh.

"They killed my mother because they assumed that I had a protector. They killed her because she was going to sign a contract." Fateh's hands clenched and he missed the sour look that Tabor gave Etana. "Shadows won't protect you from other humans."

"Good job, idiot," Tabor snapped at Etana. "Do you really want your house to catch on fire somewhere? I told you; he's untrained, uncontrolled." Fateh started to glare at Tabor for insinuating the stupid crap again about him using fire and nearly jumped when Tabor gripped his hands. There was a dampening around his hands, a cooler pressure taking the place of the heat building. He could only stare at Tabor in shock. His speech was momentarily halted as he saw the flickers of flames die under Tabor's hands.

"He can't blame us for what the humans did. They've been killing themselves over stupid shit for so long that when we come along, we're just one more stick to add to the flames." Etana gave Fateh an amused look. "So, no matter if we showed up or not, it was humans who did the final act, wasn't it?"

Fateh opened his mouth to argue, but he hesitated. Hadn't he said much of the same thing to his friends before? That humans weren't all that great; look at what they had done to each other over the years. They had chained their fellow humans and in some parts of the world, probably still did. He couldn't even use how Shadows chained humans as an argument for them being worse than humans.

"It still doesn't change the fact that she wouldn't have been killed if they hadn't seen her as selling out." His words were stubborn. "I don't care if they see me as a monster, but she was just trying to stay safe."

"You no longer care that the humans hunted you down, just what they did to your mother?" Etana leaned forward, eyebrows raised. "That's a bit of an unusual way of thinking. Most humans don't think that way. They'd have a breakdown and thoughts of revenge. Crying, even—it seems like a good option for them. I've heard several people scream because they were so upset. Those feelings of betrayal tend to linger, especially when they're aimed against oneself."

"Should I?" Fateh frowned. "It's already been a year since it happened. Getting all pissed off about it isn't going to change it, will it?"

Etana continued to stare at him, brows raising. "Are you sure you were raised human?" he asked dryly. "That's a most uncommon teenage human reaction. Believe me, I've seen plenty of them."

Fateh had seen this reaction before, from friends who called him strange and warped, who thought that he should care more about what he considered pointless. It didn't seem worth the effort to get upset over something that already happened. It wouldn't change the outcome.

"Deal with the day-to-day, that's how it should be." Tabor shrugged, and Fateh was surprised to see Etana nodding along with him. It was the first time someone besides his mother agreed with his way of thinking. Most were so concerned with the future that Fateh was surprised they didn't die from the stress of it all. The worst anyone had called him was a sociopath, and it had only been partially teasing. He swallowed hard; he wasn't sure what it meant to have these two agree with him.

"Tabor still hasn't forgiven or forgotten what happened to him," Etana said with a vaguely pitying look on his face. "Sometimes even us non-humans have regrets and feelings of pain for what wrongs have been committed against us."

"Fateh doesn't need to know about that right now." Tabor made a cutting-off gesture with his hand and glared at Etana. "I'll tell him in my own time, but he doesn't need any nightmares at this point. He's got a bucket load of shit that he has to process before I dump more on him."

"I'm still going to get revenge for what they did to my mother," Fateh said stubbornly. "Somehow, I'll make sure they see what they did was wrong." Meira hadn't been the one to kill her, but she'd incited the violence that ended in tragedy. He *would* be asking Tabor about his history with the Shadows. He acted like he was friends with them when he was in town, but there was apparently a much longer history between them that Fateh could only guess at. He looked up when Etana spoke again.

"And what if they're already contracted to their own Shadows, little one?" Etana leaned over to watch his reaction more closely. "Then what will you do? Be angry at the world and yourself for all eternity?"

"Their Shadows can't stop another human," he spat out. "They showed that clearly a year ago when they just stood around and watched my mother be killed." He glared at Tabor. "Even you didn't help. You weren't even there," he whispered, sounding like the teenage kid he still was.

"No, I wasn't there or else I would have helped. At the very least, I would have kept you out of the hands of those people who chained *you* with very real metal and kept you behind a watery guardian."

"Sometimes staying near the *scáthach* changes a person," Etana said thoughtfully. "Humans are especially vulnerable; their souls are malleable. It's like ... being around radiation. It warps and twists everything it comes into contact with and it doesn't even do it in-tentionally." His gaze was direct. "You already should know that the *scáthach* are worse than radiation in that way. They're very aware of what they are doing."

"Yeah, I figured that." Fateh rolled his eyes. "So, is that their plan? To warp all of humanity into twisted versions of themselves?"

"Only works on the pure soul, Fateh." Tabor shook his head. "Or else the humans would be a lot worse off than they are now."

Fateh sighed and looked out the window; he had no idea where they were, but it was a large-looking city, surrounded by humans and possibly tylwyth teg and who knew what else. "Yeah ... I figured," he whispered. "Being chained isn't as bad as the other possibilities." *Like that girl from the restaurant who had her soul entirely taken and was nothing more than an empty puppet.*

"Mmhmm ..." Tabor rested a hand on his head briefly. "Alright—enough of this moping and worrying you're doing. Let's eat and then crash. We've only got a guaranteed week of hospitality and then we've got to head out."

Fateh blinked. "You were serious that Etana might not be our friend in a week? How does that actually work? Friendship can't be controlled like turning a tap."

"It's not exactly that." Etana shrugged and moved into the kitchen. It was surreal how normal he acted. It was weird to think of the ... well, Tabor had said they weren't Shadows, but they weren't human, either. "It's just that we sort of ... work on opposite sides at times. Right now, we're on the same side, but next week I may have a higher bidder." He sighed at Fateh's look. "My clan enjoys being neutral." He gave Tabor a pointed look.

"Hey, I'm neutral," Tabor protested. "I go around helping both humans and the *scáthach,* but for now I'm sticking with Fateh here." He ruffled Fateh's hair. "Your soul is tied to mine now, so I don't have to worry about you selling me out—" He leaned closer to Fateh, causing him to back up as fast as he could. "Not that you would, hmm?"

Etana shook his head. "You already know that contracts are unbreakable, Tabor. Your little *partner* couldn't betray you even if he wanted to." He turned to Fateh, handing him a sandwich. "Look, you're going to have some perks along with this whole chained thing, you know."

"Oh, yes—because having my skin fried off because I brushed against cold metal is ever so awesome." Fateh rolled his eyes. "Doesn't sound like that's one of the perks you mentioned." "I wouldn't know about being hurt by metal. I'm rather fond of it—you should try it sometime." He leaned closer, waving a metal-covered hand too close to Fateh's skin for his peace of mind. "Obviously, since you're covered in more metal than what I've seen in the punk rockers store in the mall," Fateh shot back, trying to cover up his unease. "I wasn't ever bothered by it before. Who's to say I'm bothered by it now?"

Etana moved closer to him, practically touching him with his hand before Tabor moved between the two of them. "Let's play nicely, now. We don't want this place catching on fire, nor losing its support structure because someone lost their temper."

"Your kid is the youngest one here and you're still younger than me," Etana huffed. "Don't talk to me like I'm a child." He turned to Fateh, crossing his arms against his chest. "Watch it, shorty. I may look like a teenager to you, but I've still been around a lot longer than you have."

"Oh, well, that's something to be proud of." Fateh snickered. "I always brag about how old I am. No wonder you—" his words were abruptly cut off when Tabor covered his mouth.

"Enough. The both of you. Jeez, do I have to put you in separate rooms to get you two to behave?" Tabor gave him an exasperated look, but some sort of amusement turned up the corners of his mouth a bit. "And here I thought Etana was the *mature* one here."

Fateh shrugged, barely resisting the urge to say 'he started it,' thus acting like a real child. "I'll stop if he does," he conceded. *Not that was any better …*

"Whatever," Etana huffed, crossing his arms against his chest. "I don't argue with toddlers."

"Except that you just did," Tabor pointed out dryly. "We can't have you bickering like children if we're to do something together for the time being." He kept one hand on Fateh as he eyed him. "You need to calm down again. You're still too unstable."

"If I'm unstable, it's because of you," Fateh pointed out. "I never did anything strange before I met you."

"That's a lie and you know it." Tabor's voice was cheerfully brutal. "I remember first meeting you and you did weird things then, too."

"You're full of shit." Fateh stared at him. "When you pretended to be my friend, nothing like fire ever happened. That's something I would have remembered. Fire is kind of dangerous."

"You still did unusual stuff as a kid," Tabor insisted. "And you were never burned around me," he pointed out. "Other people couldn't stand to be around me, but you were just annoyed, not over-whelmed by the heat."

Fateh had no argument for that. People had pointed it out be-fore, had backed away from Tabor ... and Fateh had always just as-sumed that Tabor was holding back the heat on purpose around him. "I still don't see how I'll be stable or unstable. It's just a contract; it's not like I'm a Shadow or anything."

"No, you're not a Shadow." Tabor grinned and ruffled his hair. "You're a bit too solid for that."

"Think he'll ever be stable with that human part of him screwing things up?" Etana snickered. "You should just get rid of it now, Tabor. It really is a mistake."

"He's not a mistake, he's unique." Tabor smacked Etana on the side of the head. "And stop talking about him like he's not here. Do you want to upset the kid again?" He sighed. "He's got a human's up-bringing, but he's better than most. And again—do I need to remind you? Contract. Completely unbreakable. He's not going betray me and I'm not going to hurt him."

The look that Etana gave Fateh was cold with a small smirk. "Not if he has any ties to humanity. Humans lie and betray all the time for no reason. As long as any part of him is human, I don't have to trust him at all, even if he is a contracted pet."

Fateh swallowed hard; he was aware again of the position that he was in—of being around those who didn't play by the same set of rules that he grew up with and didn't think the same way that he did. They weren't human and if Meira and Tobias were right, *he* wouldn't be human anymore, either.

"Didn't you say much of the same thing?" Tabor's breath moved over his ear, voice pitched for him alone, even when Fateh could see Etana straining to hear him. "Before you judge us, think back to how all your little friends saw you."

Fateh paled as Tabor pulled away. He remembered; it was hard to forget being taunted for not caring. It was just one more sign that he fit in more with the 'monsters' than he did with the humans. Maybe he did know how to act like the tylwyth teg.

"Whatever," he mumbled, expression sullen, trying to hide his distress. "Look, can we just rest? I've had too long of a day and I don't want to deal with this crap anymore." *This entire day is messed up.* Everything felt distant, muted, and he vaguely wondered when it would start to hurt; when the shock would wear off. "This is not how I wanted to spend my seventeenth birthday."

"You're all of seventeen?" Etana asked, eyes bright with mirth. "That's so ... precious." He coughed at Fateh's tired glare. "Happy birthday, I guess?"

"Hm—perhaps we should put you to bed." Tabor gave Fateh a thoughtful look. "It's not like you're going to run off, now are you?"

Fateh could see the line of the chain shimmer and he rolled his eyes. "One—I said I'd be in this contract with you. I'm not going to break it. I keep my word. Even if I was some kind of asshole who re-neges on a deal, you have a leash on me, so I really don't think that's an option. And again, where would I run if I wanted to? I don't know where we've landed, with all of that jerking around with shadows that you were doing."

Tabor snickered and lifted him in the air by his collar, shaking the breath out of him before he could say any more. "I'll keep an eye on you, nonetheless," he said dryly. "I rather like having you around and you've had a rough day. Screaming nightmares is not how any-one wants to be woken up."

Fateh's head jerked around at Etana's snicker. "Or any other kind of nightmare," he pointed out. "Don't sing the kid to sleep, Tabor. I know very well your singing voice sucks. He may be a toddler, but I don't want my bed scorched because he didn't like your choice of lullaby."

Fateh growled as Tabor laughed. "I'm going to put the kid to bed and catch some sleep myself. The kid's right—it's been one hell of a day." He rubbed at his head with his free hand. "We'll talk more about this tomorrow."

Etana waved him off. "I'd say don't do anything in the bed, but you're not the type to go after something that young, even if he was interested."

"Mmhm." Tabor nodded, carrying Fateh along down the short hallway to a small room and dumping him on the bed. "Sleep," he ordered briskly. "You need it, I need it." He shook his head, muttering under his breath, "One hell of a day."

"You're telling me." Fateh kicked off his shoes, crawling under the covers. He was too tired to really think anymore and even though he knew Tabor was staring at him, he fell asleep almost as soon as he closed hxis eyes.

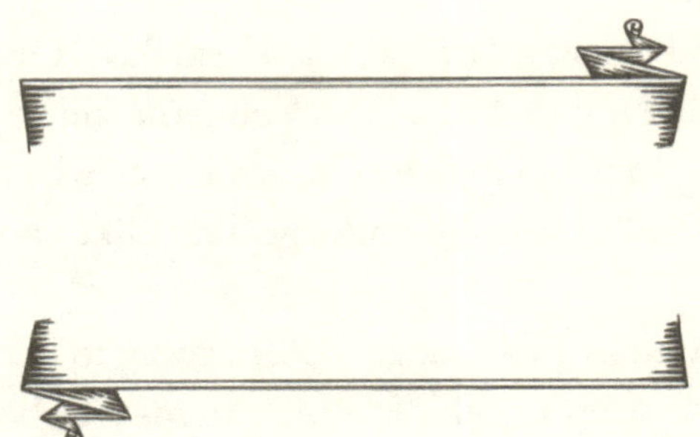

Chapter Twenty-Six

"M*om ...?" Fateh took a step closer to his mother but was yanked back by Tobias. "Mom—are you—stop it! Leave her alone!" He struggled, but he couldn't get loose. "Don't worry, it'll be okay." Her smile at him was painful, even if she meant for it to comfort. "I'll—we'll be fine. Just—" She broke off as the sharp edge of a knife was pressed to her throat.*

"I'd be quiet if I were you. We want you to watch this—watch what a monster your son is. You wouldn't be defending him so much if you saw the truth of it." Meira's voice was emotionless and Fateh could only watch in horror.

His so-called friends held him down, pressing metal to his skin flesh sizzling as the metal bore down, branding him as if it were red-hot. He cried out and his mother's eyes widened. "Fateh?" she whispered.

"He was always a monster—see?" Meira mocked. "Why do you want to defend a monster? Let us kill him now and we'll let you go."

"Mom ...?" Fateh cringed when his mother turned her face away from him and mocking laughter filled his ears as he was kicked down.

"Don't worry, monster. @e'll make sure that we take care of you."

"No ... no no no no no!" The surrounding air startled to crackle, shimmering as it did during intense heat. "I won't—I don't want to die!" His attackers drew away from him, swearing and staring at their hands, red welts and blisters already spreading across their palms.

"Get rid of him!" Meira shouted. "Get rid of him now!" Her voice took on a hysterical edge and even his mother was backing away from him as if he was a monster—something to be feared and shunned and driven away.

The smell of smoke filled his senses.

───────

"Fateh! Wake up, you stupid kid!" Fateh jerked awake at the sound of Tabor's voice. His hands on his shoulders felt too cool, almost cold, and he struggled to open his eyes to meet Tabor's. The smell of smoke that was in his dream still surrounded him.

It took him a moment to realize it wasn't just left over from the dream and that there really was smoke around them. "Wha ...?" he waved at the smoke and tried to focus. "Jeez, kid—we were only joking about you setting stuff on fire in your sleep. That must have been one hell of a nightmare." He helped Fateh sit up and looked toward the door, where Etana was covering his face and breathing shallowly.

"I didn't expect him to do it, either." Etana's voice was sharp. "Stupid aodhamair. Some of us can't breathe through this mess." He waved at the smoke. "Tabor, do something to get rid of it, would you? I know it doesn't bother you, but I'd rather not test my lungs."

"Oh right ..." Tabor winced and rubbed the back of his head, the smoke spiraling inward until it eventually dissipated. The only sign was a lingering smell of burnt wood and cloth. "Sorry about that—was more worried about waking up the kid and putting him out so he didn't cause any more damage."

Fateh looked down at himself and yelped; most of what he was wearing was singed and tattered, some still smoking slightly around the edges. "What the hell happened?" he demanded, tugging at the clothing and cringing when the part he touched fell apart in his hands.

"I figured that you had a nightmare." Tabor watched him carefully, assessing the damage.

Etana sighed. "That much is obvious, Tabor. Enough with the dancing about and tell the kid the full truth, would you? It might make it easier for him to handle himself." He held his hand over his face, voice muffled as he spoke. "Jeez, it stinks in here ..."

"The whole truth?" Fateh's brows drew in as he sifted more burnt pieces of clothing off, cringing a little as the threads collapsed completely. No one seemed to be staring at him, but nonetheless, he felt exposed.

"Ah... yeah. That." Tabor sighed, running a hand through his hair. "I guess I should have told you this sooner, but—I wanted to give you some time to get used to being with me before I dropped another bombshell on you." He looked over at Etana, who gave him a 'get-on-with-it' gesture. "Spark ... you're not really human."

Fateh's mouth dropped open; first, his friends had accused him and now Tabor was confirming it? "I ... but ... you said that this mess was because of ..."

"No—I never outright said that." Tabor shook his head quickly. "And you were doing stuff before you ever contracted with me." His gaze was direct, crumbling Fateh's argument before he opened his mouth.

"But my mom was human." Fateh frowned up at Tabor. "I know that for a fact—I mean, if I was one of *your* kind, wouldn't I have noticed it sooner? Wouldn't you guys have noticed it sooner?"

"You're a mistake," Etana said bluntly, watching Fateh as he tried to cover up with what remained of his clothing and bedding. "I've never seen anyone with an Otherworld soul and a human body—even if the body is less human than those around you."

"He's not a mistake," Tabor said sharply, frowning at Etana. "He's unique. Who's to say there isn't more of him about? We haven't exactly been looking." He sighed. "I have a feeling that the prison he was in held more of them. It's a shame I only met the troll bride. It was clear that she wasn't all human, either."

"Her name is Randi," Fateh snapped. "And what do you mean? She didn't turn to stone in the sunlight. She wasn't a troll."

"Maybe not, but the trolls picked her for a reason. They're dumb, but they can still sense when someone is unusual." Tabor turned his attention back to Etana for a moment. "Why don't you get the kid some clothes? I don't think those are going to hold up much longer." Another puff of ash accompanied his words.

Fateh cringed. He didn't want to expose himself to Etana or Tabor and he was already feeling vulnerable. "Yes, please," he whispered. "Look, I'm—I'm sorry, I didn't mean to—I didn't *know*, okay?" he asked. He stared up at Tabor. "What does it mean, that I'm ... I'm a ... whatever you are?" he asked. "I thought the fire was just something you did but you're acting like it's more than that."

"Well, yeah." Tabor sighed. "It's like this—if you believe in fate and all that jazz, something went wrong along the way and you got popped into the wrong container. It's never happened that I know of, but it doesn't mean it's a bad thing, you know. If it makes you feel better, those kids in that prison of yours were the same. Just different pieces of a larger puzzle."

"The kids who wore the bracelets were all involved with Shadows in some way. Or not Shadows; they called them all different names." Fateh's voice was soft. "So, I'm not human, but not one of you either."

"Stop using that 'one-of-you' crap." Tabor scowled. "You're one of me, thank you, and *we* are fire elementals."

"But ... you," he amended his words at Tabor's scowl, "we're human-shaped," he pointed out. "We look normal. By my standards, anyway."

"Which are very limited," Etana pointed out, holding some clothing loosely in one hand. "You've only ever seen and been around humans, so of course you're going to criticize anything that isn't." He snorted. "Just like a human to think that way."

"I'm either human or not human," Fateh snapped. "Excuse me for being raised like one. I didn't exactly have someone stop by and tell me any different until just now." He looked at the clothes and then down at the ash streaking his arms and legs.

"Yes, you can wash first before you put on new clothes. But kid—" Etana sighed. "Accept it quick or else there's going to be more accidents. I don't want my house going up like a torch because you're having teenage anxiety issues."

"I didn't realize what had happened ..." Fateh stared up at him, fear darkening his eyes. "I just had a nightmare and I ... my mother. I wanted to save her this time but my friends called me a monster—" He swallowed hard. "I am, aren't I?" he asked. "I always was the monster they were scared of."

"You're not a monster, not any more than those humans were." Tabor helped him to his feet and steadied him while Fateh found his balance. More bits of clothing dropped to the ground. "It's only how you take it, kiddo, and what you do with it." He shrugged. "Besides, mortality is overrated."

Fateh blinked at him, trying to process that for a moment. "I'm not sure if that was supposed to be a pep-talk or another sign that I'm slowly sinking into a really crummy whatever life, but ... I think it failed on both levels." He rubbed at his head. "I'm going to take a shower, get cleaned up, and then hopefully you guys will be able to explain more of what's going on here."

"Yes, yes—go get cleaned up, little Spark," Tabor waved him off. "Hopefully you'll be able to think over your ... position in life whilst soaping yourself off. I don't think I want to deal with hysterics any more than Etana does and really—it's not something you can change."

"No, I can't..." Fateh made a face and rubbed at his arms. "I do want to understand it, though." He looked sad. "I'm losing a lot lately... guess my humanity isn't all that much on top of everything else." He took the clothing from Etana and stepped into the bathroom.

He was relieved to be away from the two of them—the whole *'oh, by the way, you're not human. You should be glad because humans obviously suck'* was irritating, to say the least. He stared at his hands, covered in ash as he brushed the remains of his clothing off. The skin underneath was untouched, not even a hint of red to show he had been burned.

"What the hell does it mean, being a fire elemental?" he groused, turning on the taps. "All that stuff growing up ... all the weird crap that started happening when the Shadows showed up ..." He made a face. He instantly felt better as he stepped into the scalding hot water. He didn't want to admit it—who wanted to admit they weren't human and were the enemy that had taken over their lives? "And this Otherworld crap ..."

It was surreal to be doing something as normal as washing, and why did Etana have such ordinary things around, anyway? *You'd think if he was some sort of magical creature, he'd use magic to get himself clean. And wouldn't all that metal rust?*

As he washed his hair, the situation suddenly hit him like a hammer blow and he slid down in the shower, feeling like all the air had been knocked out of him. His mother was dead because his friends had killed her and he was now contracted with a fire elemental who said he was the same thing. He didn't care that there was a possibility that Tabor and Etana might hear him, or that he was seventeen and boys 'didn't cry' after a certain age. The hot water of the shower poured over him as he shook with sobs.

————

"That water has to be getting cold by now," Etana observed, raising an eyebrow at the sound of the still-running shower. "Do you think the kid's okay?" He was replacing the sheets on the bed, after having grumbled over having to do the chore.

"He hasn't had an easy time of it." Tabor sighed. "I admit, I screwed it up by not seeing it for certain before the contract, but jeez, if I had told him at the beginning—" He stopped as the shower turned off abruptly. "It wouldn't have changed anything. The kid would still be what he always was."

Fateh stepped out, draped in Etana's clothing, hair dripping slightly. "Yeah—but at least I'd be better prepared," he said dryly. "I might have even been able to save my mother." The sleeves of the shirt were too long and covered his fingertips as he reached up to brush his hair out of his eyes. "At least I wouldn't have set the bed on fire."

"And yourself," Etana muttered under his breath. "Still, kiddo—you still thought you were human. You might have done worse and hurt your mother or somehow yourself in the process." He shrugged. "Accidents happen, especially with the really young."

"You don't know that," Fateh protested. "You were always what you were. If I had found out earlier ..." He knew he still would have denied it, but saying that he would have *tried* eased the ache a little.

"True," Tabor interjected. "You may have figured it out sooner and accepted it, but more than likely, you would have denied it so much that you would have done more harm than good." Tabor sighed, looking worn out for a moment. "Granted, if we had never come back, you might have never known; but then again, you might have flared up and caused more destruction without anyone to save you."

Fateh blinked up at him, caught off-guard by his serious tone. "You don't ... know that," he whispered, but it was a weaker protest than before. He didn't know that, either. He could have set his house on fire and there wouldn't have been anyone to explain or stop him ...

Etana glared at him. "Stop griping about it—I thought that shower would have cooled you down to start thinking clearly. You're going to need to start taking responsibility for your actions. You're starting to show your powers and that means you should be old enough to control them."

"You don't know a damn thing about me!" Fateh stood up, face to face with Etana. "I'm just ... I know that I did this and I hate it, okay?" he shouted. "I hate not being able to control whatever the hell is wrong with me. I'd rather be broken and anti-social than be the type of person who sets things on fire when he gets upset."

"Like now, you damn moron!" Etana yelped, backing away from him. "Tamp it down. Jeez, save me from emotional fire brats who haven't gained control or maturity yet." His anger seemed to be gone, replaced by annoyance instead.

Fateh stared down at his slightly smoking hands and swallowed hard. He tried to imagine the fire going away like it never existed and soon everything was back to normal. He swallowed hard at this evidence that *he* could control the fire. "Well, excuse me. I'd like to think it takes more than a day to get used to having your world shift entirely," he huffed. "Give me at least four."

"Three, and that's being generous." Etana's mouth twitched and Fateh snickered as well.

Tabor eyed the two of them as if he was uncertain as to what was going to happen next, then shook his head. "You two got over that fast." He rested a hand on Fateh's head. "Are you going to be okay now?" he asked.

Fateh shrugged. "As well as I was before, I guess," he muttered. "There's no way that I can repress this fire stuff until I know what to do with it, is there?" He looked hopeful. "Like Etana mentioned?"

"You'll burn your soul out if you try something stupid like that." Tabor sighed. "Look, we may always be what we were, but your soul has always been what it is as well. Fire is damned hard to suppress and flares up at the worst of times unless you learn to control it. Putting a lid on it will only make it worse."

"But I can still try?" Fateh persisted. "Or you can try to make it so that I don't have nightmares or burn my clothing to ash?" The hope in his voice was almost painful and Tabor shook his head at the sound of it.

"We'll make sure that, in time, you won't go burning houses down around our ears." Tabor patted him on the head. "That will take time—when you're older and probably a bit taller, too."

"It's not my fault Etana's taller than I am," Fateh snapped, mood switching again and glaring up at the other. "I'm still a kid, you know." He looked decidedly put out at the teasing. "Is there any place that I can go get clothing that actually fits me? I'm not picky, but I don't want to look like some kid playing dress-up, either."

"That's because you're short." Etana snickered. "But yeah—I go into the city a lot. We'll find something for you that fits a little better before you go out and then do some basic shopping for when you and Tabor head off to wherever again."

Fateh nodded and stifled a yawn with one hand. "Sounds awesome. First, though—can we talk about what is actually going on here? This whole fire elemental thing that you said I am—and the Otherworld and Shadows?"

Tabor sighed. "First off, the proper name for our clan is the *aodhamair*. Only humans call us fire elementals because they don't have the knowledge of our name anymore. We're immune to fire, can create it—and because you're part of the Otherworld, you're ... ah ... allergic to those things that hurt us. Metal, salt ..." He shrugged. "It's not as bad as you probably think it is. As for the rest of your questions ..." He grabbed Fateh before he tipped over. "You're too tapped out to listen to them right now. How cold was that shower before you ended it?"

Fateh shrugged. "Can't remember. I just know all the heat was gone after a while and I didn't want to move." Tabor's voice echoed strangely in his head, sounding far away. *Probably coming from that tunnel he's shouting down ...* he thought muzzily.

"Idiot," Tabor muttered. "Cold isn't good for you—neither is copious amounts of water, but I think we can sacrifice a little downtime to make sure that you're *clean*."

"Glad to hear it." Fateh yawned again, not realizing that he was half-leaning against Tabor, more color coming into his skin as he leeched heat from Tabor's body. "Hopefully, I won't have any more nightmares," he murmured. He felt very distant from what had happened during the past couple of days as if the crying had created a block that set him apart from the actual pain of it all.

"Me too, kid." Etana sighed, watching as Fateh fell asleep against Tabor, half-supported by the other. "Tomorrow should be an interesting day." He grinned at Tabor, who was edging over to the bed, Fateh half-cradled against him and dead to the world. "Sleep well, you two."

Tabor managed a rude gesture before falling against the pillows. Fateh never stirred and Etana snickered. "Enjoy your pet, Tabor—even if he is a fire-breathing dragon underneath that scruffy human shell."

"Mm ... morning should show more of the dragon." Tabor sighed and stared down at what he had found, wondering just what he was going to do with him.

Chapter Twenty-Seven

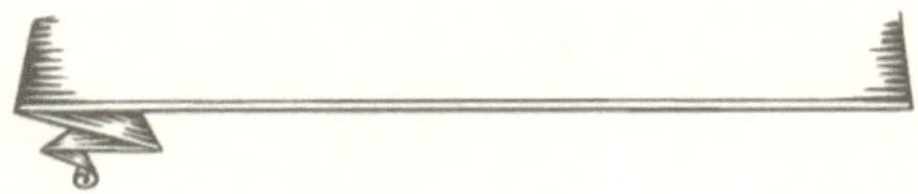

"I ... what the hell?" Fateh shoved at the warm presence wrapped around him, eyes narrowing as he realized it was Tabor—in the same bed as him and looking entirely too pleased with himself. "What do you think you're *doing*?" he snapped.

"Ah, and the dragon awakes." Tabor snickered, easing off the bed and observing Fateh, hands on his hips. "Are you going to burn down the place or are you going to hold your temper?"

Fateh stared at him and scrambled out of bed. "Why the hell were you in bed with me?" he demanded.

"Just making sure that if you had another nightmare, you wouldn't burn down your bed around you," Tabor reassured him. "Nothing more than that. You're so mistrusting of me."

"If you didn't purposely try and upset him," Etana called out from the next room, "then you wouldn't have to worry about his inability to trust. Really now—and you were lecturing *me* about upsetting the kid. I really don't want another fire started in here, Tabor. Get the kid dressed and send him out exploring."

"I'm not some kid that needs help getting dressed," Fateh snapped when Tabor looked as if he was going to do just that. "I can take care of myself, you know."

"Yes, I'm sure ..." Tabor eyed the ashy remains of what had been the first set of sheets Fateh crashed on. "But yet, you're not allowed to, are you?" he murmured. "I'd take this small piece of freedom while I can, little Spark."

Fateh flushed at the reminder that he wasn't on his own anymore; he didn't exactly need it spelled out for him, but Tabor didn't have to be such an ass about it, either. "I hate you," he snapped, grabbing the clothing Etana had left for him and slamming into the bathroom to change. Like hell, he was going to give that pervert a chance to stare at him while he changed, no matter what he had already inadvertently witnessed before.

"But I care for you so much," Tabor called after him, grinning widely as Etana came into the room. "He's too much fun to tease," he explained.

"Mmhm ..." Etana rolled his eyes. "Just don't overdo it, hm?" he asked dryly. "I really don't want to be cleaning the scent of smoke out of my house for years to come. Honestly, Tabor—I can nag him all I want, but you should know better."

"I should?" Tabor's look was entirely too innocent. "I'm looking out for Spark as much as he'll allow me. There's nothing in our contract that states I'm forbidden from teasing him. It's good for him."

"But not for my furniture." Etana rubbed at his temples. "I'm going to head into the city; check out some things. Send the kid out when you think he's ready. He's going to need something of his own to wear, especially if you're going to drag him around."

"Staying in one place is too damn boring," Tabor complained.

"And you're harder to track down if you're moving," Etana interjected. "I know you, Tabor—you've spent enough time with my family that ..."

"Yes, yes, shut up," Tabor hissed, gesturing at where Fateh was 'hiding.' "Spark can't hear this, you understand?" he whispered. "It's for me to tell him when I want to."

"You mean you'd actually tell him?" Etana stared at him in somewhat shock; it wasn't anything that he would expect Tabor to share. He only knew because his father was the one who initially found Tabor and the story was passed down the line, along with the favor that had never been cashed in.

"One day, perhaps." Tabor sighed, looking older for a moment and tired. "Just not now. I'll tell him when it's time."

"You do that." Etana shook his head before heading out the door.

Tabor looked after the place Etana left, grimacing as he ran a hand through his hair. That story—it wasn't something he'd readily share with anyone, not even Fateh. Even though they were of a kind, and they were contracted to each other, he still barely knew the kid.

He also didn't want to scare him; if he knew what the scáthach were really like ... he'd never look at the invasion of his hometown the same way again. Some things were better left unsaid until the listener was more prepared to hear them.

The sound of the bathroom door broke him out of his introspection and he smirked at seeing Fateh still drowning in the oversized hoodie and jeans. "Spark, we've got to get you something you won't be swimming in. Didn't your mother ever give you milk so that you'd grow?"

"Don't start," Fateh huffed, looking very young inside the oversized clothing. "You're not that much taller, you know," he pointed out.

"Yet I fit into my clothing, don't I?" Tabor's smirk widened.

"What little you wear of it," Fateh muttered. "Can't you at least put on a shirt? Pretend like you're something other than you are?"

"That's not how I do things." Tabor frowned. "And neither should you—normally. While we're here, though ... it may be best to keep somewhat of a low profile. Etana does things a bit differently in this town, different from what you've grown used to, at least."

"What do you mean?" Fateh's brows drew together in suspicion as Tabor reached for a shirt, expression distasteful.

"You'll see, Spark." Tabor ruffled his hair, pushing him gently towards the door. "Why don't you go and explore? I'll take care of my own things here first, then I'll meet you out there, hm? Etana said that he'd meet up with you, so be on the lookout."

Fateh still wasn't entirely satisfied, but before he could open his mouth to protest, Tabor shoved him bodily out the door.

Etana stared Tabor down, eyebrows raised at how he was acting. "You really are going to put your all into this kid, aren't you?" he asked. "I told you that he's trouble, Tabor." The two of them were taking this opportunity of Fateh exploring the town to talk. Tabor hoped for a little more than just talking, but they had to get the subject of Fateh out of the way first.

"And I told you that I contracted myself to him. It was a promise that was made before Fateh was even put into that prison." He was quiet for a few moments as he thought over his words. "And I couldn't let him get caught by those monsters that overran his town. They were close to taking him; he'd already made a deal with them so they had a taste of his blood."

That had been something that he had wanted to smack Fateh for; he'd known the right words, but he hadn't known to not let them taste his blood. Of course, it had been mutual, but Fateh didn't know what to do with the blood of his enemy. It was almost as good as having a name.

"And here I thought he was smarter than that." Etana snorted. "He's a young idiot then, just like you." He was making him and Tabor something to drink as he talked.

"And I spotted him first, so it's my job to make sure that he doesn't end up like me," Tabor retorted. "You know what happened to me and the others in my family." That was something that Etana knew quite well; it was something that *everyone* seemed to know.

"Of course." Etana smirked. "Since you came to *me* for help. You still haven't quite paid off that debt and yet here you are." He plopped down on the couch, handing Tabor his drink and smirking at him.

"Still claiming hospitality and a safe haven just as we negotiated for all those years ago," Tabor interjected smoothly. "I was smart then, knowing that I'd need safe harbor in the future." He took a long swig of his drink and made an appreciative noise at Etana's handi-work.

"I just didn't expect you to be dragging a kid with you when you came back." Etana shook his head. "All you had was a human promise to go after him in Mokosh's territory. That doesn't seem like it should be enough to go to a place that is so contrary to your own power."

"It was because he was a kid, and a vulnerable one, that I decided to help." Tabor sighed and ran a hand through his hair. "I may be a loner now, but I'm not a complete asshole. Besides, he's a type of kin of mine. Fire calls to fire."

Etana leaned against Tabor, metal bleeding back into his skin so that he didn't burn him. "More than fire calls to fire," he teased, tapping Tabor's nose with one finger. "Haven't we talked about the kid enough? I wanted to spend time with you, not with you and some kid."

"As much as I would like to ..." Tabor went cross-eyed trying to focus on Etana's finger, which moved down to tap at his lips. "I've got to ask you ..." Etana was leaning even closer now and Tabor was losing his train of thought. Etana was being *very* distracting. "Etana!"

"What?" Etana blinked innocently at him but didn't move back. "I'm tired of talking about your fire fledging. He's either going to burn himself out, be burned out by the Shadows, or he'll survive. What I want right now is *you*." He put action to words by kissing Tabor, sliding his fingers into Tabor's hair at the same time.

Tabor knew it was logical and that there was only so much time that they would have together before he had to bring Fateh back. He fumbled with his drink for a moment, hastily placing it down on the table next to him before letting himself relax into the kiss. He could worry about Fateh later. _____

Afterward, Etana smirked at Tabor as he pushed his hair out of his face. It had been a very enjoyable time for both of them. "I think

I'm going to find your little flame and bait him a little. I want to see how observant he is."

"You're going to follow him around, not looking like yourself, aren't you?" Tabor asked, rolling his eyes. "That's not a test of his observation skills, that's you being a dick."

"You like me that way." Etana simply grinned wider at Tabor's look of disgust. "You wouldn't be friends with me if I was any other way."

"Just don't torment the kid too much?" Tabor suggested. "I know he's an easy target for you, but remember that he's barely seventeen. He's *really* young, Etana."

"I won't torment him too much, but I think it'll be fun to follow him around and see what he does when he's confronted with me alone." Etana gave a luxurious stretch and Tabor couldn't help but poke him in the side, earning a scowl.

"I'm going to take a shower," Etana said with extreme dignity, standing up and pushing Tabor back into the pillows. "Then I'm going to go torment your boy."

Tabor made a face but let him go. He'd meet up with Fateh later, but it wouldn't hurt for Etana to fish out information from him. Maybe he'd tell Etana something that he wouldn't tell Tabor. _______

"I guess I can be grateful he's not latching onto me every second," Fateh murmured under his breath. *And I can pretend to be semi-normal, if just for a short while.*

It wouldn't be too difficult to do; he could slip into the crowd, hide away, and pretend that Tabor and Etana didn't exist. That he and his ... *no, not his mother ...* that he was off on his own, exploring and moving away from his roots.

As long as I can avoid people, it will be just fine. I'm just one more kid here, right?

He was at a vantage point where he could see the city spread out ahead of him. Etana lived in a very central location. He picked a direction at random and made his way into the thick of people. It was overwhelming seeing so many people, especially after the year in the so-called school for misplaced orphans.

It was also comforting to be lost in the middle of a crowd where no one was watching him. He felt for the money that Tabor had pressed into his hands before he left. It was going to be weird to pay for things again, instead of bartering like he was used to.

The crowds milling around him were ordinary—almost painfully so, compared to the tense atmosphere of 'home,' of that constant, underlying fear that something or someone was going to get taken away without warning. Fateh narrowly dodged a trio of girls, dressed in identical uniforms with schoolbags slung over their shoulders.

He stopped in front of a store that sold toys, his heart twisting slightly as he looked at ordinary items, including such innocuous things as a teddy bear and a baby doll. Nothing that he wanted or needed, but he somehow wouldn't mind having. *I am way too old to be hugging a teddy bear for comfort.*

Fateh debated going inside; it would be the most normal thing he would do since the Shadows had taken over his home. It wasn't like he'd buy anything as childish as a *toy*, but he would like the teddy bear. He wanted the comfort of something that was long ago out of his reach.

He didn't know how long he stood in front of the toy store, but it was long enough to earn some strange looks as the items in the window mesmerized him.

"So, how do you like the city?"

Fateh barely kept himself from yelping as the arm dropped around his shoulder; he couldn't keep back the jerk as he turned to glare at whatever stranger decided to make himself comfortable around him.

It was a kid around his own age, that was clear enough—wearing clothing that seemed vaguely familiar, but Fateh couldn't quite place them. *Not like I pay attention to that crap.* The smirk on his face set Fateh on edge, though—who was this kid to act in that way and treat him like ...

"Man, your observation skills really suck." The boy snickered. "You really don't recognize me when I've done a dye job and I'm not wearing all my piercings?" It was *that* tone of voice that caused Fateh to scowl.

"Etana." He really *did* look different—so very ordinary that it was a shock to try and associate him with the flamboyant person from before. The few piercings that he wore were nothing remarkable; if he was wearing any others in places unseen, Fateh didn't want to know about them.

"I told you that I could blend in," Etana pointed out. "You just didn't realize how well I could. It's much easier than you and your flashy way of going about things." He made a face. "Try and keep the temper down here, would you? You can pass easily enough, but I got Tabor to agree to stay home for a bit and let me show you around. It's easier here for people to think you're ... human." His voice went lower. "We're kinda covert here."

"Yes, because I can so very well control something I had no idea existed until last night." Fateh's look was sour. "And you can say that you're spying. " Fateh rolled his eyes. "I'm not a total idiot or a toddler, no matter what you think of me."

"If I thought you were a total moron, nothing you could say would dissuade me, so let's not go there." Etana was still easygoing and Fateh found himself relaxing. It was so much like having a friend again that it was almost easy to fall into the routine. "And if you were an idiot, I wouldn't be talking to you and letting you *know* what we were doing."

"Yes, because I'm *just* the type of person to go shouting to perfect strangers about what type of person I am," Fateh muttered. "Was just about to do that when you dropped in." He gestured around them. "I thought they could use a little excitement in their lives."

"Well, you never know." Etana grinned, dragging him along to a less crowded pathway. "You could be going through the rebellious teenager phase, ready to break against all the rules when your ... guardians ... aren't around."

Fateh flushed, arms crossing against his chest defensively. "Just because Tabor isn't here," he hissed, well aware of the 'guardian' Etana referred to, "I can still tell that he's *there* monitoring me." The chain was ever-present, the shimmering lines of fire twining around each other, a constant in his vision. "If I can sense him, he can sense me."

"True, which is probably the only reason why he let you out on your own, with only the leash to keep you two connected. I can help keep you in line, but it's a bit showy at times and not a talent that I'd care to display to everyone here. I've built up too much of a base to let it all get shot to hell."

"Then why did you let me out in the first place?" Fateh snapped. "Aren't you afraid I'm going to lose control or something?" he demanded. "You saw what happened when I had a *nightmare*."

"Keep this in mind, then." Etana leaned in close so that the network of gossip that ran across every city couldn't pick up his voice. "There are strange little birds all over the world, Fateh—but if you start sprouting fire, they're not going to whisper about misplaced nestlings, but start looking around for something more."

Fateh jerked and looked around instinctively, eyes darting to the side. He didn't want to see anyone—their cold expressions reverberated in his memory, how they did nothing at all except stare as his mother died ... He didn't know what they'd think of him. Would they leave him alone, taunt him, or worse—see him as one of the enemies?

"Here, sit down. This café has decent food." Etana's voice intruded into his panic.

Fateh was jerked to a stop in front of a small table, wicker seats worked into something more comfortable. He could hear the happy chatter of other people and the sound of silverware clinking against China was so painfully normal it almost hurt to listen to. "So, what's to prevent from ... attacks happening here?"

"Your enemy can't get here." Etana smirked, looking a lot more confident than Fateh felt he had a right to be. "It's the same concept as what you experienced with Mokosh. It can't get past the barriers I've put up. My clan ... Let's just say I believe we're the most useful against what you fear so much."

"So, why doesn't your kind just go up against the Shadows?" Fateh demanded.

"Because, child, I don't want to." Etana leaned forward, pausing only when a waiter walked by, before returning his attention to Fateh. "It's not in my nature to choose a side and stick with it. Tabor was serious when he asked if I was friend or foe." He tapped Fateh's chest. "Get used to asking that question."

"So, why are you a friend now?" Fateh asked, slumping in the chair. "I mean ..." He gestured vaguely. "I don't know how this whole thing works, you know."

"Most of the reasons I can't tell you yet; that's for Tabor to decide. My family and him ... we go far back. What I can tell you is that because I've invited you to my territory, you're safe." Etana's eyes narrowed. "Nothing gets in here without my permission and anything that harms what I consider to be under my protection will come to a nasty end." He smirked. "That, and you amuse me."

"I ... I what?" Fateh stared at him, protesting at the implication that he was something to amuse Etana. "How can I amuse you? I told you, I'm not a child and if you think that what I've been through is amusing, then you can go kiss my—"

"One moment, Fateh—" Etana cut his threat off easily as he gestured to a waiter to come closer. "Let's eat first and then we'll discuss more. There really is only so much that I can tell you. Tabor wouldn't be happy at interfering with his ... charge." The pause was deliberate and Fateh scowled, then flushed at the implication.

"Look, I don't need anyone taking care of me—" he started.

"Yet, you don't have a choice, now do you?" Etana smirked. "You decided to go along with this, didn't you? I'd make the best of it if I were you."

Fateh opened his mouth to argue again but Etana shook his head at him, conversing with the waiter. He was obviously well known here; even as casually dressed as he was he was noticeably deferred to. "What do you want to eat?" he asked, pointing to the menu that Fateh had neglected to notice.

Fateh blinked at the choices; there was a larger selection than he expected and he scanned quickly. "The Cajun chicken," he whispered, more to the menu than to the waiter. He hoped that it wasn't that obvious how skittish he was being in direct contact with a person and he gave himself a mental kick at the way he was acting. He wasn't a *kid* to be scared of something as normal as this.

Etana smirked at his choice and ordered quickly for himself, eyeing Fateh after the waiter stepped away. "Isn't it cliché that you like spicy food?" he asked. "Really, don't live up to the stereotype because I'm here."

Fateh scowled, slumping further down in his chair. "There's nothing wrong with liking spicy food," he muttered. "It has nothing to do with what I am, it's just ..." He made a face. "I've just always liked it. My mother liked spicy food, too—it doesn't mean a thing."

"I can see why Tabor likes to push your buttons. You're too easy to tease." Etana reached over and ruffled his hair. "Don't think so hard. You'll start to smoke."

"So very original." Fateh sighed, turning his attention to the streets, watching people move around, looking unconcerned with how life had changed. *Of course, they don't have Shadows here*, he thought, mood dipping lower. *They just have Etana and his family.*

"Hey—cheer up, would you?" Etana sighed, resting his chin in his hands. "You're starting to depress *me* with that look you're wearing. What's got you so down?" He nodded to the waiter as their water was set down, then turned his attention back to Fateh.

"I could list off everything, but then that'd just be rehashing all of what you already know." Fateh snorted. "You said you'd give me some more info about what's going on and what I can expect. Spill." He leaned forward. "I'd rather not stay in the dark as much as I have been, thanks."

Etana held up a finger. "I said that I could tell you *some*," he cautioned. "It's not my duty to do so and since that falls under the banner of another person, he would take serious offense at any misdirection. Besides," he leaned forward, smirking, "you don't want to be indebted to me for anything I tell you, now do you?"

Fateh blanched at the idea of being indebted to anyone else. While being in a contract with Tabor seemed to cancel out the original 'debt' he'd had, he knew that to be in debt to another would be a bad thing, especially to one whom he had been warned couldn't be trusted from day to day. "No, that's okay," he said hastily. "I'll ask Tabor."

Etana snickered. "Thought you might go that path. You are interesting, but I'm not sure I want to think of all the creative ways you could pay me back for a small piece of information."

"I should be so grateful. Remind me to ..." He blinked and swallowed his words before he finished the phrase. "Um ... yeah. Good advice." His voice caught, sticking in his throat almost painfully as he tried to thank Etana.

"Having problems?" Etana smirked, cheek resting on one hand. "It's a safeguard, you know—prevents from all sorts of nasty things happening with those too young to know better. Don't you know your legends, little one? There is some truth to them."

"You mean the whole thanking thing works even if you're not—" He gestured vaguely, trying to indicate his situation without too many words. "I didn't thank anyone when I was at home. We knew that much from stories at least ..." His look seemed to indicate what he thought of 'stories' and using them for information. "Fairy tales are for kids, you know. We never thought we'd have to take them seriously."

"Hey, I'm not that much older than you," Etana pointed out, "and I've read fairy tales." He picked at his food, talking around each bite. "Not that stupid, fluffed out, and sanitized crap, but the ones that at least *tried* to keep a hint of the truth in them." He snickered. "Some humans knew what they were writing about. Others missed the mark completely."

"Yeah—whatever." Fateh sighed and stared off at the crowds of people, clustered together like kids in their groups. "I guess I got lucky, not ever thanking. I just got shackled to someone because things got desperate." He tilted his head, vaguely intrigued by Etana's words. "So, those stories really do help you speak and act correctly?" His tone conveyed his skepticism.

"Haven't you noticed that in those stories, those who thanked the other powers received nothing but trouble? Even the smallest child knew not to thank us; it was considered a debt if they did such a thing. People have forgotten the rules." He pointed a finger at Fateh. "Remember that if you run into someone stupid enough that would need your help. Human debts can be collected and sorted for later use."

The waiter set down their food then. Etana made a sound of delight and helped himself to his food, the conversation apparently done for the moment.

"Great ... even while being lectured, I'm still insulted by you," Fateh muttered.

"You really expect anything different?" His brows rose. "Eat. Your food will get cold and I really don't want you setting the place on fire just so that your laziness doesn't cost you a cold meal."

"I couldn't do something like that anyway," Fateh mumbled, poking at his food and taking slow, careful bites. "I think the whole mess is triggered by me getting upset. I'm not willing to have a waking nightmare to do that."

"Leave the city and you'll soon have enough fuel. You've already had a taste of it. For someone who was raised as a human, some of what you see is going to give you night terrors." He smirked. "Even some of us who have been around some time have terrors when we see the Dark Court in action."

Fateh swallowed hard, not liking the implications of what Etana was saying. "I don't plan on involving myself with anything like that." He stabbed at his food. "I'll just ... I ..." He stopped, stunned. He had no idea what path his life was going to take now. It wasn't like he could sleep in and hear his mother teasing him anymore. There was no hanging out with Tobias and Meira ... his life was more in shambles than before.

"You see?" Etana was watching him closely. "You don't know what will happen from day to day. Once you leave this city, you're stepping out into a place that won't be like anything you've experienced before."

"And if I stay in here longer than we're welcomed by you, I'll be trapped in a place that will be infinitely worse than the place I've been before," he pointed out dryly. "I think I'll take my chances with Tabor. We're at least contracted not to hurt each other ..."

"And always remember that." Etana's voice grew serious. "You're lucky that you do have him, growing into your power so unexpectedly. You do realize how much worse it could have been?"

"You mean, I could have been dead instead of my mother?" Fateh snapped, flushing as he mangled his pasta more instead of looking up at Etana.

"You could have been taken by someone who would have used you, hurt you, and possibly eaten the magic that your soul is made out of." Etana didn't hide his relish in taking a bite of his food, licking up the juices on his fingers. "Ask Tabor about it sometime, he knows of what can be done that's worse than death." As Fateh stared at him, Etana waved it off. "I can't tell you—but just remember, we do take care of our own, and you're considered a child to us, no matter how you see yourself. Tabor and you are ... kin in a way. That's closer than just the normal bond."

"So, where's your people?" Fateh looked up briefly, hoping to see the expression before Etana spoke, but there wasn't any change as Etana shrugged easily.

"We're scattered and most are still back home. Some of us have our nests in various spots, but that's something we're doing; it's nothing you need to be concerned about." He smirked and stole a bite from Fateh's damaged meal. "Some of my kin aren't quite as nice as me. Age won't make them more tolerant."

"Even with someone that is part of your kind?" he asked, eyebrows raising.

"We don't all get along, Fateh," he pointed out. "Tabor and I are somewhat of an exception because we're friends. You'll find that certain people get along better with others. We aren't *always* the best of allies." He looked thoughtful. "Strange how life can turn out," he mused, half to himself.

"It's hard to see myself as being part of anything except being human." Fateh sighed and clenched at his fork, expression sad for a moment. "And ... I suppose my being human would be even worse than being what I really am. None of your kind would help me then."

"You have such little faith in humans that you think they wouldn't offer you help?" Etana tilted his head.

Fateh scowled. "Considering it's because of them that I realized what I was, no. They wanted to kill me and ... well ..." He sighed, closing his eyes. "This really sucks, you know. Just ... accepting it. It's like turning my back on everything I was."

"Not that human origins were all that great, to begin with." Etana grinned at Fateh's outraged look, gesturing for the waiter to come over. "It has its multitude of problems, for being as young of a race as it is ..."

"I know it has problems." Fateh rolled his eyes, blinking a bit when he saw Etana pay with actual money. He hadn't used it in so long that he'd almost forgotten the familiar routine of it all.

"You don't barter here?" Fateh blinked up at Etana. He thought the whole world was like his corner of it; nothing he had seen or heard had indicated anything different until he came here.

Etana's looked vaguely pitying. "I've heard from Tabor that your town was hit particularly bad in terms of the invasion," he mused. "No, little Fateh—it's not as bad here as it was where you came from and I'm sure there are other places that are much worse, but this relative peace—it's not so bad." He smirked. "Humans who are thrust out of their comfort zone tend to panic and it makes a mess. I like things to be calm and orderly."

"But very insular." Tabor's voice sounded from behind the two of them and Fateh jerked in shock; he hadn't even heard or sensed him coming. "They can't really do a lot of trade outside of the city, can they? It's like a bubble."

"They can trade out of the city," Etana huffed. "I make sure there's a market going so the city doesn't die completely. They're very self-sufficient, though." He stared off at the milling crowds and shrugged. "I make sure of it."

"Yeah, yeah—I'd go nuts in this place. All the same people, all the time?" Tabor tugged Fateh up. "It's been nice and all and thanks for the loan of clothes so Spark didn't wander around naked, but we'll buy our own, return yours, and then explore the city."

"Smart, Tabor." Etana smirked. "Coming just before your little pet got indebted." He interpreted Fateh's scowl correctly. "Oh, don't get so uptight about it. That is what you are, essentially. More intelligent than most, but as long as you're tied to him, you're a pet. You need to be trained before you can run free."

"That makes me feel *so* much better." Fateh rolled his eyes. "But I'm not a pet. Tabor's contract with me is different." He looked up at Tabor for confirmation and got a nod. "Lunch was nice—" He hesitated again, cautious of any sort of thanks. "See you around?"

Tabor was practically playing with the chain of fire and every time he tugged on it, Fateh twitched.

"Mmm ... come on, little Spark. I have a feeling you would rather have more of a variety of clothing and you don't seem the type to take energy in our way just yet." He grabbed the hood of his jacket. "We'll be going to get you food. I can't have my acquisition starve now." His smile *wasn't* kind, not with its sharp edges. "It would break the terms of our contract to let you go hungry."

"Good to know," Fateh said dryly. "So, if I starve myself, it will be your fault and not mine?"

Etana laughed and shook his head. "What an interesting little *Spark* you have. If you decide to stay around at all, come see me. Stay safe, little Fateh." Etana stayed at the table and Fateh watched as Tabor tugged him away, unsure of what was going to happen next. He wasn't going to admit out loud that he already felt safer with Tabor.

Chapter Twenty-Eight

"Truce expires next week, Spark." Tabor guided him along the busy street. "We need to be as far away as possible. Etana won't follow us, but we also don't want to put ourselves in his reach; staying in the town would put us under his jurisdiction."

"If it's such a problem to stay here with Etana's loyalties switching, why don't we buy clothing somewhere else?" Fateh crossed his arms over his chest. "I don't have money, Tabor. We stopped using that a long time ago. You should know that."

"You think that I'm so unprepared?" Tabor smirked. "I'll have you outfitted, but I'm afraid you will have to do with less than you had before."

"Oh yeah, I had tons before." Fateh's tone was wry. "If you're planning on dragging me around everywhere, I'm not seeing dragging around a bunch of crap as useful." He tucked his hands in his pockets. "We don't have to buy stuff, though. If you can take me back to my house, I can grab my clothes and food there."

Tabor was watching him as he spoke and Fateh made sure he kept his expression blank; he wasn't going to let Tabor know that the very idea of going back was painful, but if he did ... he could grab memories; anything that would help him deal with everything, to keep him sane.

"After you professed so loudly how much you didn't want to return? But if you want to go back to the viper's nest," Tabor raised an eyebrow, "we can go back, little Spark. Just be careful—we can't afford any accidents with you if you wish to remain incognito."

"Meira and Tobias probably spread a bunch of stuff around town." Fateh sighed. "I want to rescue as much from my house as I can." He sounded young and vulnerable and he gave himself a mental kick for it. "Can't exactly stay at home now anymore, can I?" he asked.

"That's up to you." Tabor shrugged. "Personally, a good nest is always nice to come back to and your little town has always been ... interesting. I hadn't been there for a few years since before I first met you ..."

Fateh stared at him. "You were in my town *before* you pretended to be my friend? When?" he demanded, staring at Tabor, wanting the truth on this, not some half-assed lie or deliberate misleading.

"Of course, I was." Tabor grinned, moving Fateh closer to the patches of shadow, watching him. "I'm hurt that you don't remember me from before. I hadn't brought it up before because I thought it was obvious."

"No. I don't remember." Fateh's voice was flat. "Do tell." The fact that this ... this ... that he involved himself in Fateh's life before he realized it only raised his suspicions more.

"I'm hurt beyond all reason." Tabor clasped a hand to his heart. "You were but a young thing during our first meeting and even if you won't believe me, little Spark, I had no real inkling of your true nature at that time. I admit I was curious, but ..."

"And what happened during this fateful first meeting?" Fateh paused by the deepening puddle of shadow, eyeing it uneasily. He still didn't like traveling by this method and he wasn't about to ask Tabor—yet—if there was something more suited for 'their' kind. He accepted it himself but still didn't want to admit to Tabor that they were the same kind. It would be too much like giving in.

"Oh, you had badly damaged yourself with some childish play of some sort and I, being the caring individual that I was—" He paused and snickered at the look on Fateh's face. "Oh, alright. I was bored and you were bleeding so profusely that I decided to add a bit of healing to you to speed your recovery along. I'm not surprised you don't remember that meeting, but surely you remember the one that happened just a scant four years ago?"

"I'd have to say, no." Fateh rolled his eyes. "Are you just making stuff up now?" he asked. "I'm already a part of this. Saying stuff to get me to come along or to make us closer really isn't necessary."

"I'm touched that you want to get closer." Tabor smirked. "No, little Spark—I'm not making it up. Truth to tell, it's the first time I actually noticed something about you. It's a pity I was on my way out of town at that time, or surely I would have investigated further."

"Whatever," Fateh muttered. "Tell me this fantastic story already, would you?"

"Mm ... it started in a bookstore." Tabor took his arm and directed him to a bench; talking while shadow-traveling never went well. "You were fourteen, I believe."

"You ... you were that jerk from back then?" Fateh's voice rose in disbelief. "You don't look anything like that guy. You looked ..." He rolled his eyes as Tabor gave him a self-satisfied look. "Normal. You looked *normal.*"

"I can change my appearance in small ways, little Spark." Tabor ruffled his hair, looking entirely too pleased with himself. "As can you, after many years and if you practice. I simply adjusted how I looked, as many of us didn't want to display ourselves to the humans we shared space with back then."

"You recognized something about me at that point and you never said anything." Fateh frowned.

"That's not true," Tabor gave him a look of mock-hurt. "I did warn you about that book. If I hadn't, it might have burned, and then what would people have thought?"

"If it wasn't for you, I probably wouldn't have lost my temper in the first place," Fateh growled out. "You aggravated me even then!"

"If it wasn't me, it would have been someone else and it would have gone much worse for you in that situation. I admit, my presence may have brought your talent a little closer to the surface, but it was always there, you know."

"Still—why didn't you say anything then?" Fateh demanded. "Why did you pretend you were my friend?"

"Would you have honestly believed me if I had told you the truth?"

"Did I believe you when you first told me?" Fateh returned, eyes narrowed at him. He dared Tabor to deny it.

"Well ..." Tabor smirked. "You did agree so very quickly, but then again—you like evidence, don't you, little Spark? If one can prove it to you, you're satisfied." He didn't look as if he wanted to move anytime soon.

"I still don't know how you've 'proved' it to me, but I've only ever seen the kids in that home do stuff like I did, and it didn't exactly have the best outcome." Fateh chewed on his lower lip. He couldn't quite distance himself from 'humans,' no matter how much he was told that he wasn't really one. *Or a mistake. That's really awesome to think about.* "I have a feeling you guys don't like to share power."

The sidelong glance Tabor gave him was amused. "No, not generally." He grinned. "Those who we give power to tend to regret it after a time. It's a shame when they don't play by the rules that we set out for them."

"Oh, yes—because you tend to make all the little loopholes *so* clear." Fateh snorted. "Those who play *your* games tend to get burned." He grimaced at the unintentional pun. "You know what I mean. Humans don't end up all that great if the tylwyth teg get involved."

It was Tabor's turn to snort. "Kid, you'd be playing with more than just the proverbial fire if you got mixed up with that mess. We're not that high up and you couldn't pay me to touch foot in their courts."

"You're still bothered by a lot of the same stuff, though," Fateh pointed out. "Salt, metal ..."

"Yes, yes—that's because we're all part of one big happy family. We're just the relatives that everyone pretends doesn't exist." He smirked. "They tend to push us to the background, even if we are their elders." He shook his head. "No respect."

"Why are you still here?" Etana leaned over the two of them. "I thought you were so very eager to leave my hospitality. All that talk about buying clothing and food for your pet was just an excuse so I wouldn't hear story time?"

Fateh jerked in surprise, but Tabor shrugged. "Decided to have a bit of a catch-up and teach the kid some history first before we went traveling all over the place. We do still have some time, after all."

"History lesson?" Etana's brows rose. "More like you disparaging our relatives again. You can hardly call yourself an elder, Tabor. I'm older than you and even I'm far younger than any of our fae relatives."

"They still treat *our* elders with disrespect," Tabor huffed, arms crossing against his chest. "Our kind was here first, you know that."

"Tabor, sometimes you act so young." Etana rolled his eyes. "They take the limelight and we can hide in our corners, watch, and build our power." He smirked. "It also helps if you make the right alliances."

"I make alliances with you when you're friendly." Tabor smirked. "I have an idea ... since we got distracted, why don't we let junior run free for a bit while we catch up? We weren't able to really do so last night ..." He flicked Fateh's nose playfully. "What do you say, Spark? Neither of us hovering over you for a few hours?"

"So you can have sex." Fateh rolled his eyes. "Why not, I think it'll be great. I won't have to watch you *or* hear you." He got up quickly from the bench, holding out his hand. "Gee, Dad ... can I have some money to buy something cool while you're hanging out with your friend?"

Tabor snorted and nudged Etana, who handed over the money that was used in town. Fateh hadn't seen real coins in years and it startled him to be holding a rope of them. "Yeah—knock yourself out, kid. Stuff here's pretty cheap, but you have to remember that you'll be dragging it all over the place. Tabor's as rootless as they come."

Tabor looked unconcerned at the comment and chose to ignore it as he drew Fateh closer, gripping his hand. "Let me take care of something before you go running off, though." A shock of coolness ran through Fateh's body as he jerked away.

"What the hell did you just do?" Fateh demanded, rubbing at his wrist. "You didn't have to molest me."

"A temporary solution," Tabor said, waving him off. "It won't last for more than a few hours, but at least we won't have to worry about your temper getting the better of you. I don't wish to find you by the sound of fire alarms." His look was serious. "And don't even ask me to do it permanently. Even if I could, it would kill you."

Fateh rubbed at his arms, feeling colder than before and slightly disgusted that Tabor could read him so easily. "You'd probably have yourself a zombie or something to parade around. An empty shell like a lot of the humans who screw up with contracts." He kept his tone light, not meeting Tabor's gaze nor meaning any of what he said.

Something in his tone must have conveyed that because Tabor just waved him off. "I'll make sure I find you when we're ready to go for real this time," he murmured, smirking. "I know I will."

"Great—just don't tell me the details after." Fateh made a face at the two of them as he left to explore and actually *buy* something for once, instead of bartering.

———

"Think he's going to be okay?" Etana watched as Fateh slipped through the crowd easily, getting lost to his senses, but he knew that

Tabor was keeping an eye on him through their connection. "If all of what you've said is true, he's not all that stable ..." He snorted. "Especially if he was raised human."

"He's still human," Tabor shrugged, "whether he was raised that way or not. He's just ..." He ran a hand through his hair, obviously frustrated. "Even I don't know what he is, really. That soul of his—it's not human at all, or else you wouldn't have been able to recognize him, and traveling through the Shadows would have killed him."

"The only thing about him that's human is the exterior," Etana pointed out. "He's certainly smarter than the average human." He watched the crowds milling around and shrugged. "And the way he pushes things away; it's *our* way, Tabor. The real question is, what are you going to do with the child now? He *is* a child, you know. Laughably so."

"Yes, yes—centuries behind you and a full fifty years younger than me." Tabor rolled his eyes. "He's barely coming into his power and what I'm going to do is keep an eye on him. He's too young to be wandering around, setting things on fire and attracting the wrong sort of attention."

"Mm ... toddlers and flames never did go well." Etana shook his head. "You can tell he hasn't accepted a damn thing you've told him, though—no matter what he says or how he acts. He still thinks of himself as human—not even a pet as the other humans are to their ... owners, but purely himself. Not even setting himself on fire cured him of that mindset."

"You're giving him too little credit." Tabor frowned. "There's something about him that accepts this whole mess." He couldn't help but grin. "But it's hidden under all the human stupid."

"Glad you agree with that, at least." Etana pulled Tabor up. "Come on—no use sitting around here. Let's go back to my place and wait for the kid to finish exploring. I'm sure we can keep ourselves entertained."

"I'm sure we can as well," Tabor snorted as he followed Etana back to his home. "You miss me that much, Etana?" He smirked at the flush that spread across Etana's face.

"I wouldn't tease so much," Etana huffed, practically jerking Tabor along. "You're supposed to be caring for me, you know. *All* my needs and without complaint. That was the favor that you chose to give away so long ago."

"Mm ... well, that was how you wanted to spend it." Tabor rolled his eyes, but the smirk didn't leave. "And who said I would be complaining over this?" His voice was deeply amused, even more so by how uncomfortable Etana was now. "I get my energy, you get what you want—everyone wins."

"You'll get more than energy," Etana murmured, leading him through the door and watching him. "You *always* say it's just for the energy and it never is. Why would you keep on coming back?"

"You found me this time," Tabor pointed out, already tugging off the shirt so that he was at least more comfortable. It was too hot with so many layers and he vaguely wondered how Fateh could stand it. He may have a human body, but his nature had to be making things uncomfortable for him.

"You've been gone for too long." Etana crossed his arms against his chest. "You were with humans too long, you've forgotten your duties to my clan. If I wished it ..."

"If you wished until the sun decided to fall out of the sky, you couldn't change my loyalties." Tabor's voice was flat. "I'm loyal to *you* alone, but that does not mean I'll change my alliances to the scáthach just because you had a whim to do so."

"You say that now," Etana began.

"And I'll say it in the future," Tabor stated, stepping up close to Etana. "Now come – let's not argue about it so much, hm?" he asked softly. "We've got other things than old arguments to catch up on."

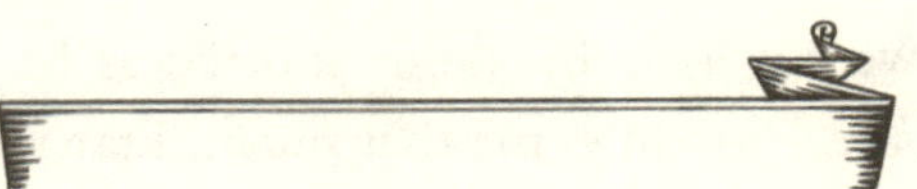

Chapter Twenty-Nine

There was a bewildering variety of stores to sort through; Fateh didn't really care what he wore, as long as it fit reasonably well and wasn't full of lace.

He finally surrounded himself with the noise of multitudes of people, going straight towards what looked fairly decent and tugging the clothes off the racks. The less time he spent here, the better. As his hands closed around a pair of jeans, his throat tightened at the memory of his last shopping trip with Meira and Tobias.

That's in the past now, he told himself firmly. *No use thinking about it.* It was useless to keep such a tight hold on it, but he couldn't help but compare this place with the shopping mall he'd gone to; he couldn't help but see how many people were here, chatting and joking and buying clothing that didn't involve cashing in old records or tapes of anything of sentimental value.

It was so different that it was almost a physical blow to his senses.

He stuffed everything into one bag and barely looked at the prices as he forked over the money. He didn't need a lot; he just wanted to keep decent. *Ha, don't buy a lot—don't weigh yourself down.* His thoughts were sour towards Etana's reminder. *Doesn't he realize how little the Shadows left us when they took over?*

Not for the first time, he wondered where the Shadows came from. They weren't there one day and the next they were everywhere. They had come after the fae and after they came, there were less fae and more Shadows.

Food was next; he *should* buy stuff that would last awhile, but he and his mother hardly ever bought a lot of food. They mostly grew what they ate. The only exception was meat and they hadn't had a lot of that for a while. He was lost in thought, trying to think of what would be good and not paying too much attention to his surroundings.

He didn't realize he was being followed.

"You must be new around here." Fateh turned around quickly at the hostile tone of voice. "We haven't seen you around before and our city isn't *that* big when you realize nobody goes out." The speaker was the leader of a group of kids—younger than he was, but all standing in defensive poses, surrounding the leader. She was unlike Meira in appearance with her curly hair and dark skin, but he didn't trust easily anymore, not after what he had been through. He didn't recognize their accents; they sounded completely different than the people he knew. *Where am I?*

"Yeah, but don't people come in?" Fateh snapped, arms crossed against his chest defensively. So what if he was arguing with kids? "Can't be all that special that you need to gawk at me."

"It is when you come in with those other things," another snorted. "We're not as dumb as they think we are." He stepped forward, sandals making a smacking sound on the ground as he came closer. "Or as dumb as *you* think we are. What are you, anyway? Human or part of what screwed us all over?"

Etana thinks he's so very undercover. Fateh gave a mental shake of his head. *Even if the Shadows aren't here like they were in my town, they've still made their mark all over the place.* "I don't know what you're talking about." He rolled his eyes. "Do I look anything other than human?"

It was the best that he could do as a reply; he couldn't just say 'no' without lying and *that* scared him more than anything else that had happened so far. *What the hell is happening to me?* His grip tightened on his bag of clothing.

"Hmph—he doesn't look like he's one of them, Meg; they're just causing problems with new arrivals like usual." The boy who seemed the most talkative stepped forward. "I mean, look at him—I could practically pound him into the ground and he's gotta be older than us. There's no way he could be one of the Others ... they're all so full of what they are." There were snickers and nods of agreement all around.

"They think they're *so* much better than all of us," Meg agreed. "I don't see how they're all that great." She seemed unconcerned with being overheard by any of the fae and getting hurt in the process. Fateh wished he had that type of bravery, but he had *seen* what the Shadows did to people who caused a mess. It didn't look like it was that bad here. Meg gave Fateh a critical once-over. "We can hide you away from those guys for a bit until they lose interest in you. What do you say?"

Fateh grimaced; if only he *could* stay hidden away from Tabor and Etana, but Etana had made it clear that he knew all that was under his jurisdiction in the town and Tabor had a leash on him. There wasn't going to be any escaping from them. He also didn't trust this group. *If my own friends hunted me down, what would this group of strangers do?* Telling them the truth was doubly out, even if it was a modified version. "I ..."

"You what?" They were practically crowding him now. "What are ya keeping secret?" Meg pushed into him, face close to his as if she could read his secrets by proximity.

"Nothing," Fateh pushed her away, grateful that he could do this normally, instead of having to worry about the newfound problems that he'd acquired after finding out the truth about himself. "Didn't you say they were watching?" He tried diverting the question again. "If they've tagged me like you've said and I go missing ..." He let his voice trail off meaningfully. He knew what it meant if a potential 'snack' or 'pet' went missing and he had a feeling that it wasn't all too different in this town, no matter what Etana said about keeping order.

He and Tabor were obviously not the first visitors to the town—but Shadows weren't the only predators, either.

The group conferred again, but the leader shrugged. "We've risked it before," he pointed out. "Now come on—and don't look stupid while you follow us. We don't want any more attention on us than we can help."

"Getting helped by the tricycle brigade," Fateh huffed under his breath. "Yes—'cause being led around by a bunch of middle school kids is totally inconspicuous."

"I'd shut it if I were you." Meg elbowed him. "You're not that much taller than we are, now are you?" Her smile was anything but sweet. "So, it can't look *that* strange."

As Fateh was practically dragged away, he wondered what Tabor would say to this and if it would be against the contract. That was the last thing he needed on top of everything else. He didn't want to contemplate what would happen to him if the contract was null and void.

The contract is what keeps me safe from him, right?

If he broke the contract, all bets were off. *Let's hope he has enough sense to realize that this isn't my fault—if he even notices what's happened at all.*

He couldn't help but notice the differences from his small town as they moved through the city to where they were dragging him. It was so different from his town that he couldn't help but focus on the elements that made it dissimilar. The size was the most obvious, but there were smaller things as well.

Like the three different schools all laid out, and the five different bakeries ... *I think Etana's bias towards food is showing with that set.* He was starting to feel more like the country cousin than before and he rubbed at his arms, trying to ward off the chill that was creeping over him. It had nothing to do with the bite in the air and he resisted the urge to tuck his hands into his sleeves or pull out another jacket.

What did Tabor say about metal? It didn't burn, not like last time—but he was very aware of it all the same. *This really sucks—humans aren't as great as whatever they are, huh? At least we don't burn when we brush anything metal.*

The shadows grew deeper between the buildings, reminding him of Tabor's shadow paths, and he was faced suddenly with a gaping entrance and steep stairs. "This is your secret hideout?" he asked dryly, trying not to let his apprehension show. He didn't know what to expect down there or from this group. He didn't know why he was going along, except for the fact that it would look stranger for him to *not* go. He was wary, however, and kept looking around, expecting one of the fae to come after them. They acted like they knew something he didn't and maybe he could bring the information back to Tabor and Etana. Etana would especially be grateful to know of any 'gossip' about his town.

"Why so curious?" Meg tilted her head back, jumping down steps two and three at a time. "We're going somewhere safe. That's all you have to know." She smirked.

Fateh chose to skid down the stairs rather than risk grasping the rusting metal railing that supported the way down. For one, he wasn't sure what it'd do to him, and secondly, he was secretly afraid it'd crumble beneath his hands, it was so old. "Gee, so honored to be let into the clubhouse," he mumbled under his breath. "Do I have to spit on my hand to seal my promise to not let the grown-ups see it?"

"You need to take this seriously," Meg snapped at him, faintly visible in the dark. "Unless you want to be completely taken—and we ain't about to have any more people on *their* side." She spat on the ground.

"We really are cautious about what we do," a soft voice said as a crackling light came to life in the room. "All the adults are brainwashed into thinking that everything's all peaceful and stuff here, but we know more than they do."

"I bet," Fateh murmured. *Unless it's like home where everyone knew what was happening because they made our home their nest.* "So, what happens when you become adults?" He leaned back, then nearly jumped as his hands brushed against the jagged metal edge of sheet metal. "Turn in your badges and friendship bracelets?" He couldn't keep the bitterness out of his voice if he tried.

"No." The girl shook her head, multiple braids swinging as she spoke, rubbing idly at the scar running across her eye and down her cheek. "We still have networks and we *do* grow up; it's not like we're the Lost Boys down here, you know."

"At least the Lost Boys usually won." Meg's voice was almost as bitter as Fateh's was. "They didn't have to fight against something that slipped in like they were casing the place and then took over without warning."

Fateh was learning to shut up before he said what he really thought. He was in a strange place, more vulnerable than before, with people who were suspicious as hell. He didn't say how humans had once conquered or what was really going on.

"Well, you're doing whatever you can now to fight back, aren't you?" Fateh shoved his hands in his pockets, wishing he was anywhere but here. He wanted to go buy something of his own to wear, wanted to get out of here and away from the bugs that seemed intent on crawling up and down his spine the longer he remained.

"We're hiding." Meg shrugged, settling herself comfortably on a stack of shelving. "If we get caught into one of those homes, we ain't ever leaving there." She shuddered. "All brainwashed to enjoy it."

"You don't want to go in one of those places." Fateh was still on edge from his time there, from the people and the tests. "They're not good at all. They don't sell people from there, but it's bad enough inside." Even if some of them enjoyed it, even if some of them felt safe—they were still watched all the time, poked and prodded. For those like him and those Shadow-touched, it was even worse.

"You know what it's like there?" Meg stared at him, eyes wide. "You were in one? How did you get out?" She stared at him. "You're not old enough to have been let out on your own." She was obviously torn between incredulity, suspicion, and being impressed.

Fateh grimaced. "I had help in escaping," he said shortly. "It wasn't exactly the method I would have chosen, though." *Having the staff brainwashed, the other kids being turned into sacrifices, and then the entire place flooding due to a loophole from the elemental that was supposed to be guarding the place? Not something I want to repeat, ever.* He looked over at them. "Still, hiding underground isn't the best thing, either. Gotta get boring—if you just wandered around and pretended like you had a home or whatever, it's not like they can confront every kid on the street."

The group stared at him, brows furrowed in identical looks of confusion. "We're registered, you idiot. Or didn't they have that in your town?" Meg asked. "They know if someone's died or been taken. They record the whole thing." She snorted. "You must have really been a country boy if they didn't keep marriage, birth, and death certificates around."

"Yeah, but do they have your pictures attached to them?" Fateh snorted. "How many people live here? If someone dies, they're not going to go pounding on your door to round up the rest."

"You really don't know how it works outside of the country, do you?" Meg gave him a pitying look.

"No, I know how it worked in my town," Fateh snapped, patience rapidly coming to an end. "There, if you were an adult, you had to register to be contracted to the Shadows. It made sure that you'd be taken care of and they couldn't kill you outright. You were chained like you were an animal. Your 'registration' is nothing compared to that."

He took a deep breath, aware of the silence. "If you're chained, your friends know it and they attack you for it. They band together, just like you're banding together. They ... they kill if your parents are contracted, even if you haven't. This—" He gestured around him. "This is hiding from something that's not all that bad yet."

"Yet." The girl with the multiple braids shook her head, expression pained. "I know what you're talking about," she murmured. "I came from a place like yours. This is only the start—or did you forget what it was like before it got really nasty?"

Fateh looked at her in surprise; he hadn't expected that—all these kids would have practically grown up with the invading Shadows. "I ..." He made a face. "It got nasty really quickly," he murmured. "They made what they called a 'nest' in my town."

"Mm ..." She still looked vaguely disapproving. "Don't judge us by how we do things. We're trying to help, any way that we can—most of us here, we're all running from something or someone." She held out a hand. "We're trying to offer you that same protection. You said that there was a chance that someone might be watching you. Don't you want the chance to be safe?"

Fateh closed his eyes briefly. "Don't judge me, either," he whispered. "You have no idea ... like I have no idea." He looked towards the stairs and sighed. "Look, the offer of being protected is appreciated, but I've got to go. I've got my own safe place." *As much as Tabor can be considered such* ... If he stayed here, there was no saying what they'd do to him if they discovered he was one of the creatures they were hiding from. He didn't know how long Tabor's 'protection' would last. He was afraid if he stayed here any longer, he'd *want* to stay, to believe in the illusion of safety, that he was just one more kid caught up in the nightmare of what went on around them.

He didn't want to be the enemy.

"Surprising if you're new here an' all." Meg narrowed her eyes at him.

"I've got someone here I know, that's all," Fateh said quickly. It wasn't a lie; he did know Etana, however little that actually was.

"Hmph—not one of those stupid Shadows, I hope." Her gaze promised something dire if he said yes to that. Not that he would be lying if he said they weren't; Tabor and Etana were adamant that the Shadows were something different from what they were.

"Can't say that they are." He was hedging his bets. *Okay, so getting around it isn't as difficult as I thought—at least in some instances.* After all, Etana said he wasn't a Shadow, but a miotal.

"Well—" She looked around her group and sighed. "If you need a crash space, we're here," she said, reluctance heavy in her voice. "Guess we can't keep you prisoner." Her words contrasted sharply with her expression; it seemed she still didn't trust him.

"Yeah—good for me. Offer's appreciated and all." He made his way to the stairs, trying not to bolt up them. The longer he stayed here, the queasier his stomach was. It seemed Tabor's protection was wearing off. "Look, if you need help ..." He let his voice trail off.

"We can manage." Meg's voice was harsh. "Don't go collecting favors on our behalf." She gestured for him to leave. "Go back to your *friend*." The way she said it chilled Fateh. It was as if she knew who the friend was, who he was going back to. "We'll watch out for you."

He was just grateful that Tabor had said they were leaving. He didn't want to deal with another set of people coming after him. Another group of kids who stared at him, judged him, and tried to figure out if he was 'good or bad.' These were different; they weren't hurt like the kids from his home were, but they were just as suspicious, just as bitter. He didn't know what would happen if they decided he was the enemy and if he stayed much longer, he was afraid that he would find out all too clearly. He stumbled on the stairs, as slick and small as they were, as he backed up them. His hands closed around the metal latch of the door, the feel of it burning his palms. He barely managed to hold back his hiss of pain as he opened it, thumping it shut with a harsh kick. Any sounds from below were cut off.

The sounds of the city filled his ears again as he hurried away as fast as he could, eyeing the buildings around him as a guide to get him back to where Tabor was. Tabor obviously could use the chain to keep track of him, but he didn't know and didn't want to know how to use it the same way. He was concentrating on the surroundings so much that he wasn't watching the space ahead of him and smacked headlong into a familiar presence, the electricity of connection vibrating along his nerves, the shock of it sending him to the ground.

"Problems, little Spark?" Tabor's mouth quirked up briefly at Fateh's appearance, reaching down a hand to help him up only to have it pushed away irritably.

"Nothing's wrong." Dust clung to his fingers as he brushed off his clothing. Standing up, he eyed his surroundings uneasily. He didn't want that group to hear him; seeing how they acted, they could still have spies around. "Why're you here, anyway?" He held out his bag; still intact. "I got what we needed to get, all but food."

"You don't sound happy to see me—I'm rather wounded." Tabor's smirk grew. "Were you thinking of staying with the kids, Spark? Trying to burrow away from me in that little hideaway they concocted?" His fingers brushed across the chain. "I can still follow you, even through the metal walls, you know."

"Nice to know." Fateh impatiently pushed back a strand of wayward hair from his eyes. "Good thing I wasn't trying to join the kiddie club." He hefted the bag. "Can we leave now?" he asked. "I've got clothing and I want to get the hell out of here."

He was starting to feel sicker than before and he wondered vaguely why Tabor seemed to be handling it better than he was.

Tabor stood in front of him, fingers possessive as he tilted Fateh's chin up. "Feeling the effects of it all, are you?" he murmured. "I wondered if that would happen, with you coming into your power all at once." He had lost his smirk for the moment.

"I feel fine," Fateh huffed and pushed the hand away again, not needing or wanting Tabor to be staring at him, pretending to be concerned. He didn't want to admit to himself what he was feeling. He was just fine before, wasn't he? Why now?

"Sure you do, Spark." Tabor ruffled his hair and pulled away from him. "Let's go get food and then we'll head back to Etana's. We can talk more there without people overhearing. I'm sure you still have a lot of questions."

"Yeah, but are you going to actually answer them?" Fateh asked disbelievingly. "Or will it cost me more than I can pay?"

"We're partners, Spark." Tabor gave him a disappointed look. "You don't trust me. That hurts." He kept an arm around Fateh's shoulder. "It's about time you learned more of the truth."

"Sure, we're partners. Calling me a pet totally makes us partners." Fateh rolled his eyes as he pushed Tabor's arm off his shoulder. "Should I even *be* in a co—"

Tabor's hand covered his mouth. "Not here, Spark. We'll talk more at Etana's house." Seeing Fateh's look of disbelief, he grinned. "I promise."

Fateh couldn't help his surprise. A promise was serious. It meant that Tabor meant what he said, and Fateh would get some real answers. "Fine," he said grudgingly. "But I'm holding you to that."

"I'm making the promise to *you,* so you can definitely hold me to it. Now, let's get back to Etana's."

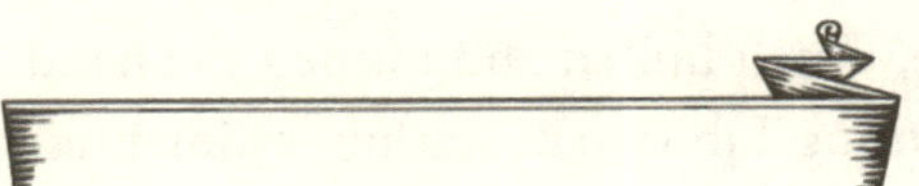

Chapter Thirty

Etana had made himself comfortable when Tabor and Fateh returned. "Done exploring my wonderful city already?" he asked. "Run into anyone interesting?" His look said that he knew about the kids that Fateh had met and was just waiting for Fateh to give up the information. Or maybe Fateh was just paranoid.

"Went shopping after our meal together." Fateh shrugged, setting his bag down on the floor. "You've got a nice city; I could almost think that nothing had ever happened to the outside world."

"That's the way I like it." Etana smirked. "It's so upsetting when the actual Shadows come into town. They're so *chaotic* that they cause a mess wherever they show up. I won't have them in my town, turning the populace into their little puppets." A look was slanted toward Fateh, who turned red at the insinuation.

"It's a shame you couldn't extend that protection to other towns," Fateh complained.

"Like your town, little aodhamair?" Etana asked, raising his eyebrows at him. "My reach doesn't go *that* far and you're a long way from home, you know. The shadows spat you out on the other side of the world. Welcome to Wanaka."

Fateh stared at him in disbelief and looked up at Tabor for confirmation, but he only nodded. "It's true," he said. "We're far away from Felinheli and those troublesome friends of yours. Far away from Mokosh and her evil little pond, too."

"I've never been so far away from home before." Fateh blinked at the unusual town name. Somehow focusing on the fact he was so far away from home made it easier to deal with the impending conversation. "Where *is* this?"

"New Zealand," Etana said cheerfully. "Fun fact, it's literally the other side of the world from your town."

"Fascinating," Fateh said dryly. He had always wanted to travel, but hearing that he was so far away from home was jarring. "Now that I know where we are, can we get onto more of what's going on?"

"That's our little Spark, getting right to the point." Tabor's voice was filled with amusement. "Doesn't want to relax after his day exploring, he just wants answers."

"Wouldn't you?" Fateh demanded, staring Tabor in the eye. "If you found out something was different about you, something that redefines your entire being, wouldn't you like to know more information?"

"What we told you wasn't enough?" Etana spread his hands. "It's not like I'm an endless fount of knowledge; I already told you that you're best off asking Tabor about yourself unless you really do want to go into debt with me." He leaned forward with renewed interest. "That can be arranged, you know."

"No, I just wanted to have a safe space to talk to Tabor," Fateh shot back. "I didn't think that talking about contracts and *aodhamair* in public was a great idea." He stumbled a little over the unfamiliar word. "Your place is the best to get a few lessons on just what is going on." He crossed his arms against his chest. "You mentioned the kids at the school, too."

Tabor sighed and slumped over, closing his eyes briefly. "You were half-dead with exhaustion and shock and you remember that?" he asked.

"Yeah, because it was *important,*" Fateh said fiercely. "Those kids were supposed to be Shadow-touched, but none of them were actually bothered by what you call the Shadows, were they? It was all something else. Water elementals and trolls and god knows what else."

"You're right that those kids weren't Shadow-touched." Tabor got straight to the point since Fateh wanted direct answers. "You've seen the Shadow-touched; they don't have souls of their own anymore, like the people who served in the restaurant where you had that *lovely* dinner. They're not like contracts."

Fateh blanched at the memory of that long-ago dinner. His mother had still been alive and they had tried to have a happy night together. He had bargained for safety like a pro, but they had still been in danger the entire time. "Yeah," he said shortly. "I've seen them."

"Well, then you know those kids weren't Shadow-touched. They're like *you*, you impossible puzzle, you."

Etana sat up straight, staring at Tabor. "You mean they had an entire building filled with half-fae kids?" he demanded. "How on earth did that happen?"

"It wasn't all of them," Fateh said slowly. "There was a small group of us that had to wear metal; I think it suppressed whatever part of us that was the ... *fae*? Do you mean the tylwyth teg? You said that we shouldn't get mixed up with that."

"*We're* not fae," Tabor said emphatically, then reluctantly amended his words. "At least, not *high fae,* not what people think of as fae. We're more primal than that, but those kids that you were with were mixed up with all sorts of fae from what I observed when you were all running around town."

"If you were watching me that closely, you could have gotten me away before things went to shit, you know." Fateh stared Tabor down, expression annoyed. "Instead, I had to stay in that hellhole for a year and then nearly drowned."

"Aw, Spark, you wanted to be in my company? That's so sweet of you to say." Tabor gave Fateh a wicked grin. "I couldn't rescue you while you were under the protection of Mokosh, remember? And before that, you were wearing metal. That would have barred you from the shadow paths that I travel."

"Not mine," Etana spoke up. "My pathways are open to metal. If I had been there, maybe I could have been your happy little rescuer."

"With your shifting alliances, you probably would have sold him to the nearest Shadow," Tabor returned. "Don't pretend otherwise."

"You're so mean, Tabor," Etana whined. "I would have kept the kid for a while, especially when he turned out to be so interesting. I thought he was unique, but you say there was more?"

Tabor looked to Fateh, who shrugged. "There was a handful of us," he said slowly. "One that said he had been contracted to a water elemental, and another with an earth elemental. Randi had dealt with trolls." He thought about Marisa and her 'clear eyes' and way of speaking and the way she saw the truth about all of them. "There was one girl that knew about us, I think."

"Oh? A Seer?" Tabor asked with interest. "It would be helpful to find *her* again. Those with clear eyes see the furthest."

"They're also the most dangerous," Etana said sourly. "You can't hide from them. They're the ones that led people to us, bringing metal and salt to burn us. We were here first, and we had to retreat to pockets of the world, smaller aspects of what we had so that we could survive."

"Now who's the one complaining?" Tabor rolled his eyes. "It's not like the metal affected you. Your kind adapted and thrived off of it. You were *born* from human greed. So don't you go yapping about 'oooh the metal burns.' Spare me."

"Hey, it was worth a try to see if you were paying attention." Etana looked unrepentant. "But seriously, humans weren't meant to see us. It's because of them that the Shadows even exist." He took in Fateh's look of shock and gave him a slow smile. "Yes, that's right. Maybe we should tell you what the Shadows really are."

Fateh stared at Etana, who only gave him an impassive look back. "What?" Etana asked. "You wanted to know all sorts of things about the fae and yourself. The Shadows took over your town. Wouldn't you like to have a little more information as to what they are?"

"They're *Shadows*," Fateh said in confusion. "What else could they be? They're some sort of fae, aren't they?" he asked.

Tabor looked away, frowning. "Do you think he's ready to hear about the origins of the Shadows?" he asked. "Shouldn't we focus on him and what he is first?"

"I already know that I'm half a fire elemental or a full one or whatever you think I am," Fateh said impatiently. "I want to know about the Shadows."

"Are you absolutely certain?" Etana asked, raising his eyebrows at Fateh. "You may not be prepared for the truth."

"I'm not a child," Fateh snapped, not breaking eye contact with Etana. "This is part of what I need to know to understand." He didn't say please and he didn't beg for the information. He had a feeling that he'd lose any respect Etana had for him if he did so.

"Oh, good. I get to break you, even if it's just a little." Etana grinned widely. "Maybe having you two stick around isn't as bad as I thought it would be."

"You like me," Tabor protested, eyes wide and innocent. "When Fateh was off exploring the town, you were telling me very vocally how much you liked me."

"Ew, don't want to know, promise," Fateh said, making a face.

"Are you sure?" Etana grinned. "You seem to want to know everything else. *I* don't mind telling you about what Tabor and I got up to while you were gone."

"You were telling me about the *Shadows,*" Fateh said firmly. "Not your sex life."

"You should get a sex life. Maybe you'd be less uptight." Etana's lips curled up in amusement but when Fateh just gave him an impassive stare back, he sighed. "You're no fun," he complained. "Fine, fine. Yes, the Shadows."

"I think he should be sitting down for this," Tabor muttered. He steered Fateh towards a couch and pushed him into it. "You'll want to sit down."

"Jeez, just get on with it; it can't be that upsetting." Fateh was getting nervous with the way the two of them were acting, though. "What are the Shadows?"

"Do you remember stories when humans would make deals with the fae?" Tabor asked softly, watching Fateh. "They'd ask for a favor or some sort of trinket, in exchange for a sacrifice of some sort."

"They got tricked most of the time," Fateh said slowly. "The bargains never ended out well for them, because the fae would twist their words and favors and make the price too high to pay."

"True," Tabor acknowledged. "The humans were greedy and didn't *think* about the consequences of their requests. They'd ask for unnatural things; power and money and safety."

"Well, safety—" Fateh shrugged, not liking where this was going. He had a feeling he knew what Tabor was going to say next, and he got a sick feeling in the pit of his stomach. "Nothing wrong with wanting to be *safe*."

"It came at the price of other people." Tabor pursed his lips. "You can be safe, but your neighbor could pay the price instead."

"Why would the fae care about that?" Fateh asked. Etana was strangely quiet, just watching Fateh for any reactions.

"They didn't; they laughed when more humans died because they didn't care about them. There was the matter of payment, however. Some humans couldn't pay the price that was asked of them, so the fae asked for the highest price of all—a human soul." Tabor took a deep breath. "Those souls—those are what became the Shadows. They're the corrupted remains of human souls They're still rapacious, still greedy, and grasping for fae magic. They long for the humanity they lost, yet hate it at the same time."

"So, the ... the Shadow-touched ... become Shadows?" Fateh's voice rose slightly. "They made deals and their souls are now forfeit?"

"Some of them became Shadows, depending on the deals they made. Others become fuel and are absorbed into the darkness that is the Shadows."

"You said they want fae magic, too." Fateh's voice was flat; his emotions were pushed to the back of his mind as he absorbed all of this. He knew he'd freak out later, but for now, he was just taking in the information. "What do you mean by that?"

Etana spoke up, his eyes on Tabor as he did so. "It's not only human souls that the Shadows try to absorb. Young, vulnerable fae, especially those with raw magic, are their favorite types of meals. Isn't that right, Tabor?"

"Yes." Tabor's tone was clipped and his eyes were dark and unhappy. "It's hard to get away from them when they latch onto you. You see why I wanted to get you away, Spark. You could have been fuel for the Shadows if they realized what you were."

"They could have taken us at any time, any of us?" Fateh asked. "Why the contracts and trades and protections?"

"They're bound to their new nature as a type of fae. If one wants a favor, they have to make a bargain. If one wants protection, one offers it. You realize that the contracts they offered were all traps, don't you?" Tabor asked. "You were screwed either way," he said bluntly and Fateh felt himself pale in shock. "Bargains with the fae, even corrupted ones like the Shadows, never end well."

"What does that say about the contract that you and I have?" Fateh asked bluntly, crossing his arms against his chest. "Am I screwed? Are you going to eat my soul?"

"I told you, Spark. It's a partnership, not a real contract. It's me looking after you since you're so new to your power."

"And what do you get out of this?" Fateh demanded. "You say that you're looking after me, but there has to be something in it for you, too."

"I don't want you to end up like I did," Tabor admitted. "Like how my family ended up. I'm doing this because I didn't have the chance to save myself or others, so I'm saving you before you get to a position where being saved is the end result."

"You're also greedy and stubborn and didn't want Fateh to be taken by anyone else," Etana said. "You were like a kid with a shiny new toy that you didn't want to share with the other kids."

"That's because the other kids would break him," Tabor snapped. "I didn't want to see that happen again."

"Oh, Tabor—no matter what, you're always trying to save people. One of these days it's going to get you killed." Etana shook his head. "You have something special and sooner or later, he's going to be noticed. What will you do then?"

Fateh closed his eyes and breathed in deeply. "Well, I guess the only thing to do is get rid of the Shadows," he said. "Sounds like it'll be better for all of us if we do."

"And how do you propose to do that?" Etana asked with a laugh. "You barely know your own power exists. You don't know how to use it and if you try, they'll eat you alive. "

"He means that quite literally,'" Tabor offered. "Just let it go, Spark. Give it a few years at least, until you've grown into your power and can fight back. Right now, you're too vulnerable."

"I can't just leave all those people there to get eaten by the Shadows," Fateh protested.

"Worry about your own kind first," Tabor said.

"Humans *are* my kind," Fateh said stubbornly. "You said that I'm only half. The other half of me is human, isn't it?"

"I said those kids at the home started out as half-fae," Tabor countered. "The longer they stayed around those forces that corrupted their lives, the more their fae nature came out. If that little bride of yours goes near any fae again, she'll turn to stone in the sun, as easily as any troll."

"And me?" Fateh asked. "Since I ... contracted or connected or whatever with you, what is it going to do to me?"

"Your fire will come out stronger than it ever has before," Tabor said candidly. "It would have eventually, especially with all those Shadows around, but with me fueling the fire, as it were, there's no turning back now."

"And you couldn't have told me this before?" Fateh demanded. "You're just as bad as the Shadows."

"Oh, trust me, little Spark, it could be much worse." He leaned closer and gave Fateh a serious look, "You could be absorbed into Shadow, your magic being leached away, little by little until only a husk of you remains. I've lost people to the Shadows, Spark. It's not pleasant, pretty, or painless."

"You would know, Tabor." Etana shook his head before turning his attention back to Fateh as if they hadn't been discussing Fateh wanting to hare off and save the people in his town. "So, there you have it, kid. The Shadows were once humans and are doing their damnedest to turn the humans of your town into their power source."

"I've got to do something," Fateh protested. How many more Shadows would emerge from the innocent people of his town? Not all of them had been instrumental in his mother's death, and they didn't deserve to be corrupted and changed.

"Get more allies first," Etana offered. "You can't do anything as you are now, but if you have more people at your back, you might be able to do something."

"And you?" Fateh asked. "Will you be one of those allies?"

"Maybe this week, but next week might be different. You can't count on me unless the gift you give is *very* high, high enough to tempt me from trading my services." Etana shrugged. "I'd rather not have my peace shattered like yours was. Sometimes that means making deals that you would find repugnant."

"I see," Fateh said slowly. "Well, if you can't help me, I think I know where we can start."

Tabor raised his eyebrows at Fateh. "Oh? You think I'll risk myself and you for a handful of humans who you barely care about and who sold you out?"

"I think you care about preventing the Shadows from spreading any further," Fateh said knowingly. "What do you say, Tabor? Want to help track down some more anomalies like me?"

When Etana and Tabor stared at him, Fateh just smiled. He had an idea of a plan. He just needed a way to execute it.

Etana snorted and looked over at Tabor. "Well, he's just like you. All temper, no brains, but a lot of heart. Alright, kid, you do your thing. For as long as I'm your friend, you'll have a safe harbor here."

"And how will I know when we're not friends?" Fateh asked dryly.

"Simple. You'll never be able to get near me." Etana spread his hands. "I won't directly harm you, but I won't offer you any help, either."

"I guess that makes sense." Fateh shrugged and then turned back to Tabor. "I know where everyone lives and Randi said that they were all going back to their homes."

"Well, well—you're going to get an interesting lesson on the type of world you're now a part of." Tabor grinned. "Sorry your trip home is delayed, but you apparently have too much on your plate to have a reunion now."

Meet the Author

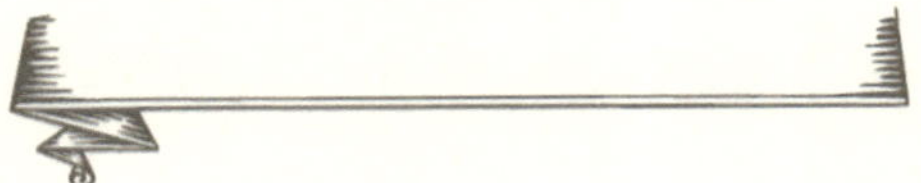

Trisha Thacker is an east coast girl at heart, coming from Virginia, but has sprouted into a desert flower after almost a decade of living in Arizona. Her two cats, Kai and Loki, are the sunlight of her life. She has told herself stories since she was a child, but she didn't start writing them down until she was a teenager, which she burned. Trisha recently stepped into the publishing world and her latest book, Sparks, was inspired by her fondness for faerie tales and was a labor of love.

Trisha loves fantasy, anime, and baking shows, but her favorite show to binge is Mythbusters. Who doesn't love a good explosion? You can find her with a cup of tea in one hand and a taco in the other while she hides from the sun.

You can reach her at trisha@trishathacker.com or her website at http://trishathacker.com